SHACKLES

MADGE MACBETH

SHACKLES

MADGE MACBETH

Invisible Publishing
Halifax & Picton

Library and Archives Canada Cataloguing in Publication

Macbeth, Madge, 1878-1965, author
     Shackles / Madge Macbeth.

Issued in print and electronic formats.
ISBN 978-1-988784-00-7 (softcover) | ISBN 978-1-988784-03-8 (EPUB)
     I. Title.

PS8645.I34G56 2017   C813'.52   C2017-905387-6
                                              C2017-905388-4

Cover and interior design by Megan Fildes | Typeset in Laurentian
With thanks to type designer Rod McDonald

Printed and bound in Canada

Invisible Publishing | Halifax & Picton
www.invisiblepublishing.com

We acknowledge the support of the Canada Council for the Arts, which last year invested $20.1 million in writing and publishing throughout Canada.

Canada Council   Conseil des Arts
for the Arts   du Canada

INTRODUCTION
By Erin Wunker

MADGE MACBETH's *Shackles* was first published in 1926, three years before Virginia Woolf's foundational feminist essay "A Room of One's Own." In Woolf's canonical text, she imagines what words and writing have been lost because women have not historically had access to the space, time, and recompense necessary for a stable writing life. "Give her a room of her own and five hundred a year, let her speak her mind and leave out the half she puts in, and she will write a better book one of these days," writes Woolf. Money, space, time. The material conditions of both survival and agency. For Woolf, these are the components for changing the status of women's lives as well as the aporias of cultural history. Get more women into their own spaces, give them the economic stability to not have to work beyond the labour of writing (and what a labour it is), and the course of history won't be righted, but it will be irrevocably and positively shifted. Money, space, time. It seems a direct enough set of needs. And yet...

In Macbeth's book the reader encounters Naomi, a married woman who has managed not only to squeeze in time for her writing amid the quotidian domestic labours associated with running a household, she's managed to make money from her writing. Indeed, through Naomi's skill as a popular writer, and her work ethic, she has moved she and her husband from a space of economic precarity—what George Orwell has described as a liminal space between poverty and upper-middle class life—to a space of relative comfort. Naomi's writing successes, along with the arrival of her aging family member who helps to cover the costs of living, makes the household upwardly mobile. No longer must she spend her time planning meals that conserve the use of cooking fuels, learns the reader. Still, Naomi's time is divided and in demand. Her facility with household management, cooking, and caregiving render the labouriousness of this work invisible to her husband and her uncle. Indeed, at one point her uncle remarks that if only an aging aunt were to move from the west coast they would have even more financial security, and Naomi wouldn't even notice the extra work. Money, yes, but despite her success Macbeth's Naomi struggles for space and time.

One of the striking things about *Shackles* is not simply the way it anticipates Woolf's axiom for women writer's success, it is also the way in which it reproduces a divisive and problematic version of White feminism endemic to the move from sufferage to second wave. In *In Search of Our Mothers' Gardens: Womanist Prose*, Alice Walker makes a crucial critique of Woolf's tacit white supremacy: "Woolf ... wrote that in order for a woman to write fiction she must have two things, certainly: a room of her own (with a key and a lock) and enough money to support herself. What then are we to make of Phillis Wheatley, a slave, who owned not even herself?" Wheatley, Walker reminds the reader, was recognized as a poetic phenomenon in her day both in spite and because of her Blackness. For Walker, Wheatley is but one example of a woman of colour who wrote and produced work of cultural import in spite of her lack of money, space, and time. Put in different words, what Walker identifies in Woolf's narrow gaze is a lack of intersectional feminist care. Indeed, so much of the critique of second-wave feminist interventions is that these White feminists argue in broad strokes for gender pay equity rather than gender, race, sexual, and economic justice for women of colour, Indigenous women, queer women, and other traditionally marginalized groups.

In *Shackles*, we see Macbeth likewise trafficking in racist analogies with the aim of pleading Naomi's case. For example, we first meet Naomi in the height of her rage over the amount of domestic work she has to accomplish before she is able to sit at her desk and write. In a moment of extreme frustration, she lashes out and hits the bed she is making up. This impotent act of physical violence—the bed can't feel her rage—reminds her of a picture she had once seen of "a black-bearded rubber trader" and "an aged Indian, cowering at his feet" unable to avoid being lashed. The brutality of the image holds Naomi's imagination in part because the Indian man has done what he can to defend himself: he has bitten the rubber-trader's leg and the two are locked in a vicious embrace. What, for me, is most haunting and telling about this introductory image is what follows: "the white man's expression held an element of brute satisfaction," and she, Naomi, yearns to wield such power over someone. Here, Macbeth reproduces the racist discourse wielded by women fighting for suffrage. In aligning herself with White masculinity Naomi identifies the coersive and violent face of heteropatriarchy, but she isn't able to move outside that restrictive and damaging paradigm. Her access to space, time, and money will be forged through attempts to reproduce the conditions available to those most legible to patriarchal culture.

Shackles is a fascinating novel of one woman's struggle to forge an artistic life amidst the intersecting restrictions of gender and economics. It is also a timely text to return to: in Naomi we encounter a cautionary—if unintentional—subtext of the perils of advancing a narrow feminist project. Without intersectional attention and racial justice at the forefront of twenty-first century feminisms we, too, will find ourselves where Naomi does. Alone, frustrated, and siloed in our exhaustion and rage.

DEAR AIMÉE

Here at last, is the book we discussed so often, and in the writing of which your unflagging interest was so stimulating a factor. I am wondering whether you will find in it any resemblance to the novel I had planned; for the characters, especially towards the end, pushed aside both me and my intention, writing their own story while I sat helpless, looking on.

ARNOLD behaved very badly. There's no denying it; and NAOMI—well, NAOMI reverted to type and exemplified woman's instinctive urge to surrender her happiness in order that she might minister to the man who pressed his need upon her.

I am not suggesting in the following pages the women are arch-angels, and men, arch-demons... amusing as life would be viewed from that angle. I would that I might help to promote a happier relationship between them by setting forth certain fundamental divergences, to which they seem mutually incapable of reconciling themselves, and which, though accepted, are not generally analysed or examined with regard to promoting a better understanding. That these are in nowise exclusive or heaven-sent revelations, will doubtless be quite evident.

Is not the crux of our social unrest due to the fact that woman no longer feels it an indecency to rebel against the immemorialised domination of man? But in refusing to yield up her will, does she not go to the other un-picturesque extreme and carry independence to the verge of tyranny—the very characteristic that she, herself, resented? Furthermore, at the uttermost end of this extreme, does she not "revert" in a crisis, refusing complete emancipation and returning to the state of submergence from which one more step would have freed her?

Woman is passing through a cultural transition. Instinctively, she is bound to the old order of things; intellectually, she clamours for the new. And vacillating, she stands between them.

On the other hand, few men will deny a preference for the old conditions, when they provided for their womenfolk without economic assistance, interference or criticism, when, as the little rhyme has it—

> "A wife should never hem and haw,
> Her husband's will should be her law."

Man cannot, at the root of him, resign gracefully his part as arbiter of human destiny. Rare, indeed, is he who can disclaim stealthy desire for an old-fashioned wife—and all that this term connotes.

Equally rare is the woman who deliberately chooses an old-fashioned husband. Even with the modern type she shakes her shackles in revolt and grasps at economic opportunity as a means of filing herself free. Her earning capacity rather than her moral right, now justifies a repudiation of the promise of obedience made at the altar.

I trust it is evident that I am dealing only with women whose temperament and mental equipment incite them to share the SOI-DISANT "larger" responsibilities of life. With the others—those who do not care for economic independence—I have at the moment no concern. The earning woman has problems that are peculiarly her own.

Her first requirement—if she would cast off the bonds with which instinct and tradition have fettered her—is to immunise herself to the lash of criticism most biting when levelled by members of her own sex. She must reverse her attitude towards her immediate environment, forgetting that she, who has produced life, is expected to sustain it. She must, in a word, be a man, entrenched behind ultimate authority, neglectful of small considerations, unconscious of the minutiae that comprise the daily habit of existence (unless they fail to run smoothly!). She must proceed to her chosen task indifferent to the claims of domesticity, of illness, of death. She must learn to exact service as her right, and the grosser forms of labour as some other person's portion. Most difficult of all, she must acquire courage to be selfish in little things and selfless in big ones; courage to inflict pain—not in the designing, crafty, malicious way of women, but unthinkingly, magnificently, virtuously, as is the way of men.

Can woman do this? Can she justify herself in her own eyes for evading the petty duties and functions which nature and tradition have imposed upon her? If so, then she has no need to make a compromise with her ambition. She can be "free." Emancipation, like everything else, is to be purchased at a price.

Is that price too high?

Your friend,

MADGE MACBETH
Ottawa, Ontario
September, 1926.

Myself when young did eagerly frequent
Doctor and Saint, and heard great Argument
About it and about: but evermore
Came out by the same Door as in I went.

— Omar Khayyam

CHAPTER 1

NAOMI breathed convulsively as she moved around the bed and tucked its coverings into place. The flush on her cheeks was not due entirely to exertion; her lips were set in grim, hard lines that indicated the strain of emotional repression. Her eyes were smoldering pits of fury.

She snatched the dimity counterpane from the floor where it had fallen, and flung it across the bed. There was something theatrical in the gesture; something primitive. It produced an instant's relief by offering a channel through which her emotion might express itself. Save for the utter silliness of the action, she would have given free play to a pent-up impulse and struck the bed.

The remembrance of a picture she had once seen flashed across her mind. It was a horrible thing, but it haunted her. She was gripped by its stark brutality... Against a background of steaming jungle, two figures stood; at least one stood—a black-bearded rubber trader. The other, an aged Indian, cowered at his feet, impotent to escape the lash descending on his naked back, the slave's yellow fangs were imbedded in the trader's leg. The picture had fascinated Naomi by its very repulsiveness—the savagery on both distorted faces, the unmasked hat. But the white man's expression held an element of brute satisfaction, and as she recalled it, Naomi wished that the dimity counterpane were a black-snake lash...

The bed, however, would not cower and flinch. It did not even protest as she pounded the pillows upon it. Calm, it lay before her; serene; insensible alike to pain and passion, mocking her hot rage.

It was her husband's bed.

Naomi moved to the window, knowing before she reached it, what she would see. Far away, in front of the old stone church and new stone rectory snuggling close— looking, with its frilly curtains and flower boxes, like a beribboned maid hanging onto the arm of a staid old man—there, before the church, Arnold would be standing, delivering two and a half—always something less than three—chocolate maple buds into the eager mouth of the Rev. Haddington Allyn's dog.

"Now," she could almost hear him say, "no more, Scotchie, old fellow. That's the last. Moderation in all things, you know... May I recall your Shakespeare?... 'Things sweet to taste, prove in digestion sour.' It is not unlikely that I will see you on my return."

Then man and beast would shake hands, impressively, and Arnold would swing jauntily around the corner, keeping perfect step to the measure of his inward applause.

But Naomi stood still, looking out into the golden morning, only half aware that the pictures she saw were of the mind rather than the eye... There was something maddening in Arnold's walk... if one watched it, moved with it, day after day and year after year. It wasn't merely vigorous, buoyant. She could have borne that. There are few women to whom masculine inertia makes a permanent appeal. But Arnold betrayed something deeper, more fundamental than vigour. There was a suggestion of complacency, self-righteousness in the way he held his head, that had become exasperating. Even had he been a total stranger, Naomi would have suspected him of being an irreclaimable egoist, a man so happily protected by an armour of well-being and right-doing that nothing really touched him; nothing got beneath the skin. Having lived with him for eleven years, there was no room for doubt or speculation. She knew. She had beaten herself against that armour, unable to find a sheltering softness for her aching and bruised spirit. Year after year she had seen it harden by his passionate conviction that suffering is the salutary treatment of a Higher Wisdom, and that the degree of permanent peace is proportionate to the measure of temporary pain. Of late, she had seen some humour in the fact that the Higher Wisdom had rather defeated its own ends by endowing Arnold with so credulous a disposition.

She recalled the months when financial disaster threatened them like a deadly miasma, spreading over the whole field of their endeavour. Did Arnold sink or sicken? Did he protest against the harshness of fate? Did he come to her for comfort or offer commendation of her courage?

By no means. He rarely mentioned his affairs at all, save to suggest some further possible retrenchment, but this admirable restraint lost some of its effectiveness in Naomi's eyes because it was accompanied by a manifest satisfaction in bearing his burden.

"We must look upon this as a test of our endurance," he once said. "Never a morning do I wake without conscious thankfulness for the strength that is sustaining me."

But he understressed the trifling circumstance, Naomi realised, looking backward, that *hers* was the strength for which he felt grateful. *Hers* were the eternal sacrifices, the self-denials. So far as the discomforts of every-day existence were concerned, life was, for Arnold, virtually unchanged.

She dispensed with a servant. She laboured over the daily menu so that the retrenchment might not be noticeable. Styles came and went unheeded while she mended his clothes, her own, rags of bed and table linen, and even the carpets.

"Did he clean his own office?" she asked herself. "Did he help with the housework or cooking? Did he even make his own bed? No! He enjoyed the fruits of my labours as unconcernedly as though *I* felt exalted at the privilege that had been given to me to become an unaccustomed drudge."

Could he suffer? Could he ache with agony so penetrating that it pierced the very core of his being? Or did not his reaction to suffering produce a self-gratification so keen that it nullified the pain and became a panacea for his spirit, thus losing all its salutary effect? If she could only know...

"Exactly how would he feel," she wondered, "if I called him up and said, 'Oh, I forgot to mention it this morning, Arnold, but you'd better get your dinner downtown. I am going away. Hugo and I have decided to fling over the traces, and we leave for New York this afternoon?' Would he experience any depth of emotion?" So much depended upon that.

Naomi found it almost impossible, consciously, to hurt anyone. Abnormally sensitive herself, she suffered acute distress at causing to others even the smallest pain. An absurd instance recurred to her as she stood at the window wondering about Arnold....

She was no more than seven years old. Her mother had called her out to the verandah where several ladies sat drinking tea. She had been kissed by each, and her appearance had been commended by whisper and facial contortion. She had no idea that her elders considered this perfectly transparent manner of communication, untranslatable to her immature intelligence.

One lady, very moist and very stout, clamped her to the rocking chair in which she sat. Naomi was a slender child and stood polite and helpless in the embrace, and presently she felt the rocker cut hard across her foot.

She made no outcry. A dread of seeing the visitor's discomfort and receiving the torrent of apology that must follow the discovery, kept her dumb. Only when her mother noticed the tears streaming down her twisted face, did she gain release. And then she rushed away from the company with a burst of well-feigned, if hysterical laughter.

Again, when she was about sixteen, she noticed that an unprepossessing youth whose racial allegiance to God's favoured family was clearly decipherable on his lean, swart features, appeared in her path each day as she returned from school. She did not realise at once that he was trailing her with a piteous, dog-like insistence that roused her compassion even while it annoyed her. But one day, he flung a little screw of paper at her feet.

"I haven't a soul in the world to speak to me," it read. "I can't imagine why I go on living at all. Will you smile at me—just smile—I ask no more?"

Naomi was not constituted to resist such an appeal. The next day, in answer to the burning look in the boy's eyes, she bowed. His mute gratitude made her a little faint. It was so enveloping, inescapable. It caught her whether she wished or not, like the waves of a rising tide. She hated herself for being unable to ignore him, but she couldn't do it.

One day in early spring, the youth left a box on her doorstep. It contained a sprig of arbutus. She thanked him. And because he stood before her, with an air that implored a little kindness, she turned and walked a few steps beside him, to the amazement and amusement of her associates.

After that, she found it impossible to avoid walking with him a little distance each day. She took no pleasure in his companionship. He was without conversation. He was shabby and reminiscent of onions and smoked fish, but she couldn't hurt him.

Her parents heard of the strange attachment and arraigned her severely.

"It's all very well to give a derelict a meal in the kitchen," said her father, angrily, "or a cast-off suit of mine or your Uncle Toby's, but admitting him to friendship, raising him to a level of equality with you—appearing with him in public—why, this exceeds any fantastic act you have committed yet! Will you tell me—I ask as a seeker after information—will you be good enough to tell me *what* you can see in this unwashed worm? You can't be deluding yourself that you love him?"

Naomi shook with fury. "I hate him!" She screamed. "I hate...hate...hate him. But don't you understand, I can't bear to see him squirm?"

Would Arnold squirm if she went away with Hugo? So much depended upon her knowing that.

Naomi tried desperately hard to be fair. Times without number she reminded herself that Arnold was good for her. She believed this utterly. But that did not make living with him any easier, and it did not add any perceptible joy to the duties she felt called upon to perform. There was the bed, for example—it symbolised a hundred and one little services which, shorn of the love impulse, became irksome, detestable, menial. Naomi had reached the point where she rebelled against certain services savouring of duteousness to her husband. And of late, he had been unusually exacting.

She didn't blame him. She derived no satisfaction from convicting him of wrong. Equipped with a logical mind, she knew that such was not the case, and also that she, herself, could boast of no spiritual superiority. No! Whatever fault there was, lay at her door... It was she who had changed, who had permitted discord to enter into their relations. She no longer loved her husband. Grudging acts of house-wifery were all she had to give, and her whole being quivered in a fever of revolt.

A clock chimed. Half past ten!

From Naomi's lips there escaped a sound that was half sigh, half moan. Every morning it was like this... She woke with the urge to write upon her; she felt that inexplicable receptivity that every writer welcomes, when thoughts pour themselves upon the keys as though dictated by an unseen speaker. It was early in the morning that she felt a heaven-sent refreshment, an energy that often enough is confounded with inspiration. It was then that she saw her stories grow.

But... there was breakfast to prepare—a simple task had she been left to the uninterrupted performance of it. However, such was not Arnold's way. He always thought of a dozen little matters that required instant recital; he rehearsed anticipated encounters with business associates; he reminded her of enquiries that should be made about sick friends; and he frequently discovered buttons whose adherence to certain garments was extremely problematical, and whose loss would leave him prey to some embarrassment.

Knowing how pronounced was his objection to undressing once he had put on his clothes, Naomi pushed aside her disinclination and went to his assistance. As a rule, some mild conflagration occurred simultaneously in the kitchen.

"I'm almost sure that I smell something burning," he had announced that morning, as she darned a weakened spot just below his collar-band. "Hadn't you better see?"

"Was I right, my dear?" he wanted to know, as she returned breathless from the kitchen.

"Quite right, Arnold. The bacon was completely spoiled. Burned to a cinder. Will you turn a little more to the light, please?"

"What a pity! If you would hurry a shade, my dear... Time does not stand still, you know. Yes, it's a pity to consume food in such a fashion. Couldn't you have lowered the gas before coming upstairs, and by so doing, saved our bacon?"

His manner was that of one whose imperishable kindliness constrained him to temper the asperity of a well-deserved reproof.

"Yes, I could," answered Naomi, "if I'd suspected that I'd be required to neglect it so long. Will you please turn to the light?"

Arnold laughed slightly. "Well, really, my dear, I'm not a contortionist. This position is extremely uncomfortable, as it is."

"And what about mine?" burst from Naomi. "Every muscle in my back is strained from trying to avoid driving the needle into your chin! It's hard enough to cook and sew at the same time, but when you make the task unnecessarily difficult, I say you're not playing fair. You know how intensely I dislike mending a garment that is rigid with the person inside it, and yet you persist in imposing on me this form of annoyance."

"Poor girl," said Arnold gently. "You must have a headache. I had no idea there would be such a bother over a few stitches. However, in future, I'll examine my clothing at night, and avoid, insofar as possible, distressing scenes like this, in the morning."

And he did, just as often as he remembered it. But, unfailingly, on the mornings when the gas was poor or the milkman late, he discovered the need for her ministrations.

If a book, a cane, or a scarf were mislaid, Arnold was certain to want it in the morning, and his eagerness to assist in the search resulted in a cyclonic overthrow of all semblance to order. By the time tidiness had been restored,

Naomi's creative impulse had been stalled and her energy dissipated. Thoughts had become fogged. Words—those precious draperies that should wrap an idea with grace and elegance—deserted her; or they fell from her patient machine like lumps of putty that no amount of manipulation could transform into becoming mantle.

Black despair settled upon her. How, she asked herself, could a woman *ever* be free? How could she adjust conditions so that the desire for self-expression might be gratified? The situation looked hopeless. Arnold wouldn't—couldn't—understand. His inflexibility of mind, his imperishable belief in the sanctity of his own convictions, rose about her like a prison wall.

She paced up and down the room, beating her hands softly together and crying, "My God, there must be a way out... there must be!" But the figure of Arnold walked with her, restraining, disapproving, somewhat affronted by this exhibition, and yet, courteous, urbane. There were times when he made her think of the suavely correct little groom, who stood on top of her three-story wedding cake and smiled.

Her thoughts flew to Hugo. Naomi was not yet thoroughly convinced that she loved Hugo. It was conceivable that his attraction for her lay in a tacit promise of emotional release. She was so tired of repressing and suppressing natural impulses. Arnold had tried to teach her that true happiness lay in a surrender of personal joy, especially when the happiness of others might be promoted by such self-denial. Whether the others deserved it or not, was a matter of no concern. He was only happy when conscious of superogatory martyrdom, and it was characteristic of him to fear joy, for, according to his bleak philosophy, misery was the only school for perfecting human nature. And Naomi used to accord him an unintelligent submission. But, gradually, she had undergone intellectual emancipation. She had lost her fear of encouraging daring processes of thought, and Hugo Main provided unfailing stimulation.

Arnold did not like him.

"A mischievous type of man," he answered, when pressed to state his reason. "If he's sincere in his radicalism—which is only another word for self-indulgence—he is an enemy to Society, to the Church. If he's a *poseur*, he deserves something stronger than contempt."

"Are not all reformers enemies to society and the church?" retorted Naomi, in small letters.

"One might concede on that point and at the same time observe that only in rare cases has the accusation been undeserved."

Nothing more was said at the moment. Each understood the implication of the other and resented it. To Arnold, Naomi's attitude expressed rebellion against social order; against himself. Naomi felt, in her husband's attitude his characteristic intolerance of anything approaching freedom of thought. It showed in countless little things... silly little things such as coloured window curtains, table linen, guest towels... Not until assured of their acceptance by people whose opinion he respected, did he permit of their usage in his own home. Once having adopted them, his enthusiasm was generous and sincere. In the matter of her dress, he displayed the same irritating conservatism. All forms of individuality were, in his opinion, questionable. Only that which has withstood the test of time, is safe for adoption.

If Arnold could suffer, she reflected, it was through criticism... even the mildest. And this was a matter of vanity rather than sensitiveness. To escape criticism, he had discovered that one must follow an established course; one must move with the mass, the commonplace.

Naomi's friendship with Hugo Main annoyed him. Secretly—or so he thought—he was often annoyed by her susceptibility to mental corruption. If loyalty had not prevented, he might even have confessed a sense of disappointment in her.

"We should be on our guard against superficiality," he once said, in reply to a spirited defence of Hugo's philosophy. He always said "we" when compelled to dogmatise and Naomi had learned that such was his kindly way of reminding her that, save for his steadying influence, she might readily become a mental flibbertigibbet...

And the worst of it was that Arnold had some justification for his position. He was so often right. Recognition of this fact did not add to Naomi's peace of mind. On the contrary. She preferred to dwell on his inflexibility of temperament, his restricted viewpoint, and his lack of sympathy with anyone who held views divergent from his own.

She wished that Arnold could understand her. His failure to do so produced acute distress. She loved his fineness, his native delicacy and good taste. She loved his exalted opinion of women and his inherent chivalry towards them. Indeed, he was chivalrous towards men, which made him an easy prey to the unscrupulous, and precluded the possibility of his ever achieving commercial success.

———

Unaccountably, her mood changed. She flew to her desk, and began to write—a terrific energy upon her—a glorious clarity of thought. Three pages of her book rolled from the machine while the characters moved before her and talked like persons in a play. She forgot Arnold, Hugo, herself. A flower of her brain was bourgeoning.

A bell rang. Naomi tried to ignore its summon, but this was impossible. Her fingers faltered, hung above the machine and the dropped into her lap. Something had been broken—shattered beyond repair. She rose and answered the telephone.

"Were you writing, my dear?" Arnold asked. "I hope I didn't interrupt anything important."

"Oh, no!" said Naomi.

"It's—er-exactly—" she knew that he was consulting the face of his watch "—exactly three minutes to twelve. I timed my call so as to leave you an undisturbed morning and yet give you plenty of warning for lunch...."

"Warning, Arnold?"

"Uncle Toby has just come in. He drove here from the station to pick me up on his way home. I knew you would want a few minutes preparation. He says he's longing for some of your bran biscuit. We'll be along presently, my dear. Good-bye."

Uncle Toby, back again! He had expected to stay away all the spring, and by then her book would have been finished. Now....

Ashamed of her lack of enthusiasm, she tried to feel genuine pleasure in his return. She wasn't really sorry; but the "superficial" part of her saw myriad obstacles that would rise between her and her work.

Already the silence of the machine fell across her spirit... the silence that is freighted, not with rest, but pain. Something vital had fled from the atmosphere of her room. She laid her papers away in a large white box as though committing some fair young body to a tomb. Death had overtaken that which but a moment since was vibrant with life, love. Laughter and song...

And so uncertain was the resurrection!

———

Voices sounded on the verandah. She went to the door.

"My dear little girl," cried Uncle Toby, opening his arms. "This is worth all the sunshine of the south! Let me look at you... I feel as though I had been away years instead of weeks."

"Just throw your things in here," Arnold broke in. "I'll take them to your room presently. No unnecessary steps for you, you know."

"My blessed children," murmured Uncle Toby, much affected. "What a fragrant twilight you offer a troublesome old man!" He trumpeted. "Open that club bag, Arnold. I couldn't resist the Dutch silver, down there. A pair of candlesticks for your dressing table, Naomi, my love. No... no... please don't thank me. Just give me a big suffocating hug... And let me tell you," he continued, presently, "that although I could scarcely wait to see you, I had an excellent reason for driving first to Arnold's office."

"You said you wanted to give me a lift home," prompted the latter.

"Nonsense! That's what I told you! Why should I give you a lift home—a vigorous young fellow who needs exercise to keep down that threatening liberality of front? I stopped for you, deliberately delaying my home-coming, because I wanted this dear child to realise that I would not interrupt her morning and interfere with her work. This, sir," he assumed an air of mock severity, "is an example in self-denial that you will do well to follow! Said I to myself, 'No matter how eager she may be to see her tiresome old nunky, she must not be interrupted when she's at her desk.' And now bring on the bran biscuit!"

CHAPTER 2

IN THE afternoon, Naomi unpacked for Uncle Toby and got him comfortably settled in his accustomed quarters. He insisted that she should change none of her plans on his account, that he was able to look after himself, but it was evident that his trip had tired him much more than he was willing to confess, and no sooner was he tucked into bed, "for a brief snooze," that he fell into a heavy slumber.

Naomi had intended to see Hugo in the evening. Arnold would be curling. But Uncle Toby's coming made a difference. After his long and refreshing sleep, he would not be ready to go to bed at nine o'clock, as was his habit. He would want to sit up and recount his gentle little adventurings.

Naomi made no secret of Hugo's visits, but she generally managed to have them in a large group or tête-à-tête. A three-cornered conversation had proven both difficult and unprofitable, especially when the corner happened to be Uncle Toby or Arnold.

She called him on the telephone.

"Well, I can't see why the prodigal's return should upset all your arrangements," he expostulated, in a tone not unlike the one Arnold used when she failed to adapt herself to *his* suggestions. "Why shouldn't Arnold give up his curling? Why shouldn't *he* stay home and listen to the travelogue while we go to a movie or something?"

"But he's *my* uncle," replied Naomi, dissatisfied, herself, with the irrationality of the answer.

"Oh, Lord!" groaned Hugo, "Can't you shake off that superstitious subservience to the ethics of possession? Can't you emancipate yourself from the tyranny of relationship?

Can't you see that *your* uncle, *your* husband, *your* child, *your* friend should not make any of these ineffable fortu-nates less free of you—or you of them—than the ordinary rank and file? Mark you," he hurried on, feeling that she was about to interrupt, "I'm not insensible to the uses of the family tie. But, little Naomi, you must not overlook the fact that a tie can strangle quite as easily as it can embrace. You, my dear, are being courteously garroted."

"They would be cruelly shocked to hear you say so, for, however appearances may be against them, they regard me as a sacred charge and treat me according to their lights."

"Aye, verily! But their lights are so dim. They are still carrying candles, unconscious of the fact that electricity has been discovered. It is this last that I want you to dis-close to them."

Naomi ignored him.

"Family life may be old-fashioned, but, after all, it's the hub around which nations revolve. I'm never very clever at arguing with you, Hugo, especially over the telephone, but the more I think of it, the more I see that this idea of free-dom is a forlorn hope. Why nothing in nature is entirely independent. Everything is bound to something else."

"Yes, but not to the extent of suffocating that to which it is bound—save in a few parasitic exceptions."

"How can you be sure? Everything feeds upon something else. Nothing has unrestricted movement."

"Ah," said Hugo, with exaggerated solemnity.

"You can't deny it. Planets aren't free of one another; nor nations, nor individuals. Animals are not free agents, and I doubt that vegetables are. Everything in the universe sub-mits to the interplay of inescapable influences."

"Vegetables?" echoed Hugo. "You couldn't have said vegetables!"

"Why not? The atoms of a turnip are held together as solidly as yours or mine. For aught I know they may be longing for freedom. But they can't have it, any more than you, or I. To achieve their end, they would cause the entire structure to disintegrate, and we superior beings would view that state with distaste... and call it rotten. It's not the law of possession, I acknowledge. It's the fear of social disintegration."

"The dear, ingenuous child," cried Hugo. "The tender young rutabaga! Perfect in form, healthy in substance, mature; and absolutely innocent of mental development. Yes, the comparison to a turnip is flawless."

Naomi laughed. She had observed that Hugo, like Arnold, like all men, probably, was less contemptuous of the woman he has overborne in argument, than elated by his own triumph. The really stupid woman is the one who keeps proving her superiority over men. It is this Parnassian Queen, and not the gentle spirit who is content to learn, they look upon as a wherriting bromide.

She would not, however, surrender her point solely to be charming.

"You have broken down my defence of the turnip," she told him, generously, "but perhaps you'll admit the case of the mother is stronger... Surely she owes a greater duty to her own children than to the children of the woman across the street? Isn't that a family tie?"

To a certain extent, Main granted it. But even this was not a hangman's rope. Primarily, her duty exists because the children are unable to look after themselves. Until that time, he conceded that she—and the father—should be responsible for the rearing of them. Children have a distinct claim upon life, he admitted, but that does not imply the need for mothers to make slaves of themselves... He approved the

English system of sending them to school at an early age...
There develops a mutual respect between child and parent
that is rarely found where children are brought up in the
home. A better perspective of the duty and responsibility
of each is obtained, and parents cease to regard children as
the imperfect reincarnation of themselves, while children
think of their progenitors as human beings instead of inefficient disciplinarians or heartless martinets.

"All this is fine as a theory," Naomi told him. "but it's so
hard to put these fine theories into practice."

Hugo complained that it was absurd to continue this
conversation over the telephone. "Giving a lecture by radio
is simple enough," he said. "But I can't talk to you this way."

"Oh, Hugo, how difficult you are! Why, even talking to
you through the telephone does me so much good... except
when you grumble."

"It's your fault," he accused. "I tell you Naomi, you are ru-
ining what even my family have conceded to be a cherubic
disposition. I *must* see you."

She argued the point, convicting him out of his own
mouth. "I thought you didn't believe in the pressure of will,
and *must* is a strong word."

Lacking a defence, he returned to his dissertation on
motherhood, pointing out that a mother's first duty is to
teach her children to do without her. "Children are just
human beings you know, put here, heaven knows why, to
experience certain physical and spiritual adventurings. The
mother who can't see this is either a sniveling sentimentalist or a jealous absorptionist, trying to gather everything
and everybody into herself, as it were. Stand your children
off from you and look at them as absolutely distinct and
separate entities! Don't spoil them by allowing them to
think that their claim upon you is incontestable; don't spoil

28

yourself by feeling that yours upon them is imponderably strong. Be individuals—not lumps of one clay!"

"It's perfectly reasonable," said Naomi, "but I haven't any children, and—"

"And there's *your* Uncle Toby."

"Exactly."

"Naomi, you disappoint me. Slavery is such an ignoble state."

"Oh, Hugo, don't begin that all over again," she cried, in real distress. "If I could only make you see... He was so good to us when we were children; and when Arnold and I needed help, he was right there to give it..."

"But, my God, why not? Isn't that just what I'm trying to tell you? Care must be given to children because they are unfit to care for themselves. I assure you no man or woman will get a heavenly crown for that! Likewise, when one is in trouble, the brotherhood idea should exist in families, if anywhere. Even a strange Rotarian, or a Mason will help you! But does he expect to hang like a milestone round your neck all your life because he has extended a friendly hand when you needed it? No! And neither should a member of your family!"

"And what about love?"

"Well, what about it? Are you suggesting that family ties engender the emotion called love?"

"There is an association of ideas, I should say."

"To the extent that the phrase 'family tie' is used to substitute for that which frequently is non-existent. Love? Why, dear girl, you can't pretend that you love a man or woman better *because* of blood relationship. If you are honest, you'll admit that the fetters of tradition have imbued you— many of us, indeed—with the belief that persons of the same lineage have a claim upon one another. But it is protective rather than emotional. Trace it back to its beginning. Possession... The cave dweller had gathered unto himself a comely wench who had borne him many offspring; he had stalked the terrible mastodon and collected a fine supply of food and hides. A stranger approaches. Is he received with grunts of welcome? Not at all. Your cave-man suspects the worst. He has provided for his family and therefore he is their master. He bands them together to fight off intrusion and they present to the stranger a stony front. Possession... provision... is the root of the family tie, if you will suffer that type of metaphor. Don't drag in love!"

He's right, thought Naomi. Family affection is a habit of mind... implanted in our infant consciousness and carefully nurtured throughout our lives. If a confessed dislike of sister, brother, aunt or uncle is accepted seriously, a flavour of indecency attaches to it. Otherwise, it is regarded as a pose, an illustration of the cynicism that relations are thrust upon us, but thank God, we can choose our friends!

Yes, Hugo was right. That bond of family grew out of man's acquisitive faculty. To hold what he had, he needed support. Who owed it him more than those for whom he provided? An effort is made to teach children to love their father because he gives them their sustenance; they must like their mother because she gave them life—often enough a sadly unwelcome gift—and they must love one another because, originally, a united front discouraged covetous neighbours. How hideous, she reflected, to explain everything!

Hugo was speaking. "Custom is a wondrous mental anodyne. Besides, progression is so unpopular. But can you truthfully state that you love your Uncle Toby better than you love me?"

Naomi caught herself before committing the banality of saying that she loved him in a different way.

"I'm answered," said Hugo. "Oh, Naomi, don't be stupid. Let me come over for a little while. I'll be there in less than ten minutes. Naomi... Naomi..."

"Hush," she warned him. "You must be careful."

"I know... May I come?"

"I'd rather not. Uncle Toby will wake any minute now, and I've so many things to do."

"You don't love me!"

"Perhaps not."

"Do you?"

"I don't know."

"Are you certain that you don't?"

She shook her head, forgetting that he could not see.

"Then listen," he went on, as though she had spoken, "come away with me to-morrow. There's no other means of proving it... If the experiment is not what we hope from it, we can separate—go each our own way. And there will be no harm done."

"No harm? Oh, Hugo, how can you close your eyes to fact and actuality?"

He didn't pretend to misunderstand her. "You mean that Arnold would not—er—take you back? I believe that is the common phrase. What if he didn't? You would have gained your freedom. The world is large. You can always write. You are independent."

Naomi began to tremble. She knew that she was flushed and that her heart thumped unevenly. She was ashamed of even this much loss of self-control. It argued a concession, a subtle response to Hugo Main's tempting.

"See here, Naomi," the man's melodious voice came to her, "can" you divorce yourself from the archaic idea that marriage is a holy covenant? Can't you see that at best it is a man-made institution, designed not to ennoble the

31

individual—God bless me, no!—but to benefit the State? Don't you realise that, just as the cave man needed a family to support his right to possession, the State needed men to prosecute her wars? Can't you remember that, as years are counted, the interference of the Church in marriage is a comparatively recent thing? What can one intelligently *sanctify*? Isn't it a simple emotional experience that, delicately undertaken, provides the intensest of all the joys life offers, and also a constructive force for greater mental and physical achievement?"

"Hugo," cried Naomi, "you must stop. A telephone is not a private instrument of communication. Besides, you shock me!"

"That," commented the undisturbed Hugo, "is at least a hopeful sign. What holy side has marriage when you look at the matter with intelligence instead of sentimentalism? Primarily, it's Nature's method for the propagation of the species, and finally, the arrangement contrived in order that two persons of presumably similar requirements, and at the same time equally harmonious differences, may find happiness and profit through intimate companionship. Mating, my dear Naomi, is a beautifully simple act, a perfectly natural function, existent in all forms of creation. That it should be considered holy in only one of them seems to be such an absurd conceit—especially when the process is virtually that which is common to all!"

"Hugo!"

"I apologise—though I have spoken a self-evident truth. So long as mates perform the slightest service either to the community or to one another, there is justification for their cohabitation. When the reverse obtains, they are merely committing—er—all those resonant and dreadful crimes of which we read so much in the Christian Bible. And the sooner the intelligentsia attack this vileness as vigorously as the intelligentsia attack what *they* are pleased to call immorality, the better place our little world will be."

Naomi sighed so deeply that he heard her.

"One thing more—and this is not a review of old arguments, it's something that came to me only a moment ago. Suppose two men seek one another for the furtherance of their financial interests and incidentally those of the community, and make a mess of the association, does the law require that they should sink deeper into a quagmire of debt and misery? No! They are helped to a separation. Suppose two diplomats or churchmen enter into an agreement that proves to be less constructive than was expected. What happens? Civil and religious law finds for them a speedy release. But marriage is different. Here, in the closest of all associations, here, where failure promotes the bitterest of pain, Heaven—that benign dispenser of human destiny—denies the pair the panacea of relief. Their partnership has to go on—unless one or the other is willing to submit to indecent and obscene conditions and thus procure a divorce. Is it holy to live in hatred, to place the body above the spirit? Why, the thing is utterly preposterous, patently intolerable!"

"That's just the worst of it," said Naomi. "We've made it *tolerable*. We've made the self-respecting course an ugly thing, a thing to be avoided."

Main reminded her of the revolution that is sweeping over the world. The little band of reactionaries, he told her, was steadily and rapidly growing.

"People are beginning to think something is wrong. So soon as enough of them act upon their conviction, the law will follow. It only requires a little courage, dear. Such respectable men and women are making a plea for saner relationships! Why won't you join them? The other night I heard a talk on Social Hygiene. The lecturer, an eminently staid and respectable man of the bloodless academician type, startled me by saying, 'We have come to believe that the only justification for the sex expression is Love. Whether it occurs in the Bonds of Matrimony or no, is a matter of slight ethical importance.' Oh, Naomi, come away with me and let me prove the radiant truth behind his words!"

"Hugo... I can't listen anymore."

"Arnold will divorce you—he may be counted on always to do the proper thing—and he will enjoy the role of injured husband... Naomi, I want you so..."

"Uncle Toby is moving," she interrupted. "He will be coming downstairs."

"When am I to see you, then?"

"I don't know. I'll telephone."

———

Dinner progressed to the accompaniment of Uncle Toby's happy prattle. Arnold played the part of the Chorus and without any hint of strain. Naomi had often marvelled at this endurance until Hugo showed her how fresh he came to these conversational treadmills; he had not been in harness all day long. His attitude towards Uncle Toby was perfect. He served him with the choicest food, he prompted Naomi when her attention wandered, and his interest in the old man's conversation never seemed to falter.

"He couldn't be kinder to his own uncle," she used to think.

"And so you grew homesick, even surrounded by a group of pleasant acquaintances?" he was saying. "Do you hear that Naomi? Was there ever such an insidious flatterer?"

"If the truth is flattery, I must bow to the soft impeachment," returned Uncle Toby, in his old-fashioned bookish way. "But I haven't told you all."

"Ah!" commented Arnold playfully.

"I saved the best till last."

"Dramatic suspense. Is she beautiful and an heiress?"

Uncle Toby showed no annoyance at the implication. Like most old men, he considered himself somewhat of an adept in the art of sweet dalliance, and the suspicion that his attentions might be humorously or distastefully regarded by the most lovely of women, did not remotely occur to him. "It is because I am seventy-eight," he was fond of saying, "that I can appreciate feminine beauty," and it pleased him to give his harmless little associations a Machiavellian aspect.

"Oh yes, she's beautiful," said Uncle Toby, "and she wouldn't want to be an heiress." He looked fondly at Naomi. "Her hair is like the raven's wing, her eyes are the colour of rich blue pansies misted by a drop of dew, her mouth albeit a trifle rebellious at times, is sweet and clean, and plenty red enough without the aid of that abominable lipstick, which I suspect she sometimes uses. The Master Sculptor has given her a lovely—"

"Dear Uncle Toby!" cried Naomi, foolishly touched by this unusual expression of affection, "You have completely forgotten my nose, ears and teeth."

The old man shook his head and smiled.

"The fact is, Arnold," he went on, "our girl is quite a famous person. You could have knocked me down with a feather when I discovered that the majority of the people down there, knew of her and had read her little stories. And after I mentioned that I had the honour of being her uncle, really I became quite the vogue. The papers sent people to interview me."

"Really?"

Naomi was sensitive to a note in Arnold's voice that expressed so clearly, for her, his contradictory emotions. He was rejoiced at each success; he wanted her to achieve none less than the highest place; at the same time, subconsciously it may have been, he resented her triumphs, her increasing independence. That hers should be the dominant personality in their ménage was a condition he refused to contemplate. The ignominy of it would have crushed him.

"What did they ask you?" Naomi demanded of her uncle.

"Oh, all sorts of stupidities, but I was equal to them—even the most serious ones."

"Why serious?" asked Arnold.

Uncle Toby floundered in trying to explain. There were two types, he noticed; one, taking a sort of superficial attitude toward writing, a very business-like attitude –nine to five, as it were—and the other, developing a strange cast of mind that seemed to believe in subtle relationship to the most spiritual and sacred forces. "They took themselves—and everyone else—so seriously," he repeated. "They referred to their Work in a tone that was supposed to command awe. Work…always with a capital W, you know…"

"Two capital W's," suggested Arnold, impatiently. Uncle Toby nodded. They placed this Work too conspicuously in the foreground, he thought, and thereby threw everything else out of focus.

"That's the trouble with them," Arnold broke in again—Naomi half suspected he was talking for her benefit. "They can't get a balanced view of its relationship to the rest of life."

"Exactly, and when they suggested that our girl must assume this attitude, too—well, I simply laughed at them." He echoed the laugh. "Shocking how impertinent some of them were! Such intimate questions they asked!"

Arnold's lips grew thin.

"But little satisfaction they got from me. I was the soul of discretion. 'My dear madam,' I recall saying to one very tenacious creature—the editor of some women's magazine in New York, I believe—'you must realise, once and for all, that Mrs. Lennox enjoys the adoration of two tireless slaves, of whom I have the honour to be one, and she is not—and never will be, please God, constrained to make writing a business. Ergo,' I said, 'she has never lost her fine perspective, she has never taken on these extravagant poses, and, more-over, she has never felt the necessity of surrounding herself with the panoplies of Art—if I may use such a phrase.'"

"Meaning the disgusting humbuggery employed by Shireen Dey," approved Arnold.

"Just so. 'As to regular hours,' I went on, 'certainly she has! We give her all the time we think is good for her. But when it comes to shutting herself away for days on end, or practicing the roles of her heroines upon us—well, she leaves all that sort of nonsense to the unhealthy, neurotic breed of writer with whom you may have confused her. I am glad of this opportunity to put you right. Mrs. Lennox is an essentially sane and moral woman. We are a happy and united family, with which her Work in nowise interferes.' And as a finale to my little address, I said, [Do not, I pray you, madam, make it appear as though my niece were a slave to a foetid imagination.'"

"I should hope not," breathed Arnold. "The vulgarities apparent in most of these interviews—"

"Don't worry," cried Uncle Toby. "I really kept Naomi's name out of them—to an astonishing extent. If there is any *blurb*—that is the word, is it not, my love?—I will be the victim. As a matter of fact," he confessed, "I allowed them to use... not her photograph, but mine!"

———

Arnold polished the face of his watch with his thumb and rose from the table. He had much to say on the subject of cheap publicity, but curling was of more immediate importance.

"Unfortunate that we have this match scheduled for tonight, sir," he said. "I hope you don" think me discourteous. If there had been any possibility of getting a substitute..."

"Tut, tut my boy!" Uncle Toby would not let him finish. "Didn't I make it perfectly clear that no arrangements should be altered on my account? Naomi is going to be at home. Isn't that enough for any man? You run along and I'll give you the next chapter at breakfast."

"At lunch," Arnold corrected. "A little rest won't do you any harm after your long trip, and Naomi will, I know, be glad to give you your breakfast in bed!"

CHAPTER 3

THE BOOK OF THE HOUR was the title of Naomi's second novel and most pretentious piece of work. Hitherto her efforts had been concerned with the type of writing broadly classified as "popular", and inclusive of fiction, children's stories, news articles, special features—anything, in fact, that promised a probable sale, and furthered what she regarded as her literary apprenticeship.

In the beginning, ambition had pricked her merely with a desire to sell her output. Arnold seemed quite unable to lay his hands on ready money, and Naomi found it utterly impossible to maintain even the most modest establishment on the pittance that he gave her. Uncle Toby's illness and removal to her home did not occur until after the early struggles were past and she had begun to make a sure, if somewhat fluctuating income.

With Uncle Toby's installation and the pooling of their finances, the sordid problems of existence were, in a measure, solved. Naomi no longer felt the necessity to plan a dinner the component parts of which must all be baked because a roast was in the oven, or boiled because a ham was cooking, and thrift demanded that no extra gas be used.

In such matters—and they are by no means the least important of a housewife's difficulties—she now enjoyed a certain ease. But the consequent obligations and responsibilities weighed disproportionately in the balance. Uncle Toby's share of the household expenses did not take the form of salary paid to Naomi, which she was free to use for her own pleasure and convenience. It provided for better food (which *she* had to prepare), for the luxury (and resultant mess) of grate fires, for a plentitude of poultry when otherwise the Lennoxes would have had to satisfy themselves with Irish stew. In short, it provided the means of raising the standard of living for all three of them, without supplying the necessary machinery for reducing her individual labours. She could not, without considerable strain, stretch her allowance to cover the wages of a good servant.

Besides, neither Arnold nor Uncle Toby enjoyed the attentions of a paid dependent. Nowadays, so many people in homes innocent of children, contrived to dispense with the services of a domestic, that Arnold had long since overcome the feeling of social inferiority with which he had contemplated this economy at first. And Naomi performed her household tasks so cheerfully and with such apparent lack of effort that she scarcely seemed to be busy at all. Hers was the art that concealed art, so to say.

Therefore, both men became fixed in the assumption that domestic duties are *not* work, that, being woman's natural sphere of endeavour, they are logically pleasant and recreative. They sincerely believed that interrupting a piece of writing to prepare dinner was a beneficial interlude.

"I often think it's a pity your Aunt Delia is so comfortably situated in Boston," Uncle Toby found many an occasion to say. "If she would only agree to live with us, you could take the place of her present nurse-companion and give up your writing altogether."

Naomi had discovered the futility of answering the old man. It was impossible for him, or her husband to understand how ardently she *wanted* to write. The assignments that came to her with increasing frequency meant, to them, brain-fag—sometimes physical collapse. They even considered her a little stubborn in accepting these unnecessary burdens and complicating what otherwise might have been a simple existence. That she should be relieved of her household tasks, at least during the fulfilling of her "rush" orders for copy, never occurred to either of them.

But perhaps a more difficult condition was the attitude they assumed towards her work, an attitude fairly well illustrated by Uncle Toby's handling of the interviewers encountered on his trip. Arnold had never overcome a sort of apprehensiveness in regard to her published material, an anxiety lest, because she had not reached the pinnacle of literary achievement, she might be considered cheap and lacking in dignity. Both he and Uncle Toby were affectionately tolerant when they were not frankly apologetic. The former always accepted praise of her as a manifestation of extreme courtesy; never as sincere appreciation. For years, both men referred to her "little stories." And interpreted their publication as a mark of special encouragement on the part of some kindly and indulgent old gentleman. That an editor's years could be scantier than sixty, Arnold learned through a series of mental convulsions. The first time he met van Taren, he suffered a rude shock. Jealousy flamed in his breast. Could this fellow in his early thirties be the erudite editor of *The Coming Day*—this fellow who made free with his cigarettes and called his wife by her first name? Thereafter, acceptance of a MSS. became, in his opinion, a personal matter between his wife and some predatory male who used official prerogatives as an avenue towards an intimacy he would not otherwise have enjoyed. He deprecated both her work, and the magazines that printed it, but he had no idea that he was jealous. He thought he was only warning his wife—the woman who bore his name—of the danger of over-estimating her ability. As though this were in the smallest degree possible from association with an editor!

Her first three stories were accepted without a return. They were poorly, but promptly, paid. Naomi was astounded that money could be made so easily, overjoyed that she could be a practical help to Arnold. Even his restrained enthusiasm did not materially dampen her spirits. She then attacked a series of plots without success, spending more than her initial returns on paper, typing and postage. She had no idea what was the matter. Arnold couldn't help her.

"Yes," he admitted slowly, "I suppose they are as good as the first ones, my dear. But even those were amateurish, immature, trifling, I never could see why they were printed at all, if you won't be hurt at my saying so. Ask the editors what is the trouble."

"I have. They won't tell me. All the slips say the same thing—that a return does not necessarily imply lack of merit, but that editors have no time to specify why the manuscript goes back. It gives one such a queer feeling," she mused, "not of wounded vanity, Arnold, as you seem to think, but bewilderment, groping. It's a little like cooking—if you understand that any better. It's as though I make you a pudding to-day which you think delicious, and to-morrow, though I use the identical ingredients, you push the stuff away as unpalatable."

Arnold closed the discussion by remarking that genius was self-evident. No one would refuse a story that contained a suggestion of it. He contended that genius was not a matter of varying degrees, but concentration of expression. "You can't be a genius without knowing it," he went on. "I mean to say, without an editor's knowing it. You are not a third of a genius to-day, and a half to-morrow, and whole one next week. Either you are, or you aren't." Personally, he could not see why anyone should want to join the rank and file of mediocre writers whose fondest hope must be limited by the acquiring of a little temporary publicity. "Too much trash is being circulated," he complained.

"But," argued Naomi, "you don't apply that theory to other professions. You wouldn't deny a lawyer the right to practice because he was not the best lawyer in the city. You wouldn't deprive a grocer of his business, or a broker, because he had a more successful competitor."

"Not at all the same thing," returned Arnold. "You are giving voice to mere sophistries. Art is once thing. Commerce, materialism, another. Commerce and its ramifications supply diversified needs—"

"So does Art. Everyone can't understand Aristotle. There are thousands of persons who wouldn't appreciate caviar, but who need and enjoy mustard pickles. Art should not be withheld from the multitude. It should be expressed so that they understand it."

"I shouldn't want to pander to the vulgar—especially when I realised I was doing so," said Arnold, and Naomi knew that therein lay the key to her husband's character. His love of the highest, the best, amounted to a holy passion—fanaticism. His was the worship of the too-exalted, the unattainable. He found worthiness in nothing less. His physical reactions to coarseness in any form were comparable and similar to those of a delicate organism to a strong food. Many things to him were sacred. Art was one. The pedestal upon which he placed it was very high. By martyrdom, he expected to attain its summit. His faith was profound and unshakeable. He was a purist, a fatalist. He was proud to be humble for he believed in a jealous God, who decreed the domination of man and the mortification of the flesh.

Regarding the subject under discussion, he refused to admit that one could *learn* to write. Music, painting, sculpture, were different. There, an artificial medium has to be employed as a channel for expression. But singing and writing were natural. One has a voice or one hasn't. One can write, or one can't. Genius, despite Carlyle's definition, was not, in his opinion, simply a matter of taking trouble.

But, although Naomi lost her happy delusion that everything worthy got into print, and that everything printed was literature, although she acknowledged the noble justness of her husband's viewpoint, still she persevered—most of the time in secret. Her triumphs she made known to him. Her failures she kept to herself. And thus there emerged in his mind a grudging recognition of her ability to win upon her environment and receive from it the reward that inevitably follows upon achievement. But Arnold's respect for Naomi's writing was fluctuating and uncertain—dependent upon the degree of condemnation or praise she received from outside. He was the type of man who could walk into an art gallery and pick out the best paintings of an established school. But of the moderns, he was no judge at all. Similarly, he could direct Naomi to the best in literature as late as the Brontës. But whether Conrad was a great novelist he could not yet determine. Had Arnold delivered himself into the hands of a Psychoanalyst, he would have been amazed to learn that, while consciously he was proud of his wife's literary prominence, subliminally, he resented it. Indeed, he hated it.

After months of torturing and inexplicable failures, Naomi received a letter which read—

"I like your story very much and will be glad to publish it if $20.00 is acceptable to you. Will you submit something else—I would suggest something rather more pretentious?"

That was the turning point. She sold about fifty percent of her output that year. The next was even better. She developed the sense of the saleable—and for a time this satisfied her. Then the thrill produced by seeing herself in print became almost extinct. The excitement occasioned by the coming of a magazine containing one of her stories, passed. Naomi told Hugo that when the family ceased to fall hungrily upon her "stuff", mailing it all over the country to immediate relatives and to remote connections of the St. Johns, she knew she had arrived!

But the curse of ambition was upon her. No sooner did she surmount one obstacle than a remoter and larger one allured her. She developed the desire not merely to write and sell, but to write and sell literature. In this, Arnold encouraged her, but his method was more stifling than provocative.

"Write something big and fine," he would say, "something that is not a preachment, but a prophecy, and will lift the people out of the ruck in which they flounder. Pseudo-science and a protest against orthodoxy have beguiled them into forgetting Christian principles and their application to our daily life. A renaissance of the spirit is coming, Naomi. Nothing is more certain. Why should it not be yours to light the torch?"

Why, indeed, she thought, feeling very like the gentlemen who, becoming embarrassed by the expectant scrutiny of his host's little children, asked why they were staring at him. "We are waiting for you to begin to be funny," said the children, and Arnold's attitude towards her was in effect the same.

"Of course, you realise," she told him, "how simple is the little task you have set me! Why not say, 'Be Socrates, Plotinus or Tolstoi', and have done with it?"

"I am only trying to show you where, in my judgement, your work will do the greatest good, my dear. You shouldn't be content with simply writing stories. They should have a purpose, and a high purpose. I am so anxious for you to do big things, so anxious to see you take yourself more seriously," he cried.

Naomi checked the bitter retort that rose to her lips. Taking herself seriously in the atmosphere of her home was, she longed to protest, utterly impossible. Seriousness of purpose was strong within her. What she lacked was time and opportunity to execute that purpose. But no one, unless Hugo proved the exception, could understand that.

"I am not in a hurry for this stuff," wrote van Taren, whose youth had so deeply affronted Arnold. "Take your time over it. Latterly, your work sounds as though you had dashed it off between dances, as it were—when you had a few moments to spare and nothing else to do."

CHAPTER 4

WITH stern seriousness of purpose, and high resolve, she had begun *The Book of the Hour*, and during Uncle Toby's absence she had completed about half of it.

That it would not meet with Arnold's approval, Naomi was well aware. His eternal plea was for a bringing back of old conditions, a revival of the past. He could even find extenuation for the vice of a bygone day. But Naomi, under Hugo Main's tutelage, was a convert to modernism. She was content to base neither her religion nor her norm of conduct upon a dead Hebrew literature. Living experiences were her concern, and of these she had written in her book, which was a protest against the spiritual and emotional enslavement of women. And now Uncle Toby had come back, and she must see that he was given his breakfast in bed!

"Coward!" She accused herself. "Why do you submit? Why do you not confess your faith—assert yourself as a complete and independent entity instead of a mere grudging dependent? How was it," she asked herself, "that she *could* submit, that she *could* compel herself to subserviency with this hot rebellion blazing in her soul and the innate conviction ever present that she was taking the wrong course?"

The continual war between her body and her spirit was an amazement to her... While she told herself that she would not perform a certain task, yet automatically her hands consummated that very act. It almost seemed that there was something hypnotic in Arnold's control over her—if the actuating force could be relegated to Arnold.

Why did she not state her case, at least, and make an effort to obtain a greater degree of freedom and understanding? Was it because she had been disciplined in the belief that a woman's mission is that of peacemaker, that family disturbances are not only vulgar, but wicked? Was it because she shrank from wounding Uncle Toby and incurring Arnold's cold displeasure? Was it inherited cowardice, a bequest from the cave-man's mate who respected the movements of her lord's strong arm, who watched her bearded brute with cunning and was quick to anticipate his pleasure? Was it woman's ineradicable desire to please, which is perhaps but a subtle form of fear? Partly, but not altogether. There was something more; something that all her logic and sense of justice were powerless to overcome; something that was never clearly revealed, but the grip of which was as relentless as instinct, itself.

Why, she mused, should an inscrutable Providence decree that woman endure the ceaseless friction of life's worrisome little things? Why must familiarity with the trivial round and common task be her unshared portion? Man blandly transfers a part of his burden to the shoulders of the weak. Woman, therefore, should enjoy a reciprocal relation with the strong. But, she doesn't. Experience has taught her that man's back is not adapted to the bearing of a myriad trivialities. He would as soon wear a sackcloth shirt, and his irritability increases in inverse proportion to the pettiness of his load. The woman of wisdom protects her men from the attribution of daily annoyances.

But why? Was this shrinking from the irritable word an echo of another day? Was this her civilised way of dreading swift and certain reprisals?

How Arnold could make her suffer! How he could twist her sensitive spirit without uttering a harsh word, or ne-

48

glecting any of his habitual gallantries. Naomi was at a loss to understand why, when she did not love him, his approval was so necessary to her.

Even the most censorious examination failed to disclose any serious enlargement of the Ego or overdevelopment of vanity's claim.

"I think I'm afraid of thought waves," she confessed to Shireen Dey, the afternoon following Uncle Toby's return.

"Sensitive," Shireen pronounced. "Nothing strange about that. You look a fright. Have you been working since dawn?"

"I haven't been working at all. That's the trouble."

"Why?"

Naomi told her.

"So the old nuisance is back again?" Shireen clicked her tongue sympathetically. "What a pity!"

"How dreadful those words sound," thought Naomi, "and yet they translate exactly what I am feeling."

"Sensitive," the other repeated. "Almost psychic. Emotional cross-currents produce in harmony of thought, exactly as statics interfere with a clear radio wave. There's an idea," she cried. "I'll work it in, somewhere, some day. Now, you, Naomi, are a receiving set, and the local broadcasters, Arnold and Uncle Toby, get in on the air, between you and the message you are particularly anxious to hear. That's what their thoughts do to you..."

"I suppose it is."

Shireen forgot Naomi's problems for the moment and was concerned with her own creation.

"That radio illustration is not really bad, is it?" she demanded. "Up to date, and expressive, don't you think?"

"Excellent."

"What were we saying? Oh, yes...speaking of anger, 'Get as furious as you like,' I often say to Doolydear. 'Shout at me with a blood-red voice'—you know men's voices do get crimson when they are angry, don't you?—'but,' I warn him, 'never dare to scold me in your mind! If you have a grouch or a grievance, speak up like a man, Doolydear. Eventually, you'll find you're wrong and give in to me. Meanwhile, however, you'll have got it off your chest and feel better. But the main point—THE MAIN POINT is, that you won't interfere with my work.'"

"You're lucky to be able to have it out with him," said Naomi.

"The same with the servants. 'The moment you feel anything but happy here,' I always say to them, 'pack your belongings and get out. I can't work in an atmosphere vibrating with suppressed rage, and I have no time or patience to coax anybody back into good humour.' Positively, Naomi, I can hear and smell that particular quality of displeasure in the air."

"Yes, I can too."

"It suffocates me," Shireen went on, wishing her secretary were present to take this down.

"Suffocates," repeated Naomi. "That's it!"

"'Strike me,' I say to Doolydear, 'strangle me, if you must! I know you wouldn't dream of it without some terrific urge—and you mustn't repress it; that's bad for you... But don't you *dare* to raise a finger against my brain children! Tampering with their little unborn bodies is just as dangerous as tampering with a physical child. On the one hand you murder my body, on the other, you murder my intellect.'"

"Sometimes I'm tempted to give up the whole business," said Naomi. "I used to write happily, but now I don't get much joy out of it."

"Then why keep on?"

"Well, there's the money—although that's not everything.

It isn't enough to make me independent—if there's such a state for a woman. But it *does* make Arnold place a different kind of value upon me. It exalts me from the level of being merely *his woman*!"

"Good God! None of us ought to be that!"

"And besides, it's hard to drop out. I can't imagine myself issuing announcements to state that 'after May 8th Mrs. Naomi Lennox will discontinue her literary work. No assignments reaching her after that date will be considered.'"

"How deliciously silly you are," laughed Shireen. "You do me a world of good. Your flippancy refreshes me, for I realise that I take myself very seriously—which is wearing, as you know. I wish I could regard everything impersonally, as you do."

Naomi said nothing, but she smiled as she wondered what Arnold would have thought had she begun to take herself seriously in Shireen's way, setting the stage for her literary performances and demanding that everyone about her play their contributaory roles.

"Exactly what do you mean by taking yourself seriously?" she asked.

Shireen veered away from the query. "Oh, it's difficult to express in just a few words. One has to be in the mood, to answer these big questions adequately. It's a sort of feeling, I should say, a sort of recognition of one's responsibility, a desire to fulfil one's trust. Of course, I don't pretend to place myself side by side with George Eliot," she went on, and from her tone Naomi suspected that this was the exact position which she had allocated to herself, "but I know that I look at life broadly, just as she did. And by giving up everything to my work, I can't fail to get a little bit—even the weeniest, teeniest smear of life-stuff on my canvas. *You* always seem to write with your tongue in your cheek!"

Naomi wanted to explain that humility gave her this manner; she had neither the encouragement of the litterateurs who were competent to judge the best in current letters, nor the appreciation of the crowd. She was just a little writer who tried not to become pontifical and offensive. But, instead, she asked—

"Do you find writing easier now than when you began?"

"Oh—er—yes, I think I might say yes. Experience gives one a certain fluency, and points of technique become almost mechanical, don't you agree?" Shireen changed her position and abandoned herself to poseful thought. She attitudinised very frankly, but with such grace and charm that everyone forgave her. "I'm so interested," she said presently. "Each new idea seems so miraculous, so divinely beautiful. As soon as it strikes me, I rush in and tell it to Doolydear and he has raptures! And then, perhaps, I'll tell it to cook... You know, she's frightfully intelligent, Naomi. I suppose a stupid person can't be a good cook... Often, when no one else is about, I call her and try a new scene on her. It's quite touching, the way she responds. Then, maybe, as I drive, I amplify it for my adored Alex, the new chauffeur...So, you see, by the time Miss Heathcote arrives, I have everything well developed and rush it out as though a boy stood at my elbow waiting for copy. Then, presently, it's a book! My publishers and interviewers are making rather a feature of the rapidity with which I turn out my work. The day of meditation is past. Thought processes must be speeded up to keep pace with the times. You remember I wrote *The Child of Passion* in twelve days, six thousand words a day!"

"And I hope to produce *The Book of the Hour* in six months," said Naomi. "Sometimes, I nearly collapse trying to do five hundred words a day."

"You do too many other things."

"Possibly. But there seems to be no help for it. Do you recall *The Blue Bird*, and the scene where the children are waiting to be born? Sometimes, I feel that my mind is a sort of brain-heaven where thoughts are waiting for birth, but the actual deliverance has become such anguish that I can hardly endure the pain. The simplest paragraph costs me hours of labour."

"Ah-h-h, you are influenced by your mid-Victorian mentor, my dear. Profound salaams. No offence meant—none taken, I 'opes! As you were! But you spend too much time on your style. Plunge in! Say something—the style will take care of itself!"

"But it won't. That's just the trouble! You see, Shireen, I haven't your blazing imagination, nor any flair for the exotic and gnomic things you write."

"Thank God! One competitor less."

"I never was meant to be a writer at all—"

"Says Arnold, I suppose!"

Naomi shook her head. "Not so much, nowadays, but *I* know it. I can compare myself with other writers."

"Nonsense! No one can criticise and tabulate them-selves impartially. They are bound either to over or under estimate."

"Even so, I know I have no original thoughts, no brilliant thoughts, no profound or ennobling thoughts. As you say, they would carry themselves. But my little utterances must be artistically set or they would be worse than tawdry. That's why I am giving so much attention to style."

"And is your new book polished and burnished to the last comma?"

"As well as I know how."

"Does Arnold like it?"

"I haven't read any of it to him."

"Hm-m-m," observed Shireen, "that means he wouldn't! Does Hugo like it?"

Naomi thought that he liked the idea, but considered she lacked force.

"I'm not surprised. Hugo is fond of a raw beef salad. Delicacy and lavender-scented antimaccasars are about on a par, in his opinion."

"Well, I don't want to be coarse," Naomi said. "I don't want my book to be one of the ten worst smellers."

Shireen sat up in mock indignation. "Excuse me, madam, but aren't you standing on my foot?"

Naomi laughed. "I didn't mean to. Because a book sells by the hundred thousand, it does not necessarily follow that it reeks."

Shireen complained that Naomi's implication denied a best seller the title to literature. "My *Child of Passion*, for example... Come now, be frank!"

"Well, I don't call it literature," confessed Naomi. "The masses of people who clutched at it almost before the ink was dry, wouldn't have enjoyed it, had it been. But it's a glowing story, Shireen. A flaming piece of occultism. If it were better written, I would class it with such a book as— let me see—as Peter Ibbetson and, oh, my dear, I envy you your gift and your persistent use of it."

"The final persistence of the saints," said Shireen, half annoyed. "I am humility itself, and grateful e'en though you praise me with faint damns."

And then Hugo and Julius came in.

——

"Didn't you bring anybody else, Doolydear?" pouted his wife, after having been kissed by both men. "You know, if there's one thing more than another that stifles my creative impulses, it's being bored."

"Gracious lady," murmured Hugo.

"Well, there's no use pretending. *You* want Naomi..."

"And I follow an inviolable rule never to make love to one woman in the presence of another," remarked Julius, helping himself to a large piece of cake.

"You never did make love," complained his wife, with petulance that was not wholly feigned.

"Emotions, nothing. Primitive appetites, if you like. Eating, drinking, sleeping—look at you now! That's your third piece of cake. Doolydear, you're disgusting... and your waistline... What would you think of me if I looked like that?"

"Oh, my love! Incomparable woman!" Murmured Julius, dropping on one knee beside her. "Is it true? And when will it be?"

"Beast!" said Shireen, flicking him lightly across the face. "You will shock our puritan guests."

Julius dusted off his knees, retrieved his cup and sat down. "You asked me what I'd think," he said, "and that's what!... Oh, by the way, here's your new contract... and, yes, a statement of royalties. May I please have a dollar, my dear?"

Shireen uncurled herself, flew to him and perched on his knee. "Tell me at once," she cried, "did they agree, and are the sales bigger than they were last year? No details, please, Doolydear, they always give me a headache. But tell me the facts—the facts!"

"Everything is O.K. I got the terms you wanted, and the sales are thirty per cent better. What it is to shine in the art of selling!" These scenes were not unfamiliar to Naomi. Shireen Dey's business was public property. She had no private life. At first the absence of reserve offended Naomi, but by degrees she grew to envy the uncomplicated honesty of it all. The contempt she had felt for Julius Dey when their friendship was young, faded away as reason was brought to bear on the situation. The Dey ménage was not unlike the echo of an ancient matriarchate in which the division of labour between the two sexes was reversed. What housekeeping was done, fell to Julius' share. Had there been children, he would have been their nurse and companion. Shireen not only earned their living, but took the position that is usually accorded to a man, in the present-day civilisation. Everything revolved around *her* needs or desires. Her work was paramount. Julius felt no humiliation in serving her to the obliteration of his own personality. He was the wife; she the husband. He was her business manager, kept her books, arranged her contracts and supervised her sales. He was the buffer who stood between her and the jars that occurred on life's uneven highway.

"And why," Naomi asked herself, "should there be anything ignominious, from the masculine viewpoint, about this arrangement? If Shireen could provide more easily and abundantly than her husband, why should she not be assisted to do so? If, therefore, *she* proved to be a better man than Arnold, why should she not demand a similar arrangement in her own household?"

Subservience to custom was the answer, in a general sense. Particularly, Arnold's temperament stood in the way. She knew that he could never tolerate a condition which made him less than master in his own home, and it was this attitude that Naomi could never hope to subdue. Indeed, she had not yet persuaded herself that her own talents justified such a demand.

———

"You look very tired," Hugo commented, as they left the Dey's house.

"The outward expression of invisible rage, perhaps," she answered.

"No," he said. "You are exhausted by the futility of fluttering. The old starling idea, you know!"

Naomi admitted there was something in it. Hugo had a curious faculty of penetrating her mind and expressing things which hitherto had been but vague emotions. "Perhaps you're right," she said. "The strain of continual control, the effort of self-discipline *is* exhausting. Besides, at the moment, I am consumed with envy of Shireen Dey."

"You needn't envy her! You could command all that she does. I would be to you all that Julius is to her—and more, Naomi. The constructive value of a love like mine, of a union such as ours is bound to be, is incalculable. Can't you realise what this repression is meaning in your work? What it is denying you?"

Always, she felt the force of Hugo's argument. In theory, it was unassailable. He was right. Self-control and self-discipline drained her of energy which would have carried her far had it been directed in other channels. Not that she was uncomfortably conscious of physical fatigue. She still possessed strength to prepare food, make beds and bear trays up and down stairs. But weariness crept over her mind. It was no longer alert to follow her direction. The *élan* and joyousness that was so spontaneous a few years ago, now required careful coercion. She often felt that in calling upon life's springs for refreshment, she found that they had gone dry.

"You work so hard to be happy," Hugo continued. "That's foolish, for happiness comes without effort to those who have the courage to take it. Oh, Naomi," he cried, in the tone that vibrated in the very soul of her, "don't waste any more time in following this phantom of duty. Believe me, my darling, it will lead you nowhere!"

"Doing one's duty is not to be termed following a phantom," she objected.

"In your case it is. I don't deny the need to perform one's duty, you know. I only contend that the Catechism neglected to point out the direction in which one's supreme duty lay."

"There's the Duty to God, and to one's neighbour…"

"Quite so, but vastly more important is the Duty to One-self."

"Oneself?" echoed Naomi, intrigued by this new idea.

"Exactly. Why should you think yourself less in need of consideration than the woman across the street? Let's drag in the poor, overworked Soul. Who is going to develop yours if you don't develop it yourself? You aren't fit to be your brother's keeper if you don't prove a fitness to keep yourself."

"Yes, but—"

"This business of voluntary martyrdom… Were you dispensing Destiny, would you condemn your neighbour to bear the burden of denial that you impose upon yourself? Would it please you to watch the spirits of all the other sensitive women being broken? Would you provide for them," he added, with the shadow of a smile, "an Uncle Toby and an Arnold?"

Naomi shook her head.

"Well, then, why treat yourself worse than you would treat a fellow being? Will you hand over a crushed and broken creature to your Maker? Do you believe that it is virtuous to maim your body? No? Well, where is the virtue in wounding and maiming your soul?"

"The old idea of salvation through suffering, I suppose."

"Hindu mothers sacrificed their babies by laying them in the lap of red-hot metal gods, flinging them under the Juggernaut, and into the Ganges. Do you think that such sacrifice was acceptable in the sight of God?"

"No, we've outgrown that. Besides, that wasn't *self*-sacrifice."

"There is no *self*-sacrifice," said Hugo. "There is no sacrifice that does not involve pain to someone else. Do you think Christ's mother, and His closest friends enjoyed his Crucifixion?"

"Hugo!"

"Hear me through," cried Hugo who, like all men, disliked having his judgement anticipated and his pronouncements taken as read. "Would you crawl into the presence of your Maker shrivelled, withered, joyless? Would you dare?"

Naomi looked straight ahead, saying nothing.

"Picture it... He is waiting to receive you—to hear an accounting of your stewardship... 'What is this?' He asks, as you drag wearily to the foot of the Throne.

"'A human being,' a spirit answers. 'It is Naomi Lennox.'

"'And what have you done to the lovely body I gave into your keeping?' God demands. 'By whose leave did you ill-treat that which you merely held in trust for Me? Where is Happiness, that joyous companion I appointed to walk with you throughout your span of life? Answer me!'

"'Master,' you whisper, raising dull eyes, 'Happiness bade fair to possess me, and I, fearing to be possessed, killed the companion you appointed to walk with me... It was then that my body withered—'

"'And your soul?!'

"' My soul?' you cry. 'Is it withered too? Is it not then, refined, purified, more acceptable in your sight, by reason of all my pain?'

"'What philosophy is this? Are you perchance a Yogi, deceiving yourself into the belief that only by suffering and the exclusion of Joy, salvation is to be obtained?'

"'Variation of that idea does prevail,' you answer. 'Were we not set an example by the Crucifixion?'

"'No,' He thunders. 'Naomi Lennox, hearken to my words! I am not desirous of human sacrifice. I can't endure the sight of pain. And when next you choose a perfect body as a Temple for the Soul which is a part of Me, and which ultimately must return to Me, I charge you to hold it sacred; care for it tenderly even as you cherish your loved ones. I am Love. Fanatics have misrepresented Me as a monster of cruelty and hate. They have taken My name in vain. They have taught that suffering and anguish are virtues. But I had not thought that you would be so deceived.'

"'Is it then right to be happy,' you murmur, 'to keep Joy and Laughter in our lives?'

"'If only My disciples would preach that gospel! If only the world would understand... Why do little birds sing—flowers yield their perfume? Why does the sky paint the glory of the sunrise and the promise of the sunset? Why do babes laugh and gurgle in their cradles? Why the muted music of My forest streams and the symbolic grandeur of the storm? Why to women wear fair forms, if not to experience every phase of happiness? Could not I as well have made mankind unsightly, crippled Nature, withheld Beauty from the world? Could not I as well have given beasts dominion over the earth and suppressed the rise of man?

"'Think you, O sinful woman, that I enjoy the waste of martyr's blood, and that a broken spirit is pleasing in My sight?'

"'I have been so instructed,' you reply. 'I had been taught that only by the subduing of the flesh might the spirit shine; that only by the flagellation of the body might the soul expand.'

"'False Doctrine! You have encouraged sighs instead of laughter; darkness rather than light. You have retarded the progress of the world by restricting your own efficiency, and adding to Humanity's shoulder the weight of your own unnecessary pain. Leave me! I would be alone with my disappointment. I weep, for I had cherished such high hopes of you.'

"That's very like what will happen when you go to Heaven," said Hugo, in conclusion.

"But striving for happiness is such a selfish pursuit," Naomi argued.

"My God!" breathed Hugo. "Isn't striving for misery, worse? Besides, as I previously remarked, there is no *self*-sacrifice. By sacrificing *yourself*, are you not torturing *me*?"

"By surrendering to you, would I not be torturing Arnold and Uncle Toby?"

"I doubt it! But, in any case, your care of them prevents them from making any sacrifice, and consequently, according to your doctrine, you are imperiling their hopes of salvation. You are making life too smooth for them."

"There's Arnold, now," said Naomi. "Don't come any farther."

"When can I see you, then, alone?"

"I don't know. I'll have to telephone."

"Will you come out with me to-night?"

"Don't insist, Hugo, please. I've a sort of a feeling that I can work."

"I'm going West on Tuesday—Naomi, come!"

"I don't know. I—I—" she struggled for self control, glancing apprehensively at Arnold, who had slackened his pace in order to avoid a meeting with Hugo Main. "I will telephone in the morning," and she left him, hurrying forward to meet her husband.

CHAPTER 5

THEY walked in silence, Naomi forcibly conscious of Arnold's displeasure. Shireen's words came back to her. She felt that he was scolding her in his mind. If he would only say something—explode, give her an opportunity for defending herself.

"I've been over to Shireen Dey's," she said, trying to overcome the absurd sense of guilt that had settled upon her.

"So I gathered," returned Arnold, falling a step behind to allow a group of elderly ladies to pass.

"What politeness," remarked one of them, loudly enough to be overheard.

"She has exceeded her last year's sales by a third," Naomi persevered.

"Indeed."

"And she's got the very contract she wanted from her motion picture people. Julius was so pleased. He has been working at it for ever so long."

"Ah."

"You know," Naomi struggled on, "writing so much—and so successfully—as she does, entails an incredible amount of business management. Julius is really a very busy man."

Instantly, she realised her mistake. Although reference to Dey's activities had been made in absolute innocence, with no motive other than combating the frigidity of the atmosphere, Naomi was conscious that Arnold saw it as a direct reflection upon himself, a covert suggestion that he should perform similar services for her. Before she could dispel his impression, he broke in.

"I should think he could find a worthier pastime. If work is neither interesting nor necessary, sport offers a gentlemanly occupation. He could be no end of a golfer or cricketer without forfeiting his self-respect. But this footling with a woman's contracts—bah! Naomi, I wonder that you can bother with such people!"

"But Arnold, I assure you Shireen couldn't attend to that mass of detail herself. Why even my pitiful little correspondence gets beyond me at times. I have to lay everything else aside until I can dispose of it. What must hers be? Hundreds of letters—from people who have loved her books and want to tell her so; new publishers who hope to put her on their lists; motion picture people of all kinds, agents, producers, actors—why, you can't imagine! Julius maintains a regular, well-ordered business."

"I'm sorry to hear it."

There wasn't the least suggestion of "red" in his voice; he might have been referring to the illness of a friend. But there was in his manner of speaking a quality that made Naomi think of a hermit immured in a tight-shuttered house, determined to see nothing that took place outside and to hear as little as possible. Often, when she tried to argue with him, she was conscious of a mental barricade that he flung up between them and through which the meaning behind her words could never penetrate. He listened with his ears rather than with his mind.

"I don't presume to dictate to you in the matter of your friends, my dear," he continued, as they mounted the steps of their home, "but I think you know that I don't care for the Deys or any of their associates, so if you keep up this intimacy under those conditions, you must forgive me for not pretending a vital interest in their affairs."

Naomi put dinner on the table, and then, feeling an un-usual assertiveness, returned to the discussion.

"We were speaking of Shireen and Julius," she said. "You told me that you didn't like them. Well, I'm curious to know what you would feel if I objected to some of your friends."

"You would be within your rights, of course," defended Uncle Toby.

But Naomi demanded a more definite answer. Assuming that Arnold would admit to friendship only those whom he considered worthy, would he not feel a sense of disappoint-ment at her lack of perception, discrimination, if she failed to find them as delightful?

"Yes, it's quite possible," conceded Arnold gravely.

"And would you admit a lack of perception on your part, when you found yourself unresponsive to my friends?"

"Take care my boy!" warned Uncle Toby, playfully, as one who is anxious to keep the peace between two quarrel-some children. "Our girl's a first-rate debater. She'll drive you into a trap."

"Why certainly—provided I considered them worthy of your friendship."

"By which you imply that I have not your fine perception in the choosing of friends."

"Look at the point without bias or prejudice. You must admit the charge. Not you only, but all women. Their judgements are inevitably faulty. It's a matter of constitu-tion, not principle."

"But Arnold... such sweeping statements! They paralyse me. I can scarcely think... such prodigious absurdity... In the first place, why 'inevitably faulty?'"

Playing with a few crumbs, Arnold gave the impression

of gathering a handful of hysterical incoherencies and holding them steady upon the table. "Because," he said, "in the nature of things, women have been denied the opportunity for estimating and judging men. Until very recently, as time is counted, they have been sheltered and cloistered creatures, spared the necessity of doing any intensive thinking for themselves."

"Even so, at least you will grant them an intuition."

"Too much. Intuition is a poor substitute for reason. I venture to say it is fifty per cent unreliable."

"Then you stubbornly hold that women are mentally inferior to men?"

"I should scarcely like to put it that way," returned Arnold. "'Inferior' is an unpleasant and misleading word. I should say that women's minds are not so highly developed, which is quite a different matter, as they themselves are quite different beings. But, speaking of friends, I have asked our curling team to drop in this evening, most informally. Do you think you can manage something—anything, in the way of a light supper?

Supper? And she had been trying so sedulously to nurture the little flame which told her she would be able to write to-night! A cold despair took possession of her. She foresaw the evening squandered, and, looking further ahead, she visualised to-morrow morning occupied with clearing away the debris...

She was tempted to cry out, "Oh, Arnold, not to-night! There are thoughts knocking against the door of my mind that must be released... By to-morrow, they will have gone back into their little caves and I won't be able to coax them out."

And in her imagination, she could hear his amazed retort, "But, my dear girl, I'm not asking you to interfere with your work. Surely a few sandwiches?... a pot of coffee?... and there's plenty of cake, here on the table!"

The impulse to protest died almost as soon as it was born. She knew from bitter experience that Arnold could never understand. He regarded any form of imaginative effort in the same light as the tangible routine work of his own office. That is to say, he was prepared to admit that interruptions or delays were annoying. Should he be called from a search through his file, he could appreciate the fact that time would be lost in a review of work that had already been done, but, after all, the document for which he searched was there, it only remained for him to turn over a sufficient number of papers to find it again. He could not, therefore, put himself into Naomi's place, nor feel the force of her argument when she explained that an idea, creeping shyly into the realm of consciousness, must be trailed and captured, otherwise it passes out into the limbo of neglected thoughts and is probably lost forever. He could not understand that delays and interruptions in creative work were always productive of mental chaos, and were frequently fatal.

Naomi had tried to "be normal," to adapt herself to his views and the conditions that bound her life. When Arnold came to her with the proposition that he would take Uncle Toby for a long walk on Sunday afternoon so that she might have an uninterrupted time for her work, she tried, conscientiously, to produce results, in order to show her appreciation. But, somehow, nothing "came" on Sunday afternoon. Nothing, that is, save a racking headache due to the nervous strain of trying to accomplish the impossible. For a long time she would not admit that the thing was an impossibility. She tried to acquire the habit of writing as one acquires the habit of eating.

"If you need any help," he called to her, "let me know. But nothing elaborate, mind. Don't go to any trouble."

———

The visitors had all assembled before Naomi had finished washing the dinner dishes. There was one alleviating circumstance, however, for which she was duly thankful. She was not expected to receive the men, nor to take any part in the evening's entertainment. Arnold liked to posture somewhat after the manner of an oriental potentate—a man, independent of women and able to command them. "Stag parties" were proof unto him that he was a devil of a fellow, and he even allowed himself the recounting of a wanly pornographic story when "out with the boys."

After the dishes were finished, Naomi made the sandwiches. Then she prepared the coffee and arranged cups and plates and glasses on a tray. And all the while, she kept telling herself that she wasn't tired… and that she mustn't be sorry for herself nor feel that she was put upon… that presently, she would go upstairs and do an hour's work before the party broke up and Arnold came to bed.

Instead of which, she tidied up her bureau drawers and laid out her husband's suit ready for the presser in the morning.

———

When Naomi heard Arnold coming upstairs, she closed her eyes and lay perfectly still.

"Oh, were you asleep, my dear?" asked her husband turning on the lights. "Dozing, eh? It's only—er—" (rasping the winder of his watch) "—it's only just twelve. I got them off early."

"Not, I hope, on my account."

The words were unintentionally sarcastic, but Arnold was insensitive to the irony in them. From the bathroom, he disclaimed any consideration for her, and in conclusion remarked that it was a very jolly party. Naomi murmured a languid satisfaction and longed to ask him to be silent.

"Bancroft's such a rattling good fellow. I like him more each time I see him. By the way, he brought a friend to-night. Some chap named Sharp, from the West, I believe. Said to me, as he was leaving—but perhaps you heard…?"

Naomi had, but she said nothing.

"It was just as they were going—he turned to me and asked, 'I suppose you can't claim the distinction of being related to Naomi Lennox, the writer?' Said I, 'That all depends upon whether you call a wife a relation or an infliction.' The boys were vastly amused, and *he* said… Oh well, he said all the eminently fitting and pleasant bromidisms. But his manner *was* funny. He became embarrassingly deferential towards me. You would have laughed… such absurdity!"

Through closed eyes, Naomi watched him arrange his clothes on the *chaise longue* and kneel beside the bed. He knelt there an unusually long time and she wondered what he was praying…

To herself, she said, savagely, "There you go… bowing the head and bending the knee before the remote and jealous being you call master… a being who knows not love, but demands eternal sacrifice and suffering… There you go… grovelling on your face and calling yourself a sinner… and not believing a word of it!

"But you are… you are! You don't know God… the true, living God You don't know the God of sunshine and flowers and laughter and gay human hearts. The idol you worship is a heathen deity… like Shiva, the Destroyer, and you would propitiate him by offering the broken body of others... Presently, you will come to me... a woman you profess to exalt, but actually degrade... and without consideration for *my* physical or spiritual path, you will make me your THING! I serve you with my hands all day and with my body at night... and you preach to me of sacrifice...

"Go on... pray... pray that you may never be healed of your comfortable blindness..."

He rose and eased a passing irritation at the waistline, snapped off the lights and opened the window.

Naomi lay rigidly, scarcely breathing. She was trying to force upon his inner consciousness the realisation of her renitence, her aversion...

The effort was unavailing. Arnold came towards her, a great black bulk against the thick background. He hand groped along the quilt until he found the opening between the two sheets, then he turned back the covers and crowded in beside his wife.

"Bancroft was telling me about meeting some of the new Laborites in London last month," he chattered.

Naomi wasn't listening. "How can he talk?" she thought. "Why doesn't he feel that I can't endure his touch, that I *hate* him?"

She was conscious of a wild impulse to beat him with her fists, to kick, to scream. Her nostrils were assailed by the faint odour of toilet water and toothpaste. She tried to move her head. Arnold's pyjamas were buttoned tight to the throat. They were thick and fuzzy. The soles of his feet were hot. His hands were efficient and determined.

He was crushing the breath from her body. He was ravishing her soul. Without tenderness or by-your-leave...

"...and he said that Sir—er—at the moment the name has escaped me—as a Member of the Cabinet, would..."

Naomi felt deadly ill. The smothering blackness seemed to lift her as in a vice and whirl her round and round. She gasped. She was choking.

"...and men of his calibre are bringing exactly the right element into the Government, so Bancroft says... which means..."

He talked on, in broken, jerky sentences. Insensible to the sacredness of his privilege, he was unintentionally brutal in his abuse of it. He would have been shocked to realise that his request for the most ordinary trifle would have been met with greater gentleness and courtesy than he displayed in demanding the most precious possession his wife had to give. Nor had he taken into consideration the fact that a different aspect on his part would have stirred this woman's emotion into a living, joyous flame. No! He reduced the supreme act of love to a mere physical function which he performed as soullessly as he took his morning bath.

"... Bancroft was most optimistic. It was a treat to hear him talk..."

Silence.

Freedom came to Naomi with offensive suddenness. There was in Arnold's abrupt departure that which made her sense of humiliation and defilement complete. Even as she drew the disordered covers over her, she heard him say from his own bed—

"Jove, but I'm tired! A lot of fellows talking... one scarcely realises the strain at the time." He yawned. "Night, my dear. Sleep well..."

Naomi buried her face in her pillow, overcome by self-loathing. Hugo's words rang in her mind...

"Prostitution cannot be sanctified—either by custom or the church. The woman who submits to an unloved husband, is not a whit better than her professional sister of the street."

She felt soiled... unclean... unclean... And there was to-morrow night... and the next... and the weeks, and years... And Arnold's God approved of him, and gave him fortitude and strength...

Marriage, to him, meant this incontestable right over the woman he had taken to himself, and the idea that Naomi might hold divergent views never occurred to him.

An irritating rhythm of sound caught her ear. She held her breath and listened.

Arnold was snoring.

CHAPTER 6

IN THE morning, everything went wrong. The telephone began to ring before she was dressed.

Arnold cast a button and she cut her finger sewing it on. Winter had put forth a last spiteful effort to thwart the coming of spring, and the water-pipes were frozen. So was the milk.

Breakfast was a hideous scramble, during which Arnold kept his watch in the table and his eyes on his watch. His remarks were sympathetic, but his manner belied them, for Naomi felt that, beneath his impenetrable cloak of urbanity, he was accusing her of negligence, lack of foresight; blaming her for this *contretemps* which, by some inscrutable process of masculine reasoning, he felt was her fault, and which in an efficiently managed household, would never have been allowed to occur.

"It might be just as well to provide against these triffling annoyances," he said, "by filling some pans with water each night and by taking a little extra milk. I seem to remember, in our home we used to scald it to keep it from turning sour. This bacon's very thick, isn't it?"

Naomi did not speak, although she knew that her silence would be misinterpreted. In the old days, Arnold had frequently rebuked her for sullenness, unable to distinguish between this trait, which he despised, and the triumph of self-control which saved his wife from bitter and savage recrimination.

Arnold was never sullen. Naomi had to admit it. But she reminded herself, as she filled his cup, that he had little or no provocation. "Sullenness," in her case, was the result of misunderstanding, inconsideration, unjust accusation—utter inability on her husband's part to see that his exactions were both impracticable and absurd. Scald the milk! Fill pans with water!

He wouldn't argue. He wouldn't listen to explanations. Explanations were, to him, excuses, and he hated people to make excuses. He leaped to a conclusion and, disregarding contributory causes, fastened upon the effect.

"I prefer to get at the root of the matter," he was fond of saying, and having got there, the incident, for him, was closed.

"We've no water. We've no milk," his manner implied. "There's the situation in a nutshell. It's for you to see that I'm not inconvenienced like this again…"

But he wasn't sullen.

Having not the smallest desire for food. Naomi sat at the table and tried to eat. Arnold disliked being forced to feel that she served him. He preferred to live in the comfortable delusion that meals just happen—of course, accidents are brought about!—that a household runs in its routine grooves as easily as twilight follows day. He couldn't bear to hear the creaking of machinery or to come face to face with the fact that someone had to keep all those wheels in motion. He confessed to Naomi that all pleasure in his first trip to England was destroyed after seeing the stokers at work in the hold.

He folded up his napkin neatly, brushed a few crumbs into his plate, took up his watch and went into the hall.

"What time will you have lunch?" he inquired, with the implication that under present disordered conditions, he was willing to adjust himself to her arrangements, even at great personal inconvenience.

"At the usual time," she said, "if that suits you."

"I'll make it suit," he returned, politely, and then, with his hand on the door, he observed, "Wasn't it fortunate that I insisted upon Uncle Toby's staying in bed this morning? He's spared all this confusion. I do hope that both the milkman and the plumbers will have come before he's ready for his breakfast. I hope so, too, for your sake, my dear."

"Thank you," murmured Naomi. "Good-bye."

He was gone. Naomi stood perfectly still, her eyes closed, her head thrown back, her hands tight-clenched at her sides.

"I can't endure it," she said to herself. "I can't go on."

She began to tremble. Her heart thumped in great uneven beats as though something inside her were sobbing. She would have given almost anything to cry. It was fortunate that Uncle Toby had been spared this confusion!

A spasm of rage seized her. She swayed and caught at the bannister for support. Why should she spend her life protecting two men from the countless annoyances that beset her every hour? Why should she exhaust herself in a continuous effort to play up to Arnold's temperamental variations and, as Shireen said, "woo him into a happy frame of mind?" Why shouldn't he sometimes adapt himself to her vagaries of temperament and, by so doing reduce her domestic tribulations?

"You must learn how to take me," he had once said, half playfully, "and when you understand my moods and discover how to deal with them, we will get along like a pair of turtle doves."

Sublime egotism! She thought, bitterly. Superb masculinity! When had he ever tried to understand her moods and learn how to deal with them? When had he ever troubled to order his conduct, so that it would relieve, rather than increase the friction? If he had ever done so, the result was not visible to the unassisted eye. On the contrary, at the very times when she was most sorely tried, when her nerves were raw and quivering, his manner, if not his actual words, reproached her. "Take yourself in hand, my dear," he seemed to say. "You are behaving childishly. All of us must practice self-control, submit to discipline." And she had surrendered... surrendered... so that her whole life had become an expression of the text, "Not my will, but thine, be done."

But she couldn't go on. She lacked strength to continue the struggle. In the old days, she used to believe that Arnold was always right and that she should compress herself to fit the limited confines of his hard-and-fast conventionalism. But now she knew that however right he might be, she could never accommodate herself happily to his narrow standards and that henceforth her outlook would always be at variance with the viewpoint that he held.

There was the case of the silver spoon. Several months after their marriage, Naomi discovered that one of the spoons was missing. Untried in the fires of connubial purgatory, she made the unfortunate mistake of mentioning the circumstance to her husband. The result was as startling as it was unexpected.

"A silver spoon?" echoed Arnold. "Not one of our wedding presents?"

She flushed and shook her head.

"Not one of *my mother's* silver spoons?" he persisted.

"Yes,"

"Lost?"

"I—I—can't find it."

"How long has it been missing?"

She didn't know.

"You don't know? But Naomi, really... I can scarcely believe you. Was it there yesterday?"

She couldn't say.

"Extraordinary! Simply incredible! Don't you count your silver every morning?"

Vainly she tried to show him the absurdity of such an occupation. He wouldn't listen. His mother had made a tour of the house every day—inspecting silver, linen, china, provisions. Not a bottle of jam could be removed from its place in the cellar without her being aware of it, he boasted. "By this system, she had silver to leave us," said Arnold. "Whereas *you* might allow half the house to be carried away and never miss it."

"Housekeeping was different in those days," explained Naomi, bewildered by his lack of understanding. "Like everything else, it has undergone a change of method. The chatelaine of the middle ages, dealing out the day's rations from a locked buttery, is as obsolete as a spinning wheel."

"But you *must* keep track of our possessions," insisted her husband. "You *must* know from day to day where we stand!"

"Do you count your office supplies each morning? Do you measure the ink in the big bottle, weigh your boxes of paper and check your envelopes?"

"Now you are growing excited and childish," reproved Arnold. "That is not at all the same thing."

"But I assure you, it is."

"Excuse me, Naomi, it is not. I have something else to do. You haven't. Housekeeping is your job. If you allow things—valuable things—to disappear—well, it is obvious that you don't *keep* house! However, my dear, we will say no more about it. Experience is a hard teacher and I am sure you will profit by this lesson." He patted her tight-clenched hand and smiled, somewhat pontifically. "We'll have to re-member to limit our dinner parties to eleven, or perhaps I can pretend that coffee is bad for my nerves."

How she hated him for that last—that seeming to make

the best of her mistake when, from her point of view, she had done no wrong at all. It was an attitude that became fixed as the years went on, and failing to dispel it, Naomi surrendered to it in silence that was always misconstrued as sullenness.

———

With a frank disregard of time—thus establishing their status as members of the leisured class—the plumbers, who had promised to come early, did not put in an appearance until nearly noon. Naomi could make no headway in the kitchen, so she emptied ashtrays, swept burned matches from the floor and cleared out the grate.

"This is the last time," she kept telling herself as she poked at the dead, grey coals. "I simply won't go on. Not because the work is killing me—no—it's Arnold... his utter lack of comprehension where the routine of the house is concerned... his kingly acceptance of my labours without the remotest conception of what they cost me, and the sublime way in which he takes my cheerful service for granted... It's all wrong! It isn't fair!"

Hugo's half-mocking, half-sympathetic face rose before her. She wondered what, after eleven years of married life, would be his attitude towards her. Would he gracefully resign himself to an unappreciative acceptance of her ministrations, requiring, in a polite and passive way, that she sacrifice herself mentally and physically to provide a comfortable, an economical home for him?

"Are all men alike?" she asked herself, "or is Arnold a conspicuous exception to the rule?"

As a matter of fact, Arnold did not like to see her perform household tasks. Few things irritated him more than to come home and surprise his wife at work. He wished her to be waiting idly in the living room or on the verandah, utterly disassociated from the less ornamental phases of their existence. Hugo, discovering this characteristic in the early days of their acquaintance, did not allow it to pass without comment.

"Exactly!" he blazed. "In the first place, a pretty woman is easier on the eye than one who shows the effect of culinary labours. In the second place, the average man can kid himself into believing any blasted thing he pleases, and seeing his woman all dressed up—like a horse on parade—he says to himself, 'Ha, ha! I have made this creature the queen of my castle!' which titillates his vanity and gives him the devil of a fine opinion of himself. He's a generous provider, forsooth, and a damned shrewd chooser... for, of course, he goes to the grave secure in the belief that any one of a dozen women would have flopped into his arms with little or no encouragement.

"The reverse side of the picture is devastating to his self-respect. He is not only offended by the spectacle of his woman flushed and greasy and unbecomingly garmented, but he sees himself as the creator of a scullery-maid rather than a queen! His own status is lowered. He is rebuked by his vanity—some call it conscience—and forced to the realisation that he is not such a fine fellow after all. Patently, he is not an adequate provider, and worse than that, he has been a damned bad chooser. Look at the woman Jones got... he could quite as easily have had her!"

Naomi suggested that he was hard on men.

"You bet your boots, I am," he had agreed, violently. "I know 'em too well, that's my trouble. Soon as I hear a fellow hold forth on women's rights, equal wage, and such like, I put him in the 'Pedestal' pigeon-hole and despise him. He's the sort of man who kneels to a woman in the drawing-room and then flies to his club to avoid seeing her slave for him in the kitchen ... He's the sort of man who forgets that he married for mental stimulation and spiritual ecstasy. His wife is a neglected drudge throughout the day, and conspicuous on his horizon only between the hours of ten P.M. and morning. God forfend that I should ever put a woman on a pedestal!"

How sincere were these explosive utterances, Naomi asked herself, and how would they work out in daily practice? How, exactly, would they apply to her—if—if she went away with Hugo?

They saw one another so seldom. There never seemed to be sufficient time to reach the end of a discussion. He drew radiant pictures of their life together, but she was unable to follow him for lack of details which would go towards making up that association.

"We are always left hanging in mid-air, so to speak," he complained, "We never seem to get anywhere... Are you coming to me, or are you not?"

She couldn't decide. She was racked by indecision. There were so many things that she wanted to discuss and have settled. This very matter, she reflected, clapping her hands softly together and holding her breath to avoid inhaling the dust—how would they work out the problems of their daily existence? How solve the riddle of the myriad *little things*?

If she could only feel as some women did in the circumstances, that by going to Hugo, life's ultimate goal would be attained! If she could only arrive at the state of mind where nothing else mattered... Unfortunately for her, so many things mattered. She would have to make so many arrangements... That was the part she hated—thinking of Arnold and Uncle Toby and of leaving them provided for and comfortable. If only she could be kidnapped some night and made to go...

At this point, a faint whisper, that Naomi called conscience, lifted up its voice in warning. She tried to analyse it and failed. Hugo had converted her to the belief that in leaving Arnold she was committing no wrong—that freedom was her right—and he offered her that freedom. But could she grasp and hold his offering? Was it not, after all, a myth, a pixie, a will o' the wisp that flitted beyond the darkest reaches of a woman's life and would not be overtaken? Was she not striving after the unattainable—implacably bound by that inherent, instinctive woman-thing that surrenders, even protestingly, to the domination of man? Would it not develop that presently Hugo's requirements, though immeasurably different from those of Arnold, would clutch and fetter her with virtually the same chains as those she now wore? It was this that worried her and made her indecisive.

She carried the ashes to the kitchen and was revolted by the unsightly collection of unwashed dishes on the table. And presently others would be added to the number, and that would mean she must spend most of the afternoon in disposing of them. And then, there would be dinner to prepare.

"I won't do it anymore," she cried aloud. "It isn't fair. I'll have a maid. Arnold *must* agree. I'll *make* him listen—show him a chart of the day's routine... He'll have to admit the unreasonableness of a system that leaves him entirely free to pursue his calling and at the same time enslaves me to the point where I can't proceed with mine at all..."

While rebellion was hot within her, she telephoned an advertisement to the papers, and immediately felt a shade uneasy at what she had done. Somehow, she seemed to have committed herself to a definite and radical change; a change that, by reason of her aggressiveness, took on a somewhat unpleasant aspect. Naomi did not flinch from the truth, even though it condemned her. She admitted that a good maid would be a means to an end… in imagination, she saw a competent and trustworthy woman moving quietly about the house and commanding, by virtue of her dignified salary, a respect that Arnold Lennox's absent wife had never enjoyed. She hated herself for conjuring up this picture. It gave the whole affair an aspect of sordid scheming. Naomi couldn't scheme to go away with Hugo, no matter how difficult things were at home. If she went—if she ever went—the thing must just happen.

She dragged herself upstairs and began to make Arnold's bed—a victim of that peculiar phase of anger which always attacked her when engaged in this task. She hadn't at all the same feeling when washing his plates or darning his socks. She wished she could summon sufficient courage to leave it unmade or to say to him in the morning—

"While I get our breakfast, my dear, suppose you make our beds. That's a fifty-fifty division of labour and will enable me to get to my machine a few minutes earlier each day."

Such had been Hugo's suggestion.

But she couldn't do it. Once she had tried and the words strangled her. Arnold's displeasured amazement would have caught her like the fumes of a gaseous poison.

Oh, she knew that this was cowardice and that to conquer it she must strive to pluck hyper-sensitiveness from her disposition. Hugo accused her of weakness, and, she suspected, despised her for it. She despised herself. But naïve delicacy prevented her from sinking to the level of the quarrelsome fish-wife who, disregarding the golden rule, achieves her own ends regardless of method, and is happy in their achievement.

Naomi feared that she could never master sufficient courage to take the step that tempted her; and presently,

Hugo would grow impatient of her silly chasséeing, her mental and spiritual curvettings, and go away alone—or with someone else!

She dropped on her own bed, exhausted by the strain of it all. "Surely," she cried, "even the sternest God could not expect me to endure such elemental misery... Surely this is not the price of doing right?" Hugo had said she was being garrotted and that release lay in her own hands. He had accused her of committing a lingering suicide and adjured her to *do something*!

Well she would! She would do something. She would give him up. That would be one thing settled. If she hadn't the courage to go away with him, at least she had sufficient strength of will to give him up. This dangling wasn't fair— to either of them. And, having made this decision, Naomi succumbed to an unprecedented passion of longing for the man. Her very spirit ached for him... the sound of his voice, the touch of his hands... Never had he seemed so necessary to her; so ineffably dear.

CHAPTER 7

UNCLE TOBY rang his bell. Naomi carried up his tray, placed it before him and retreated hurriedly from the room. She was in no condition to bear his affectionate scrutiny.

The plumbers came at last and took possession of her house, exercising resolutely up and down the back stairs and contriving to be just wherever she hoped they were not. After a bit, they shut themselves in the bathroom, presumably because there they could talk undisturbed, there they could smoke and discuss their favourite screen stars and hockey heroes.

Promptly at noon they disappeared, leaving tools, bronze fingerprints and the reek of the blow-torch behind them. But the pipe was not yet thawed.

Naomi went upstairs to make Uncle Toby's bed.

As a rule, some chivalrous spirit prompted him to leave the room while she was working there, although, had the matter been brought to debate, both he and Arnold would have denied a menial aspect to that form of service. On this particular morning, however, when her most ardent wish was for solitude, Uncle Toby elected to keep her company. His cheerful little inanities strained her to the breaking point. She was afraid to speak lest she should laugh, and her laughter surrender to tears.

"How is work going this morning, my love?" the old man asked, examining a fern that grew on the window-sill.

"If you mean writing, I haven't been able to get around to it."

"Oh, well," he responded, brightly, "there's time enough. The day is young. Who was it said that rest is a change of work?"

Naomi hurried downstairs to prepare lunch—a sketchy meal, truly, but in the circumstances, the best she could devise. Arnold regarded it with perceptible if mute disfavour, and in his effort to prove how thoroughly he understood the disorganization of the household, rasped her nerves to the verge of hysteria by such remarks as—

"I *should* like a little mustard with this ham, but owing to a frozen water-piper, we mustn't ask for it, eh, Uncle Toby?"

Or—

"We're lucky to get even this, sir, 'pon my soul, yes... Incredible what trouble too much water, or too little, can occasion. Are you really getting plenty to eat, or can you suggest something else? I am sure Naomi has all sorts of good things tucked away in the pantry..."

And, just as they were about to leave the table, he observed,

"We should be thankful that this doesn't happen often, Uncle Toby, but, I'll wager that our reward will be handsome, at dinner. Indeed, I believe we could do very well with a cup of tea. What do you say, my dear—a nice cup of tea about half-past four, to compensate us for this frugal luncheon?"

Naomi thought she was going to summon sufficient courage to refuse. "Well, Arnold," she forced herself to say, "this afternoon will be very full. I won't be able to make any headway in the kitchen. Even last night's 'remains' are untouched, and the plumbers do leave such a mess."

"I quite understand," interrupted Arnold. "You needn't bother. *I* will make the tea! If you will just see that the cream isn't frozen, I will attend to the rest... 'Mr. Arnold Lennox requests the pleasure of Mr. Thaddeus St. John's company at a tea party, etc.' Goodbye, my dear." He brushed his lips across Naomi's hair. "I hope you will have a happy issue out of all your afflictions. But, whatever happens, don't let household troubles get on your nerves."

Naomi worked without a break until Arnold came in for tea. She had arranged the tray and had seen that the kettle was boiling.

"There now," cried her husband, as he wheeled the tea wagon into the living-room, "we'll show her how to have a party, won't we, Uncle Toby? Women make such a fuss about nothing." He handed her the toaster to adjust, and asked for some jam. "Don't look so forlorn, my dear. All of us meet with temporary inconveniences... 'The man worth while is the man who can smile, when everything goes dead wrong...'"

What could she say? What words could she assemble strong enough to interpret for Arnold the situation as it appeared to her? She did not ask for praise or a too-high estimation of her daily tasks. But she had arrived at the point where the purblind discounting of them was no longer bearable. If Arnold had only said, "I know you've had a devilish day, old girl, so don't worry about us... Tell me what I can do for you..."

Such an attitude, however, was not conceivable. He was firmly convinced that, having poured boiled water into the ready teapot and wheeled the wagon into the living room, he had performed all the necessary labours connected with the ceremony of serving tea. That any previous preparation had taken place, or that any subsequent work was necessary, he waived stubbornly aside. "You can't make labour out of putting a few cups on a tray," he would have said, had Naomi tried to explain, and further argument would have been useless.

He would have understood that she must not be expected to lift heavy burdens, strain at a swollen door or window, scrub floors or beat carpets, but that she should not work all day at lighter tasks, was something he could never appreciate.

In the domestic ménage, Arnold was always the god out of the machine.

"There's a moral taint in a person who is not content to work," he often said. "Of course, I don't include invalids or the physically unfit. But normal human beings should be glad to work. We are God's servants, not mere butterflies."

———

Contrary to popular opinion, the mellowing influence of food on material man is not inevitable. Certainly, Arnold's response to the elaborate meal Naomi had prepared, was negligible when she introduced the subject of her proposed domestic change.

"I confess I am surprised," he said. "Don't you think I might have been consulted?"

Instead of arguing the point, Naomi asked, with a wildly pounding heart, whether he could increase her allowance.

"It's only for a time," she pleaded. "Only till such time as my freedom can be transmuted into revenue. Of course, the experiment may fail. If I can't get a thoroughly competent woman, I am better off with nobody. The average servant would only give me somebody else to look after."

Arnold stiffened. "That's a rather unfortunate expression, isn't it? One would think that your Uncle Toby and I were a pair of bed-ridden dependents."

Naomi felt the chill of despair creeping over her. Already, she stood in the shadow of defeat. It was always like this. Whenever she could nerve herself to a reference to her difficulties, this was the inevitable result. Arnold, after one glance at the obstacle she pointed out to him, shut his eyes, made a wide detour, and not only denied the existence of any obstruction, but straightaway discovered in his own path a barricade at which he halted, and which so far as Naomi was concerned, was quite discreet from the main discussion.

"Oh, Arnold, please don't be so sensitive! Please don't require me to be eternally on my guard with you! Can't you understand that I, too, have human feelings... raw spots... and that you touch them very often?"

"I?"

"Yes, you! Only this afternoon, you took me to task for looking 'forlorn,' when, with just a shade more sympathetic observation, you would have seen that I was tired to the very verge of hysteria..."

Arnold took refuge behind the bulwarks of masculine irrationality. "You make work for yourself, my dear. I've noticed it often. You lose your sense of balance and do so much utterly unnecessary pothering. This, naturally, induces a state of nervous irritability, the effects of which we *all* suffer. Forgive me if I speak plainly, my dear."

"Speak as plainly as you like, but try to listen to me when I allow myself that same infrequent privilege. Listen, I beg of you, with not only your ears, but your mind."

"Aren't you a little theatrical?"

"I can't go on like this. Granted that I *am* nervous and irritable, I must have some relief—some remedy. I am disciplined until the old, self-inflicted scourges no longer bite. I'm not complaining..."

"I'm glad to hear it," cut in her husband, distantly.

He made no effort to conceal his displeasure. Naomi's attitude was, in his eyes, utterly unwarrantable, proof positive of her attempt to evade a proper share of life's responsibilities. Lacking imagination, mentally unmalleable, Arnold could not distinguish between joyous occupation and dilettantism. Enjoying a task, robbed it, for him, of dignity and reduced it to the level of a pastime. Work, he believed, meant honest toil, necessarily irksome; a channel through which the conscientious might express a living principle by submitting to the discipline of duty. He didn't like to work. No one did, morons possibly excepted, and he could not forgive Naomi for straining against the insistent shackles of domesticity.

Never having known the tormenting power of creative impulse, he was unable to appreciate the urge that consumed her. But he did know that in her place, he would have fought against the desire to write, he would have crushed this form of self-indulgence, and returned to tasks that promised less temporal pleasure but surer spiritual redemption.

Besides, to confess a distaste for housekeeping was, in his judgement, a serious indictment against the character of a woman; and a wife inclined towards skill in letters was apt to neglect these numberless little attentions due the man whom she had been enjoined by the Church to cherish.

"No," Naomi repeated, "I'm not complaining... at least, not as you interpret the word... I'm not exaggerating a trifle, or imagining a grievance that does not exist. My case is clear—I never have any leisure. Every hour is crowded with housework or heavy with the necessity to rest. Consider to-day...You may say it was an exception, but I'm tempted to deny it. The exceptions are restful days, especially since Uncle Toby has come home."

"Naomi, for heaven's sake, stop!" Cried her husband. "I can forget that you've said these things, but surely you—a right-minded woman—never can! Leaving aside your natural affection, leaving aside the claim of relationship, which I trust you acknowledge, his financial contribution is something you can't overlook."

"Ah!"

Naomi uttered a little cry. She was not prepared for the mention of this, the most delicate topic that could arise between them. Years ago, she had discovered Arnold's reluctance to talk about money... particularly his lack of it; had learned that it humiliated him to confess his limitations. His theory—for others—amounted to this: that a bare sufficiency was a little more than man actually required, and in all her deprivations and denials, Naomi was supposed to prefer doing without those things he could not provide. An expression on her part, of anything less than contentment was tantamount to criticism; was construed as an attitude that accused him of being both ungenerous and incapable.

He had been drastically opposed to taking anyone into their home as a means of relieving the financial stringency, and only by stressing Uncle Toby's helplessness, had Naomi gained his consent. Having given it, however, it was characteristic of him to extend the invitation himself, and offer the old man in all sincerity, an unconditional home for the remainder of his days. How the expense of a semi-invalid was going to be met, was a problem he gave himself no pains to consider. To have accepted a monthly cheque would have made him feel like an inn-keeper and denied him the gratification of believing himself a hospitable and large-hearted man. Ordinarily, he preferred to ignore Uncle Toby's contribution to the household, to dismiss it completely from his calculations, a circumstance which Naomi was glad to concur. For, in referring to it, Arnold's manner held a covert suggestion of repugnance at the indelicacy that enabled her to accept it; or a satisfaction that whatever her other annoyances, at least she knew no strictures in the matter of money.

"Listen to me, Arnold," Naomi urged. "For years we have

avoided the subject of money. You would have it so. I sub-mitted. I couldn't bear to hurt you..."

"Hurt me?"

"Well, embarrass, then. I couldn't bear to show you how inadequate was your provision, even though you were doing the very best you could! That would have hurt, wouldn't it? And wouldn't it have hurt to see how I scrimped and pinched, and found even then, that earning something more was necessary... and I began to write? But now, won't you look squarely at the situation. Would you like to see my bills, or will you accept my statement that Uncle Toby is no longer a help, but a charge upon the household?"

Arnold smiled faintly.

"It was your idea—our having him, I believe?"

"I know it, and that's not the point. When he came first, his allowance was a relief. I don't deny it. What it cost me to take it, I won't try to explain. I couldn't. But time after time, I used to clench my teeth and promise myself that some day the food it bought would not taste so bitter."

Arnold observed that he did not quite see the drift of this extravagant disquisition.

"I'm trying to make you understand," said Naomi, "that to maintain our present standard of living I must have more money, and that if you cannot supply it, I must. Furthermore, I require relief from the eternal exactions of housekeeping, and to this end I have engaged a servant."

"Your Uncle Toby," began Arnold, but she interrupted him.

"In the beginning, his cheque seemed large, but year by year it has shrunk as prices have soared until to-day it amounts to less than a third of our household expenses. Increasing the amount evidently has not occurred to Uncle Toby, and I would starve sooner than ask him... This applies also to you, Arnold. You give me to-day what you gave me five years ago, and the deficit is made up by me. Every cent I earn goes into the common coffer, and never save for a brief and unhappy period have you been constrained to eat poor and unpalatable food. Do you think," she hurried on, "that without my contribution we could afford the bootleg stuff, a plentitude of new-laid eggs, and crate-fed poultry?"

"Say no more!" Commanded Arnold. "This is too unutterably painful. Presently you will be saying that the bacon is mine, the coffee is Uncle Toby's, and the roast our joint possession..."

"No, no!" She ignored his bitter jest. "You *must* hear me out. You *must* try to understand. It isn't that I don't want to contribute. I do... I do! But to make this possible, I *must* have more time to write. Otherwise, these little luxuries will be cut off and we will all miss them. Going back to my original point, I can no longer write *and* carry on the housekeeping."

Arnold made a characteristic detour.

"Why not? Why less now than in the past? If you examine yourself honestly, will you not admit that, infected by the general unrest amongst women, you find housekeeping distasteful? You know we all must work."

"Of course. But shouldn't we be allowed to choose what kind of work we will do? Would you, for example, be content to spend your days picking up an old lady's handkerchief?"

"Provided that such was a necessary form of service, I would. Provided, that is to say, the old lady needed her handkerchief and couldn't pick it up for herself."

"We'll take a little more extravagant example. Would you be content to wave a fan above the head of some oriental sheik all day long?"

Again Arnold chose to take her literally. "No," he said, "that is a different matter. As usual, you've missed the point entirely. The only justification for life is service—SERVICE—doing needful things for other people. It is that which dignifies housekeeping and, if I may say so, robs your writing of any claim to special consideration. When you order your home, you are serving individuals, the community, and broadly speaking, the world. When you write little stories, you are serving your vanity, your greed for money, and yourself!"

"Oh, Arnold, that's not fair—I picked up the old lady's handkerchief—I served—for years, and I don't think I ever whined about it. But now, will you blame me for wanting to be relieved of that occupation, especially when the old lady will be served quite as well by someone else? *You* wouldn't like housekeeping! I am so happy writing—I am ambitious—I want to get on. *Can't* you understand?"

"Perfectly," said Arnold. "I will try to manage a little more... and now, if you will excuse me, I think I will go out for a bit. This has been a very distressing half hour and my head has suffered."

He bowed with cold courtesy and left the room. Naomi sat still and stared with vacant eyes at the closed door. "What's the use?" she cried, within herself. "Oh, what *is* the use?"

Never, in any vital discussion, had she accomplished her object. True, she often seemed to carry the day, but Arnold always left her oppressed by the burden of defeat. Her triumph was an empty one.

It was her own fault, she thought. She was too frightened and self-conscious to handle these situations well. What a silly comparison—picking up an old lady's handkerchief—fanning an oriental sheik! How could she have been so stupid and absurd?

She was always trying to make Arnold see her point without hurting him, without actually holding up the mirror to his failure. She was always trying to spare him the abrupt discovery that he had hurt her. She couldn't say bluntly, "For years, I've encouraged you to make a slave of me, and now I'm going to have freedom—to work at a task that is more congenial."

She couldn't bring herself to say that, even though these round-about speeches irritated him and made him less sympathetic towards her "superficiality and radicalism."

As a child seeks comfort from a fairy tale, or a girl from a stirring romance, Naomi went to her desk and began to turn over the pages of her manuscript. She made a correction. She amplified a paragraph. A new sentence slipped from her pencil; then another... In some darkly mysterious way she found that, despite numbing fatigue and spiritual discouragement, the creative instinct was alert. She could write. Was that the reward of suffering, she wondered? Did darkness light the lamps that glowed on life's great highway? Could Arnold's bleak philosophy be the surest, after all?

Her fingers flew. There was no hesitation, no uncertainty. Whence she derived the physical strength to sit upright and transcribe the thoughts that surged into her mind, she did not stop to question. This was the mood she had once described to Hugo as being that in which, without interruption, she could write a good book at a sitting.

"Naomi!"

She gave a startled cry and looked up to see Arnold standing in the doorway. His tone implied that he had spoken several times without attracting her attention.

"Well, what is it?" Perhaps there was slight edge on her voice.

"I am going to bed now."

There was nothing epochal in the announcement. Naomi had heard it countless times before. Moreover, she had acted in compliance with its thinly-veiled summons. Had Arnold been born a century earlier and in a different social station, he would have achieved the same effect by finishing the chores, reading aloud a chapter from the ponderous family Bible, bolting the doors and windows and then, picking up the lamp, he would have said to the mother of his eleven children, "Now we'll go to bed."

Thereupon, she would meekly have laid aside her eternal mending and followed her overlord to the connubial couch. Arnold's manner was but a polished modification of his prototype, and Naomi's attitude had been always strongly reminiscent of the other woman's.

"Oh," she usually said, "is it as late as that?"

"Past eleven," her husband would reply, polishing the face of his watch with his thumb. "I've given you ten minutes' grace."

"All right. I'm coming." And she had tried to hide the reluctance with which she laid away her work and followed him. In this way, many a good story had been ruined.

But to-night, she wouldn't stop. She would teach Arnold to respect her work—to realise that at such times she could not be at his beck and call.

She bent above the machine and struck the keys blindly, with an air of intense concentration.

"I say, I'm going to bed now," he repeated.

"Very well."

Amazement almost robbed him of the power of speech. "I—I—just-er-thought I'd tell you," he stammered.

"Thank you. Good night."

He recoiled as though she had struck him. Naomi had a fleeting glimpse of his face before he closed the door and left her in the throbbing silence of the room. Again, the seeming victory had been hers. Again, the effect was that of defeat. Although his physical presence no longer confronted her, the sense of his predominance lingered—the harmony that he had left was more vivid than his definite presence in the room. She found herself disturbed as by some persistent and irritating noise—like the whine of a swinging door, or the clatter of a restless blind, or the whirr of an electric fan... Her mood was shattered... No thoughts would come... She was conscious of nothing but Arnold's cold displeasure.

Defeated, she closed the machine... undressed in the dark and crept, miserably, into her bed.

CHAPTER 8

"YOU may have observed," said Hugo, on the following evening, "that my actions are guided by joyous impulse rather than a fixed and considered norm of conduct that is based upon a bookfull of rules and prohibitions. For example, I do one thing to-day and undo it to-morrow; I say one thing in the morning and revise it to fit the changed circumstances in the evening. This variability partially explains my charm. There is one rule, however, in my code of ethics, that is more or less fixed—I rarely tell the woman I love how tired she looks. No need explaining why... To a person of sensitive disposition, there must be an unpleasant suggestion of imperfection that... Naomi, Naomi, what have you been doing to yourself?"

"Interviewing prospective servants. I've had fifteen applicants to-day. They came singly and in pairs. Their ages varied from seventeen to seventy, and their capabilities, judged superficially, seemed to exist in inverse ratio to the wages they demanded. You wouldn't believe how many flawless women there are, floating, homeless, about the city."

"My poor girl," said Hugo, in the tone that melted her hardness, made her long to creep into his arms and sob out her woe upon his breast, "I suppose you've spent your entire day—and strength—in being snubbed by the unhelpful Lady Help."

"Just about. I began to suspect, from the questions some of them asked, by their general attitude, in fact, that place-hunting was, to them, a sort of mild excitement—er—like window-shopping to some women; like trying on hats."

"And the result?"

Naomi shrugged. "I'm no prophet. Perhaps I expected too much. I've had a picture of Shireen continually in mind, but, of course, there couldn't be two houses like hers. After the stream began to pour in, I felt rather as though I'd thrown a boomerang that had returned to smite me."

There was a moment's silence, broken by a suggestion from Hugo that the gentlemen of the household had not received the idea of change with conspicuous enthusiasm.

Naomi tried to laugh.

"The atmosphere all day has been so frigid that, if its present temperature continues, we shan't need to take any ice at all this summer."

Hugo made an inarticulate sound deep in his throat. Then, "Where is Arnold?"

"I don't know. He announced that he was going out, without saying where."

"And Uncle Toby, of course, is in bed?"

"I think so. As soon as Arnold left, he said he supposed I wanted to write and went upstairs."

"And now I'm here bothering you and taking up your time."

She touched his temple with a gentle forefinger—a strange little caress he had never encountered in any other woman.

"No... I couldn't have worked to-night. Do you know, Hugo, I've come to the conclusion that freedom—for a woman, at least—can never be seized—appropriated— captured by struggle. It must come through the voluntary and cheerful generosity of others. Freedom is a gift that must be thrust upon one. One must possess it almost unknowingly, like air and warmth. For example, to-night I was left alone. But I didn't feel *free*. Quite the contrary! I felt deserted, confined, imprisoned—like a child who is locked in a room to be punished."

"And can you tell me—even approximately—how long you intend to endure this self-imposed and futile state of Yogism?"

"No, I can't tell you... Until I summon sufficient strength to break away, I suppose. Oh, Hugo, I know how it must appear to you! I know you must despise me. I despise myself for this terrible mental and moral flabbiness. But I simply haven't any courage."

"You are wrong," said Hugo, quickly. "If you'd only recognize the truth. You possess a greater degree of courage than anyone I know. But it seems to me that you have allowed sentiment to overcloud your reason—that you confuse courage with endurance, which is quite another thing. Naomi," he said, suddenly, "do you ever lie awake thinking about me—pretending that I—not Arnold—sleep close beside you, within reach of your lips, your hand?"

She gave a mute assent.

"Well, tell me," he persisted, "exactly how does that make you feel? Happy or miserable, resigned, mutinous or ashamed?"

She wasn't sure. Probably she tried to shut him out of her thoughts, for the sake of peace. She didn't consider it a healthy occupation to dwell overmuch upon dreams that were too wonderful to come true.

"There you are!" cried Hugo. "Sentiment would have us believe that dreams are something beautiful, remote and unattainable, while reality, is drab, close at hand and impossible to escape! Why don't you think? Why don't you experiment with this contention—try to discover whether it is accurate or whether it is untrue? No one has ever made a step forward without blasting some accepted fallacy, outraging some revered tradition. I think I know what you feel—it's the weight of those damned old verbotens guarding the conduct of the 'sweet, pure, woman'—the terrible monster that frightens her into enduring the unendurable."

He rose and sat down in a remote corner of the room, his back towards her.

"I can't think, to-night, with you so near," he explained, "and I must think...We have so few opportunities to talk... we must get something settled."

Naomi was on the point of crying, "Yes, yes! That's what I decided, too. I'm going to give you up—then something will be settled."

But she was an instant too slow. Hugo rushed on.

"Talk to me, dear. Open all the hidden doors of your being. Let me feel what you are feeling." He leaned forward and took his head between his hands, speaking as though he groped for phrases that had been learned, but were now forgotten. "Here we are, two rational people, faced with a crisis that will mould the remainder of our lives. Presumably, we wish for the same outcome. Obviously, we are held apart by a matter of principle. I contend that we should see alike... No, no—please! Let me make my point... I don't argue that the ordinary debate inevitably convinces the losing faction that their opponents are right... but I argue that this is not an ordinary debate, and, given opportunity to reveal ourselves to one another, perfect understanding should be achieved. Either you come to my way of thinking, or I come to yours. Either I am convinced of the impossibility of the course that I propose, or you admit that it is feasible and act upon that conviction."

"I can never hope to convince you by argument, Hugo," said Naomi. "Emotions cannot be translated into words, and my inhibitions are, I suppose, emotional, utterly divorced from reason. My reason is perfectly in accord with your arguments. I just don't seem strong enough to co-ordinate it with my actions, that's all."

"Try!" he urged. "Try harder, and keep on trying. Realise that knowledge is the ability to distinguish the right course, combined with the strength to pursue it. Talk to me about the sort of thoughts or feelings that restrain you..."

Broadly, she told him, there was the fear that realisation would be a disappointment, that they would find closer association productive of the same old problems revealed in a different form.

"In other words," he interrupted, "we will tire of one another, and find the Paradise that looks so enchanting from this distance, rather a slummy place, after all."

"Yes, that about covers it," she said.

"Slums can be avoided. Education shows us the way. Couldn't ours be converted into parks and playgrounds, Naomi?"

"I don't know. We can't set the pace for progress... Yes, yes, I know what you would say... We can do our bit. But is it a happy state—that of the reformer? I may know I am right, but does it follow that the world—even the small circle crowding my immediate corner—will approve of me? The lash of moral discipline will cut me wherever I pass... people will turn their heads away... And I never pretend to be indifferent to Public Opinion."

Main swept aside this point by reminding her that divorce is becoming an act as respectable as marriage; and Arnold would certainly divorce her. Besides, her friends henceforth would be outside the ambit of parochialism; they would not be gregarious morons. "Your place is among the intellectuals—to use a much abused word," he said, "the writers, the thinkers of the time. Are they not notoriously advanced, whatever that may mean? Do they care a button for traditional and dogmatic conventionalism? Can you imagine Shireen Dey looking aside as you passed? She would be the first to promote you to a higher place in her esteem."

Naomi could not bring herself to confess that, deeply as she prized Shireen's friendship, she missed from it something—some elusive element—that gave life a finer meaning, that made clean purpose the more worth striving for. There was no opportunity at the moment to trail the nebulous thought, or confine it in words. It was just a drifting emotion... Shireen compassed the present; no more. She offered no promise of continuance... The moment was rich and vivid, but Naomi liked to speculate upon tomorrow. Somehow a picture of the future with none but Shireen upon the canvas was not altogether a strengthening factor in Main's argument.

"I suppose, then, you would not admit the possibility of finding yourself under a cloud? You can imagine no change in your business or social relations?"

Main was genuinely amused.

"Not the slightest."

"I knew a chap who was dismissed from a Bank, and one who was cashiered from the Army because they ran away with other men's wives."

"Fortunately," murmured Hugo, "I have no intimate connection with either of these exalted institutions. And while we are on this topic, let me say that although I am not a wealthy man, I have what people are pleased to call an independent income. My movements are not subject to the zealous interference of an individual or a group of individuals. I am in the expressive vernacular, my own boss."

"I know that you are not the slave of an office, but surely, Hugo, you have business connections, business associates?"

"Well, my dear girl, the market—the Stock Exchange—does not concern itself with morals. This is an axiom. Besides, any men with whom I do business, are not likely to carry hypocrisy so far as the bridge or billiard table." He flung a match upon the hearth, caught her eye, and put it neatly upon an ash-tray. "I can offer you a decent home," he continued, "in which your privacy will be respected, exactly as I would respect that of another man. I don't want you to 'keep house for me,' Naomi. I want to make you a home. I am inordinately proud of you, ambitious for you. I am impatient to surround you with the sympathetic environment in which you can express yourself, in which you can work. I am eager to use whatever talents I may possess to further your advancement, to see you occupy a prominent place in the literary sphere. I never tire of picturing myself as your Mr. Gaskell."

"Where would we live?" asked Naomi faintly. Never before had they brought their discussion to this point, to a consideration of the *modus vivendi*. Never had Naomi seen the path so free from obstacles, the sky so bright.

"Anywhere, or nowhere. If you turn your affairs immediately over to me, I will go straight to New York and learn the selling game as Julius Dey has learned it. If not, we'll just put the wardrobe trunk wherever you like, and feel you can work. I may have to be away quite a bit, but surely this fact must react as a point in my favour. It should mean an added sense of freedom—not desertion or punishment."

Naomi said nothing.

"Is there something else?" he asked gently.

"You will probably call it the expansion of my religious complex, but I am wondering if any good can come of such selfishness—on my part, I mean."

"I don't call it selfishness, or if I did, I should cheerfully admit its justification. Every creative artist should be forgiven that course of action which the unappreciative might regard as selfish but which I—and the artist, surely—define as spiritual self-preservation. Oh, woman of mine, I wish I could make you understand how much I want to do for you!"

Naomi was silent a moment. Then she asked,

"And will you explain what I am to do for you?"

"You are to give me the companionship that I desire more than anything on earth. You are to give me—when you will—the realisation of a love that is at the same time a spiritual refreshment and a physical force, both constructive and re-energising. I will draw from you the happiness that I pass back to you. You will complete the arc of my being, as I will complete yours. In a comradeship such as I foresee—a comradeship based upon equality, mutual respect, and intelligent selection—there will not be a lonely road at the end of the journey... a straight line that leads to oblivion. We will be as a circle, individuals in an endless chain... This thought (badly expressed, I admit), annihilates for me the dread of old age, enforced solitude, as the world rushes heedlessly by. The appeal of the flesh may pass, but there is no end to the stimulation of the mind. Understanding, sympathy, communion—these will be our food, our daily sustenance. And if we are permitted to go down into the twilight of the valley together, how thankfully will I cling to your hand. If not, how passionately will I cling to your spirit!"

"It sounds so simple," the woman murmured.

"Because," Main told her, "the things I want of you are those you can't help giving. Arnold, on the other hand, demands a painful distortion of your whole cosmic system, so to say. You might as easily shrivel your arm, or bind up your feet. With him, you are denied expansion. You are repressed. You are the victim of continuous pressure. This is as sinful for you, who submit, as for him, who commits. Can't you see that life's only worth living when its pleasures are greater than its pains?"

She shook her head. This was the part of his philosophy that frightened her.

"Why not?" he flared.

"What if you found that life with me was not predominantly pleasurable? What claim would I have upon you? I mean that, with a tie so slender, I should never draw a breath without the fear of losing you."

Naomi realised, even as she spoke, that these words illustrated a throw-back to the mental attitude of primeval woman. How ineffaceably these ancient traditions had branded her! How slow was her emergence into the light of a higher culture, a larger freedom! What, she asked herself, was the essence of her problem save an expression of woman's historical dependence upon man, her submission to brute force, her inherited sense of obligation? She couldn't assert herself with Arnold. She couldn't conduct herself as an equal. To do so was to incur his displeasure. To hold a divergent view stamped her as unreasonable. To triumph in argument was unthinkable. Seared upon the consciousness of both of them was the archaic fiat requiring that, to man, woman should yield up her will. His must be the voice; hers, the echo.

What did this mean? It meant a reversion to type—caveman type; it meant stagnation of the spiritual movement for women; it meant that she was a theoretic progressive and a practical back-slider; that, in order to preserve peace and the *harmony of injustice*, she must forever submerge herself and assume the unheroic role of an Ego masseuse. Coming back to the starting point, here was she, a woman of intelligence and education, believing in the doctrine of progress, yet possessing insufficient courage to confess her creed, not only in public, but private; conducting herself as though the preponderate purpose of life lay in preserving Arnold's mental and spiritual equilibrium. A high ideal, truly! She played when he wished to play; she was quiet when he wished to rest; she was vigorous when he wanted exercise. And to show any disinclination was to be sulky or unreasonable. She was no better than a dog. Not so good!

"I think I see," said Hugo. "Speaking as a woman of the Stone Age, you argue that, having captured me—with greater cunning than honesty—you must devise some way of preventing my escape when I discover the fraud... My God, Naomi, wouldn't you be glad to have me go if I wished for release?"

She didn't answer.

"Speaking as a sentimentalist, I suppose you are not confident that I love you."

"Sometimes."

"Why? Because I admit having loved other women—because I don't swear that I shall never turn my eyes in any direction but towards you?" He rose and approached her with the peculiar suggestion of ferocity that always sent a quiver through her body. "Look here," he said, "if I swore that no other woman could ever interest me, would you believe it?"

"No."

"Does any intelligent woman ever believe a man who takes that oath?"

"No."

"Then why—"

"I suppose because it gives one a sense of security, economic permanence, perhaps. I don't know. One wants to hear it even though one knows that it should be classed among a gentleman's lies—something gratifying to the ear, if palpably untrue."

A sharp spasm of jealousy shot through Hugo Main.

"Man is eternally searching his past and speculating about his future," he said. "What riches life would offer if he could only be induced to realise the present. Tell me—did you enjoy this sense of security, economic permanence, during the flaming days of Arnold's courtship?"

Naomi admitted that she did. Looking back upon that chapter of the past was like looking into Bluebeard's Chamber, where all the mutilated bodies of Arnold's beautiful lies were hung. She remembered how exquisitely he "made love by talking," how tenderly he sermonised on the glory of their life together, how infinitely touched she was by his delicate and high regard; exalted and not a little awed to feel that she possessed the divine qualities with which he invested her. Yes, how exquisitely Arnold had made love by talking!

"I can imagine..." Hugo cut in upon her memories. "I can see it all—sloppy sentiment—words—words-words... Talk and more talk about inspiration, the sanctity of the marriage-tie and ideals... My God, why can't women see? What does this high-sounding eloquence amount to? What did it do for you? I'm reminded of Ibsen's advice to one of his characters who persisted in bleating about ideals—'Why use these foreign terms?' he demanded, in effect, 'when we have perfectly good and descriptive words in our own tongue'—why ideals when what you really mean is lies?"

"Hugo, your bitterness is not only cruel, but offensive. You prate of consideration, sympathy..."

"And use the surgeon's scalpel. I only want you to recognise the degradation of being exalted. For I don't exalt you Naomi—which really means that I refuse to consider your social status, your mentality, your duties apart from mine. We are equals, comrades, entering into a reciprocal agreement so rational, so fine, that it will stimulate the high emotionalism that religion is supposed to promote. Using a cant phrase, we will enjoy a *spiritual communion* that is impossible between the 'exalted' woman and the man who exalts her."

Naomi raised her lips, ineffably soothed by the nearness of the man, by the flow of his rich, full voice, by a sort of mental warmth that enfolded her. She was never aware of this sensation with Arnold. She never had been. Arnold's speech was precise and crisp. His voice was chill. His flesh was hard and cold.

They kissed lingeringly, and Hugo did not want to let her go.

"And suppose I should fail you... I failed Arnold, you know. I am not at all what he thought I was."

"He didn't think about you—that's the point. He thought about himself, unconsciously, if you like, but definitely, none the less. Most of us do. I do, but the difference is that I know it, and admit it, and try to live it down. I don't want to be a tyrant. I don't want a slave. I want a companion."

"Hugo," murmured Naomi, "don't go on... I have something I must tell you."

"Hear me out, then I'll listen. I don't think you are the finest woman who ever lived. If I did, I wouldn't aspire to win you. You would be too fine for me. I don't offer you days and nights filled with love-talk. Ours will be a life of hard work, and hard play and dreamless sleep. We will be true to one another, loyal to our friends and tolerant towards those who are not. But we will not live by rule and a senseless adherence to traditional obligations that build barriers between us instead of bringing us into closer harmony. There, now, I've preached my sermon and feel better. What have you to say?"

A curious intoxication robbed Naomi of the will to speak, to move. A warm giddiness stole over her, such as she always experienced in a hot-house crowded with exotically perfumed blossoms. Hugo's voice rolled over her mesmerically. She wished it could go on forever.

"I'll say what should have been said when you first came in."

"I'm listening."

"I've decided to give you up." She felt the convulsive movement that ran through his body, and somehow, took a crumb of comfort from it. "I know myself well enough to realise that when it comes to packing a bag and locking the front door—I'll never do it. Oh, my love, my love... I want you so. I want to come. I want to be happy, but I just can't do it."

"You can! You shall! I leave for the west on Tuesday and you are coming with me!"

"No, no!" She struggled in his arms as though his words had sufficient power to abduct her. And, as she fluttered and strained against him, Main held her the tighter. Involuntary, was this act of *maleness*, this instinctive urge to assert his superior strength and reduce the woman-creature to a state of submission and obedience. The instant that he became conscious of his action and its significance, Main loosed his clasp. He dropped his arms, allowing her to go free.

But Naomi didn't go. If she recognised her liberty, she made no move to use it. She lay against him, inert, possessed of not one lucid thought, and yet aware of all his words implied. Fashioning no picture of their future, Naomi knew an instant's supernal ecstasy, as though their spirits met and mingled, discovering the very essence of happiness, the love that passes all human understanding.

As by common consent, they both rose. There was in their attitude a suggestion of the last round of the struggle. Hugo broke the silence. He said,

"I wouldn't stoop to coerce you. If you feel that you cannot go, that settles the matter—for the moment. But giving me up?" he managed to laugh. "Silly child, those are just empty words. You can't give me up, if you mean get rid of me; you can't prevent me from telephoning, telegraphing, writing you. If, when I ring the bell, you peep at me from behind drawn blinds and refuse me admittance to your house, I will stand on the street corners and waylay you. I will wait a thousand years, if need be, until you are convinced that love and decency go hand in hand, and that—" he broke off and seized her rudely in his arms. He had intended to bring his argument to a logical conclusion, but the words trailed off in broken sentences that had little to do with reasoned deliberations. He lost himself in a gust of passion and incoherency that earned his later contempt and Naomi's tenderer regard.

"Oh, come—come, my little love," he cried. "Life will never be free of pain till you are mine—mine! You do love me, darling... Kiss me—give me your beautiful lips again... Ah, my lovely one... the touch of your sweet body... your breasts... let me kiss them, too... oh, Naomi, my love, my love..."

"Sh-sh-sh, dear heart," she cautioned. "Uncle Toby will hear you!"

"Say you will come," he urged. "Oh, for God's sake, don't put me off again! You want me? You love me?"

Her clinging lips answered him.

"Say you will come... swear it..."

A clock chimed. They started and stood apart, quivering and yearning for one another with their eyes.

"You will come?" he repeated.

She inclined her head.

"Very well." The words were scarcely audible, but he heard them. "Good-bye... until Tuesday."

"Tuesday," he breathed. "Tuesday..."

CHAPTER 9

MEANWHILE, Arnold was tramping the streets, hotly reviewing the scene of the previous evening. It had clogged his mind all day; it had become so enlarged that everything else was crowded out. And the larger it grew, the smaller he shrunk, until there was little remaining save a fierce and blinding fury. First, she had defied him, and later she had dismissed him. "Thank you," she had said. "Good-night!" Such a position to have been forced upon him! By his own wife, too!

Neither he nor Naomi had referred to the incident during luncheon or dinner, but he manifested his displeasure by ignoring her and showing an exaggerated courtesy towards Uncle Toby. Her attitude towards him was anything but humble. One might have thought that she would have evidenced some penitence, made overtures that were equivalent to a request for pardon. Nothing of the kind! She paid no unusual attention to him at all. The whole circumstance was intolerable!

He was eager for solitude and the restoration of his self-esteem. Unconsciously, he was intent upon enjoying his anger. He wanted to be angry, to remember that his authority had been questioned. He wanted to be roused to the pitch where he could express that dominance which should mark the conduct of every self-respecting man. Without knowing it, he agreed with Ingersoll, who said, in a widely different connection, "There exists no more degrading doctrine than that of mental non-resistance." To render benefits for injuries—especially those inflicted by the female of the species—was, Arnold felt, to ignore all distinctions between actions. He who behaved towards a docile wife and rebellious wife alike, possessed neither love nor justice. Non-resistance was the attitude of him who had not the spirit to resist. It was either a confession of weakness or the deliberate repudiation of a spiritual obligation.

Resistance in this case, he decided, must take the form of manifest displeasure. This, he had found, was the most effective means of disciplining Naomi.

The part of disciplinarian was not a happy one, he reflected. It would be much easier, pleasanter, to let matters slide, to acquiesce, to do nothing. But the easy course was the primrose path. Resolutely, Arnold veered away and sought out the bramble.

As the saner, the stronger mind, he clearly saw his duty towards his wife—that it was for him to develop those qualities which he was disappointed not to perceive in her after their marriage, but which he still believed she possessed. He tried to remember that Naomi was a child, a mental tomboy, a charming harum-scarum, whose appearance was deceptive because she had adopted grown-up clothes when she should have been wearing pinafores and rompers.

"Ballast... restraint... a sense of responsibility..."he checked off his wife's requirements, as he walked along, "a keener realisation of woman's place in the great universal plan. I *must* not allow her to develop into a radical, a free thinker, a cheap imitation of a man."

The sharp frost of early morning had surrendered to the blandishment of spring and the night air was cool and fragrant, with a lush earthy smell. Arnold drew a deep breath, refreshed by, and yet unconscious of it.

This matter of the servant, now... His thoughts flowed on in more or less well-defined sentences. Of course, it wasn't so serious—not the thing in itself. He had considered the proposition, more than once—especially after reading one of those offensively intimate Personalities that had featured Naomi recently in the Press. No earthly reason, so far as he could see, for stressing the fact that she did all her own work, as the article was so vulgarly phrased. All her own work! Marvellous, indeed! She was referred to as a sort of super-woman, for doing all her own work! A super-woman—or a martyr, by God!

Arnold unbuttoned his coat. It flapped loosely about him as he tramped on.

Didn't he do all his own work? And didn't he work for her, besides? Nobody mentioned that! What did they think he was, anyway—these bumptious, bobbed-haired women who poked their powdered noses into his affairs and offered him gratuitous insults in return!

And Naomi didn't discourage them. That was the secret of his bitterness. She accepted these undeserved tributes at his expense. She didn't play fair. There was lacking in her a trait that he had taken absolutely for granted, a trait he had supposed that every decent woman possessed— domestic decorum.

But Naomi soon disabused his mind of this belief. She wasn't even loyal. He had been indescribably shocked by the discovery. He always would be. Judging from the fiction of the day, all women were disloyal, damn them!

Arnold walked faster.

And greed? By God, they were greedy... simply insatiable...Give them decency and they'd ask for comfort; give them comfort and they'd ask for luxury; give them luxury and they'd howl for extravagance.

Deceitful, that's what they were—hypocrites. You never could be sure just what was going on in a woman's mind. You never knew when you had her. You could slave the best years of your life for her and in the twinkling of an eye, she would turn against you and attach herself to some other man—some man who held out towards her a richer prize.

There was this fellow Main... making Naomi feel abused, put upon... poisoning her unstable mind with all manner of revolutionary thinking... giving her a false sense of values, laughing most likely, behind his hand at the way in which Naomi gobbled his flattery and asked for more...

Of course, he wouldn't stoop to jealousy. Besides, he had perfect confidence in his wife... She might be foolish, but never actually depraved. At the same time, he wished with all his soul that he could get the fellow out of the way. That accomplished, he could cope with her disloyalty.

He supposed women couldn't help it—that it was the inevitable result of their dependence upon man. Woman was inbred with a sense of cunning, the necessity to curry favour. The more desirable she made herself, the greater was her power. By hypocrisy and not by truth, did she hold sway.

But the realisation was bitter—bitter. It was well-nigh intolerable, when one had to apply it to one's wife!

He tripped and plunged on. What had he been thinking about? Oh yes, this matter of the servant. How much more appropriately would the suggestion have come from him. *There* was an instance. He put his finger on it with sour triumph. There was a case of her lack of domestic decorum. *He* should have spoken of it. Then Naomi might have demurred, declaring that things were all right as they were, that after all, she was only doing her bit and that it was a pleasure to serve with her own hands so considerate a husband. At that, he would have insisted that a maid should be installed, after which she should have yielded and everything would have been pleasant and cheerful.

But what had happened? She had ignored him. She had assumed control of him and the house and all that was his, in an extremely high-handed fashion and then sought to exonerate herself by flinging in his teeth a long list of grievances. All of which, Arnold felt, was a serious transgression against the laws of propriety that should govern the conduct of any wife towards her husband.

His pace quickened.

In deference to his self-respect, he could not permit this occurrence to pass unnoticed. To do so would be to confess himself incapable of resistance in the first place, and a failure in his duty towards Naomi, in the second. It would be easier, of course, to do nothing—was that the tempter's voice?—but he would conquer this inclination towards moral flabbiness, he would take Naomi in hand.

Arnold was walking rapidly now, and, subconsciously, wishing he had left his coat at home. The stars shone above him with a languorous brightness that seemed to waver in each lilac-scented gust of wind. Motor lights flashed past, somewhere near a Victrola blatted jazz while half a dozen youngsters danced neck-and-neck. To all this, Arnold was oblivious.

He must take Naomi in hand. Disagreeable as it was, he must make her conscious of his authority. Arnold did not agree with William Morris when he said that no man is good enough to be another man's master. Man has always been, is, and will always be master over woman. History, religion, science prove it. Nature makes certain immutable laws which even science can't defy. This was one of them.

As for the servant... of course, they should have one; a nice respectable, elderly woman would add a very pleasant tone to his establishment—especially when he was entertaining.

"Oh, I *thought* I heard you come up on the verandah," he invariably said, when he went to the door.

He didn't like opening his door. It would have been gratifying to have been capably served the other night when that fellow Sharpe was brought to the house. Sharpe was the type of man who noticed things. Arnold could almost hear him telling of his visit in some such words as—

"Spent an evening with Lennox...topping fellow. Yes, his wife's the writer, you know... Awfully jolly little home, he's got; nothing ostentatious, you understand, but artistic, comfortable. A regular home, with old-fashioned hospitality; *you* know what I mean—a gentleman as a host... that sort of thing. And such a jolly old dear of a servant... likely been with the family for years... After she'd served us, she curtseyed and asked, 'Is there anything more I can do for you, sir?' and Lennox answered in the tone that—er—well, just *the* right tone, you know, the tone so few people achieve nowadays, 'No... no, Harrison, thanks. You may go to bed, now. We shall not require anything else.'"

A big black bulk rose out of the earth and barred his passage. It was Scotchie, the Rev. Haddington Allyn's dog.

Arnold took note of his surroundings. The windows of the Parish House flung their soft radiance into the quiet darkness like so many distorted moons, over whose pink face, coarse black cobwebs were etched, with here and there a leaf of ivy.

The sound of decorous applause drifted out into the fragrant street, and curiosity snapped the thread of his thoughts. He wondered what was going on. Then a woman's voice sang through the stillness like the throbbing of a harp string. Arnold was conscious of a peculiar thrill, a response to that note, as he twisted his head slightly and waited for the rest of the song.

But no song came. The woman was merely speaking, speaking in the most moving voice that Arnold had ever heard. Although it was monotonous, although it was confined within the range of a few low notes, it was freighted with that diapasonic quality one sometimes encounters in an actor; or a priest who intones his words. There was in it a promise of wider harmony, as though presently it would break into more tuneful channels, soar into a melody that would touch the soul.

For a moment Arnold listened, so completely enrapt that he forgot to wonder who was speaking. All at once, he remembered... Allyn had announced it on the Sunday previous. Miss—Miss—Hilda... what the deuce had he said? Miss Lydia—no, that wasn't it. Lydia didn't harmonise with that voice... Miss Hester—yes, that was the name. Miss Hester Ashburn, a Field Worker, had returned from Siam—or was it Assam?—from somewhere, anyhow, and would relate her experiences in the Parish House... Miss Hester Ashburn, evidently was speaking.

Arnold had given but listless heed at the time. He didn't even bother to determine what a Field Worker was, and as he stood there drinking in the richness of her voice, he tried to tell himself that he wasn't interested.

A Field Worker! He didn't like it. It had an earthy, agricultural flavour. Missionary was no better. Carrying the Gospel to the heathen was an excellent practice, he agreed, but, taken individually, missionaries—feminine missionaries—were repellent to him. A rapidly-sketched picture of Miss Hester Ashburn formed upon the canvas of his mind—a tall, spare woman, cramped into a stern black serge; gray hair dragged back from her high forehead and showing the passage of the comb through its sparse strands. Spectacles. Sallow skin. Unpleasant teeth. But her voice... It charmed him; literally, that. It provoked in him a desire to see the woman who possessed it, even though disappointment must be his reward. He crossed the street and tiptoed through the vestibule, dropping into a chair at the very rear of the Hall.

Then he raised his eyes to the platform and received a shock.

A golden cloud, an orange flame, swayed there beneath the harsh glare of a too-powerful electrolier. Miss Hester Ashburn was scarcely more than a girl, a slender, milk-skinned girl, whose mass of reddish hair caught the light from above only to intensify it and throw it out to the farthest recesses of the room. She wore some sort of yellow silk robe that billowed about her at the slightest movement and produced an effect that was unearthly, ethereal.

Arnold made no attempt to follow her words. He cared not a button what she was talking about. He was caught up in a curious emotional tide that carried him beyond the zone of speech; that dulled his senses like a strong narcotic; that drugged him with the music of a woman's voice and the dazzling light that gleamed from a woman's hair.

He had been seated for several minutes before he realised that Allyn also occupied the platform. His personality had suffered an almost complete eclipse.

Presently, Arnold began to struggle against this penetrating pleasure. He was always suspicious of happiness, whatever its form. He tore his eyes from the speaker and sought out familiar faces in the audience, wondering, resentfully, why all good women had to be so distressingly plain. His eyes rested upon the two Brobdingnagian females—sisters—who were happily ignorant as to the reason they were called pillars of the church. Nothing more suggestive of palæolithic art has yet been discovered in human form. They were possessed of that terrible and devastating energy one associates with the moving of a glacier, and they dedicated this turgescent gift wholly to the church. They attended every service. They bore implacably down upon every meeting. Religion, as expressed by them, was as grossly intemperate as the uncontrolled thirst of the man addicted to his bottle.

Arnold watched the Thurlow sisters, sitting upright and immobile, listening stonily to the rich melody that seemed to hold everyone else in thrall. He wondered what they were thinking; what kind of thoughts ordinarily occupied their mental realm. He wondered if they ever thought about men, and the darker emotions that were supposed to lie remote from the estate accorded to a virgin.

He stared harder. What was this? A stain, the colour of brick-dust, crawled slowly over the profile of the elder sister. She moved ever so slightly, as though some internal tumult had communicated itself to her external envelope. What was going on, he asked himself?

The assemblage, which had hung rapt upon the speaker's words, sank back and shuddered. Arnold forgot the Thurlow sisters. He forgot everything save the blazing vision of the girl upon the platform. He did not even connect what she was saying with the flush that scorched Miss Thurlow's cheek. His entire being was aquiver in response to the music of a stranger's voice, music through which he caught occasionally a few words.

"Children," she was saying, "mere children... forced into wife and motherhood by men old enough to be their fathers—their grandfathers! You cannot imagine the inexpressible horror of their stunted little lives... You cannot remotely conceive of their suffering... Why, I, myself have nursed a little girl through four terrible days of hard labour...

and then watched her slip into the merciful arms of death. You must realise, if you pause to consider the matter, you *must* realise that there are physiological reasons that explain the shocking condition of eastern women, those ghastly child marriages... I won't dwell upon the subject, but we *must* educate them. We must show them a better way."

Arnold was distracted by a sudden movement near at hand. He tore his eyes from the platform in time to see Miss Thurlow lean suddenly forward, snatch a Leaflet from her rack, and begin to fan herself. A spot immediately beneath her chin throbbed heavily. Arnold watched her with a sort of horrid fascination.

"Curious," he reflected, "that the mere thought of sex-expression should stir that granite pillar!" What dark and secret longings lurked deep within her zealous soul? One might have thought that at her age, consideration of such matters would be purely scientific; that they would leave her cold, untroubled. But this revelation... Miss Thurlow! How soon did emotions atrophy from inanition, he wondered? Did denial intensify them, and give them longer life? Was Miss Thurlow ashamed of her unappeased appetite? Imagine... Miss Thurlow, of all people!

He speculated upon her in the light of marital relationship... upon the quality of her personal charms. Often, when scarcely realising it, he considered women in the nude... as he passed them on the street, he stripped them in imagination, free of clothes. At the same time, he was affronted when Naomi acknowledged even the most harmless sex-consciousness by some such observation as, "I was the only woman in the car," or "there wasn't another woman in the room."

Yes, he mused, of course Miss Thurlow would wear corsets... stiff, unyielding corsets, out of which she would rise, white and majestic, like a gigantic loaf of bread. And the other sister would overflow her casing too, looking and smelling faintly like a junket pudding.

He shuddered.

Taken *en masse*, a congregation, a meeting such as this, exalted him. Religionists, as a collective body, produced an atmosphere that gave him spiritual refreshment. Splendid, devout souls, he might have said. Fine examples of high-living and Christian piety. But, individually, he despised them. He could not have spent an hour in their company without developing towards them all the venom of the potential assassin.

Miss Thurlow! Of course, she had a filthy mind, all covered over by that granolite exterior. Over-sexed, she was, albeit well-controlled. He hated her.

His attention was whipped back to the speaker.

"I am addressing you frankly," she said. "There is no other way. I am appealing to you—" her eyes seemed to fasten hard upon him "—in the name of Christianity, humanity, common decency! You can't turn a deaf ear to my cry. If any of you can go into the Field, I implore you to return with me. There is an appalling amount of work to be done. But if you cannot go, then give me generously of your abundance, that this mission of mercy may continue. Who, in this audience, will refuse the prayer of my little girl-mothers? Who dares confess indifference to the lives of little children?

"I have said enough. Is there anyone present who will open my subscription list with one hundred dollars?"

There was silence, embarrassed, suspenseful silence. Heads moved ever so slightly, in dignified curiosity. How had this appeal affected one's neighbour?

The stillness grew oppressive. Stifling. As in a dream, Arnold felt himself drawn to his feet. He was amazed to find himself standing. This was madness, a stern voice whispered. He couldn't afford a contribution of one hundred dollars!

An instant's wild misery dazed him. But it passed as he captured a measure of self-justification. Here was a true sacrifice; what it would cost him, God alone would know! Here was a gift worthy of his Maker. Besides, he had been called upon publicly to acknowledge his Master, to confess his faith, and he had soberly answered the call.

He saw a great light break over the girl's face. She made a strange little gesture towards him with her flowing sleeves and then folded her hands close against her breast as though to crush the emotion that struggled there. For one dizzying instant, Arnold felt as though she had taken his body into her warm embrace, as though his head lay within the circle of her arms, under the amber radiance of her bright, gold hair.

The Rev. Haddington Allyn started to his feet. There was a general movement throughout the room. Arnold was conscious of two large, flat faces upturned to his.

"In Miss Ashburn's name, Mr. Lennox," said the rector, "I thank you. Your response is handsome, and I trust that your example will be followed—Ah thank you, Mr. Rostetter... Miss Wylie, will you be so good as to take down the names and the amount of the subscriptions promised? Mr. Rostetter said—er—exactly! Fifty dollars... a very generous sum, sir... Have you written that, Miss Wylie? Who else now? Miss Thurlow? Ah, I knew that you would not fail us... how much did you say? Twenty-five... thank you. What amount does Miss Agnes contribute?

Every head was turned in the direction of the Thurlows. Arnold saw a swift, worried look pass between them. Then with a suggestion of recklessness, the younger sister rose to her feet and promised another twenty-five.

"Splendid!" Commended the rector. "Did I not tell you, Miss Ashburn, that you would be well advised to open your campaign in our little parish? Did I not declare that here we have a living Christianity—a religion that finds expression in deeds, not mere labial protestations? Er—we have not heard from many gentlemen..." The Rev. Mr. Allyn took up a position on the platform where he could see around a pillar in the middle of the Hall. "Isn't that Mr.... Ah, yes, I thought we would hear from you, Mr. Greenlea. How much did you say? Twenty-five dollars? Thank you."

Another painful silence followed. Those members of the audience who had subscribed tried to look disinterested, and those who had not, kept their eyes down, as though fearing to be mesmerised by the rector or his guest. An atmosphere of discomfort was perceptible.

"Well, well," cried Mr. Allyn, smiling. "What seems to be the matter? Has our little flame of generosity flickered out so soon? Surely there is someone else who wishes to assist in this humanitarian endeavour. Five dollars, Mrs. Croy? Why, of course, it is acceptable. No amount is too small, my dear friends, if it is the largest you can afford. Two, Mrs. Tulley? Another two... Did you get that last, Miss Wylie? Really, I am touched—I beg your pardon, Mrs. Dunn... speak out... don't hesitate... One dollar? We take it with gratitude... Now what about the rest of you who wish to subscribe one dollar? Dear me, Miss Wylie, your prowess with a pen is being put to the test... Look at the hands that are raised back there... Mrs. Slater... yes, I recognise you... Many thanks... Mr. —er—" the rector looked embarrassed. "Mr. —er—"

"McCaffray," prompted the gentleman.

"Of course! Mr. McCaffray. How much sir?"

"One—" began McCaffray, "—one-dollar a week for a month!"

The rector clapped his hands. "There! Isn't that splendid? Why did we not think of so sane a method before? *Now*, what about the young people? Can you not save a small sum each week, my little friends, deny yourself a movie, and adopt Mr. McCaffray's wise system? Come, now, who will pledge a dollar?"

A small child stood up. Arnold saw in her an incipient Miss Thurlow. He watched her with hostile eyes.

"Laura Bingham!" The Rev. Mr. Allyn might have been St. Peter introducing the elect into eternal bliss. "I am not surprised. Laura is the leader of our Sunday School, Miss Ashburn. Thank you, my dear child. And who is that, Miss Wylie? Ah, Peter Malcolm... a good Boy Scout. God bless you, Peter. The grown-ups should find it difficult to remain seated after this..."

Arnold did not know how long the frenetic competition lasted. He was scarcely conscious of his surroundings at all. But months later, the remembrance of it distressed him. Indeed, he recalled it with genuine repugnance. In Allyn's geniality, there was perceptible a strong quality of professionalism. The way he whipped his parishioners' pride and set them vying against one another was disgusting. It was as though he offered them this chance of making good their credit in Heaven. There was no co-operation in that, Arnold reflected. Precious little humanitarianism. There was vulgar competition, and the hostility that develops when one group or individual endeavours to gain supremacy over another. And Hester Ashburn... he acknowledged an expression of cupidity in her eager eyes; he recalled how cleverly she played up her lovely young femininity. The whole thing was revolting!

But, at the time, none of this was apparent to him. He watched the play of light and yet more light on the girl's face, and thought of sunshine and stained glass windows and log fires, and the hot flame of glacier ice, and all manner of extravagant fancies. And, suddenly, there was a deafening babble and much confusion. A crowd of people surged towards him and then divided. In the aisle thus formed, Mr. Allyn and the girl approached. Arnold's heart hammered sharply. He felt a curious sense of oppression with her nearness. She was looking directly into his eyes.

"I know that Miss Ashburn will want to thank you personally, Mr. Lennox," the rector cried. "May I present you? Here he is, Miss Ashburn…"

Arnold bowed. Mechanically, he stretched out his hand. The gesture was one of groping rather than salutation. He felt the quick hot clasp of fingers that were unbelievably strong.

CHAPTER 10

THEN they were alone in the spacious, shadowy street. Arnold was still quivering with, struggling against, emotions that were foreign to him. He could not seem to touch solid ground as he walked. An absurd idea possessed him. "All these buildings," he thought, "are made of vapour. If I touch one, there will be no resistance. Even that tree—this post—even we, ourselves, are insubstantial, like objects in a dream." Conversation, words, banalities—the cohorts that had always mustered to his call in times of stress, deserted him. He could think of absolutely nothing to say.

"Pull yourself together," some inner voice admonished, harshly. "You are behaving like a stupefied jackass. Pull yourself together and be normal."

But he couldn't pull. There was nothing to pull against. He couldn't overcome that sensation of insubstantiality—of floating to music, wrapped about with two flame-coloured sleeves.

"Either I'm going dotty," he told himself, "or I'm ill." Aloud, he said—

"You must be greatly pleased with the result of your meeting. I thought the response was very spontaneous, didn't you?

If Hester Ashburn suspected the effort behind his words, she gave no sign. Certainly, no similar restraint embarrassed her. She broke into a rapturous appreciation of the audience in general and Arnold in particular, that set his pulse throbbing.

"It is to you that I owe the success of my mission," she declared. "Your example fired the rest of them. If I could tell you—if I could only make you feel—share—my joy."

They moved into a pool of light, and Arnold turned to his companion. Her face was transfigured. The fire of fanaticism burned in her eyes. She was smiling at him, not mirthfully, mischievously, youthfully, as Naomi sometimes smiled, but raptly, unearthily, as a martyr might have expressed her holy joy, her selfless sorrow, her piety and exaltation.

"She has suffered," he said to himself, taking, had he but known it, a strange satisfaction in the discovery, "God, how she must have suffered!"

They stepped up to the curb. He caught her arm. She made no move towards freedom. Their gait was rhythmic, slow.

"You had extraordinary courage to go out there," Arnold remarked.

"On the contrary," Hester returned, quickly. "I had none. That's exactly why I went. I ran away."

"Ran away? To India, and a mission? It seems impossible!"

"Oh, please don't think me better than I am! That would be supreme irony."

"I think you are quite splendid," said Arnold, somewhat more at his ease. "That is not an idle compliment. Your work speaks for itself, Miss Ashburn."

"No, no! It was easy… it was a refuge… In undertaking it, I sacrificed nothing—unless it was my parents! The difficult course would have been to stay at home. I must tell you." Her words rushed on in that deep sing-song melody that moved him so poignantly. "I was an only child, shockingly spoiled, self-willed, passionate. I can't remember having been denied a single wish, up to the time I was twenty."

"Oh," murmured Arnold, suspecting what was coming.

"Then I fell in love—with a man nearly twice my age, a man who was everything I thought he ought *not* to be, but I loved him."

They were walking more rapidly; his hand still touched her arm.

"We were engaged—oh so stormily engaged," the girl went on. "Then—then—out of a clear sky, I mean, without the excuse of a quarrel, you understand, he went away—he jilted me."

"The cad!" cried Arnold. "You were well rid of him."

"We were mutually unsuited to each other. But, of course, I couldn't see that at the time. First I played with the notion of suicide... yes, yes, I did... And then, in the most miraculous way which would take too long to tell you now, I had a chance to go to India in the service of God and the Church."

"But your parents," began Arnold.

"Naturally they opposed the idea. They did everything to induce me to change my mind, offered me every sort of distraction. But I wouldn't listen... You understand, my motive was entirely selfish, at that time? Believe me, Mr. Lennox, it was! I wanted to get away, to bury myself, to acquire some bizarre—yes, I think bizarre is the word—interest, that would serve as an anodyne and make me forget. I don't know why I am moved to talk to you like this—a perfect stranger."

"Sometimes a perfect stranger possesses perfect understanding," suggested Arnold, less sententiously than he had intended.

"Yes," she agreed. "Yes, you are right, and after what you did for me to-night, I want you to understand. Where are we? I should be going to the hotel—wherever that may be."

They laughed.

"I'm afraid that, as a pilot, I leave much to be desired," murmured Arnold. "The fact is, I have been so interested in what you were saying... We are not very far. Would you like me to try to find a taxi?"

"Oh, dear, no! If you only knew how I love this—this refreshing air, this sharp change after my years of heavy, paralysing heat. I'd forgotten what our spring nights *could* be like. Am I taking you too far out of your way?" she asked, suddenly.

Arnold scoffed the idea aside, and led her back to what she had been saying. "In spite of your denial," he told her, "I feel that you have behaved with rare courage. Leaving out of the question such dangers as disease, uprisings, native hostility, and intrigue, you must have suffered countless hours of spiritual torment-homesickness, discouragement, indecision. Your face betrays as much."

She thanked him for his understanding with a glance, still protesting that cowardice kept her at work. "But I like to think," she added, "that through my white-hot pain, I was led to God."

"Through suffering, we all are," said Arnold.

"Of course," the girl went on, "my life seems to have been continued on another planet. The readjustments... the dreadful revelations... You can scarcely imagine! My spirit endured a dozen crucifixions..."

"...and resurrections," interrupted Arnold.

"Yes, perhaps. At all events, I came to a closer intimacy with my Master, and that is what really matters."

Arnold's agreement was utterly sincere.

"I think you have been splendid," he repeated, "a conspicuous example to your sex. Unfortunately, one meets few women of your calibre, to-day."

"I am nothing," she contradicted softly, "nothing, that is, save a clumsy instrument through which the Divine Will tries to manifest itself. When this radiant truth enters into the consciousness, it floods one's being, Mr. Lennox; all discontent, discouragement—all pain is swept away. The

earth becomes as Heaven, and all its creatures are like-
nesses of God, Himself. I don't mean to imply," she broke
off, "that I have attained to any such perfection of the spirit.
All I am trying to express is, that I can see what the Master
wishes to do for me, and I am trying my poor best to help
Him. Do I bore you with my professions and confessions?
Do you agree with me, at all?"

"Answering the last question first, I agree so completely,
Miss Ashburn, that I seem to hear my own thoughts set
forth in words. You are like my higher, better self speaking.
We are companions in spirit, at least." There was a little
pause. "To answer your first question—well you would
not care for compliments, and anything I could say would
sound like that."

"Oh, please—don't chatter with me," cried Hester Ashburn. "In the first place, you would take me at an unsportsmanlike disadvantage, and in the second, I shall probably
meet other men who can only do that!"

Her voice, though low, seemed to carry far out into the
quiet night. Arnold felt a sudden sense of annoyance. The
spell cast by her presence was, momentarily, broken. He
disliked the thought of other men "chattering" with her,
holding her less highly than he held her, subjecting her to
the irreverent attentions they paid to other women. Why,
some gross fellow might even walk home with her like this...
his hand beneath her arm.

All at once, Arnold was very conscious of her nearness,
the soft rubbing of their shoulders, their hips; and, not
infrequently, he knew contact with the slender limb that
refused to keep step with him, flashed close to him and
away, beneath the filmy silk of her gown. He was intensely
aware that the curve of her breast lay within reach of his
fingers, that every little while, in her fervency, Hester Ash-

burn pressed his hand tighter to her lithe, warm body, and that the sweet flesh of it swelled and surrendered to the pressure.

Some coarse brute might take advantage of this, Arnold thought.

They passed a man and woman standing in the shadow of a building. There was something defiant as well as furtive in their attitude, in the way they drew apart as he and the girl approached, in the way they watched them with suspicious, resentful eyes.

A hideous thought took possession of Arnold's mind. He saw himself as he looked to those two creatures skulking in the shadowed doorway; he knew that, mutely, they were charging him with the same relationship towards Hester Ashburn as they held towards one another. And they were hating him—for his superiority, his wider opportunities for pleasure. It was as though they had said—

"Oh, yes, of course you sneer at us, trying to crawl out of sight in this dark hole! You have no need to walk the streets with your woman; you have no need to haunt the parks, and keep an eternally alert eye open for the coming of a cop. You're a swell, you are! You can go to a hotel, or one of those places run just for the likes of you! We have nothing but this..."

He released the girl's arm so violently that she was startled. She could scarcely be expected to know that he was crying within himself—

"How shocking... how revolting... and yet that's always the way... No one understands me! Friends and enemies—they're all alike, blind... blind! People are always thinking the worse of me, imputing to me motives that are utterly foreign to my character. Those dreadful creatures, there... Oh, why can't someone see me as I really am?"

Then, because he didn't want to take Hester's arm again, and because he could offer no adequate reason for his action, Arnold fumbled for his handkerchief, and concerned himself with it for a long time.

Presently, the recollection of something she had said moved him to speech again.

"You don't believe that we can escape—or shall I say transcend—suffering, do you? Don't you think that so long as we wear a human form we must submit to human restrictions?"

"Only in a measure."

"Then you would argue that the human being can achieve salvation while still living upon this earth?"

"Ye-es—I think that might be possible."

Arnold shook his head. "You have become strongly impregnated with mysticism, then! Aren't you closer to the teaching of Buddha than Christ?"

"No, no," she cried, "you mustn't say that! But it's too big a question to be thrashed out here. My mind is distracted, and I am a little tired. I can't lay my case before you coherently, and I don't want you to think... Buddhism," she repeated, gravely. "I suppose you are saying that we must suffer, and keep on suffering, to become sufficiently refined. It is not enough to be absent ourselves from life and its turmoil, as Gautama did."

"Certainly, it is not enough to avoid suffering. Of course, if the renunciation of human contacts is the supreme sacrifice..."

Hester interrupted him. "But don't you think it might be possible for some of us to get life's measure of pain crowded into a short period—let us say two or three years? Or, putting it another way, can we not plumb the depth of suffering all at once, rather than spin it out over a period of time?"

"Not to the extent of rendering us immune forever afterwards. Of course, I can conceive of a certain trial being so heavy that all others would seem trifling by comparison. Perhaps that is what you mean?"

Hester's denial was slow but firm. Her hand slipped up Arnold's arm and clung there as she added emphasis to her words by the pressure of her fingers.

"No! Or, at any rate, that is a sordid way to state it. It seems to *ignore*, almost"—squeeze—"the *spiritual*"—squeeze—"element which is the *keynote*"—squeeze—"of the whole thing!"

For answer, Arnold returned to his first contention. "The mere fact that people suffer is bound to produce pain for others," he said. "You can't get away from that." Then suddenly, "Take your own case—don't you suffer? Don't you suffer for those unhappy children of whom you spoke so eloquently tonight?"

"Ah," cried Hester, shaking his arm, "that's just what I *must* try to make you understand... Of course I suffer for them, and I try to help them. I help them because I am not utterly and absolutely broken by my pain. It doesn't get inside me, and tear at the very roots of my being. I am in a measure detached... able to look on and reflect upon the better of two courses... Oh," she broke off, "I can't make it clear without making myself a monster of egotism and selfishness. You *mustn't* think that because those things are happening to *me*, I can bear them better! What I mean is that nothing that could happen to *me*, would matter so much that it would prostate me. The dreadful agony I endured before, was due to my not knowing God... being engrossed with Self..."

"You are very young to have done with suffering on your own account," commented Arnold. "For your sake, Miss Ashburn, I wish I could share that faith."

"Oh, don't think me arrogant, defiant, please! I would not shirk a heavier Cross if it were offered, and you are not to think that the life I lead is smooth and untroubled."

"It is a martyr's life, I should think," said Arnold.

"No, not quite that, but I really try to do that work that comes ready to my hand. Only—here I am, back at the starting point again—there is peace between me and the pain."

They had reached the hotel. Hester held out her ungloved hand. It seemed abnormally long and white and slender, and Arnold was conscious of a curious desire as he looked at it.

"I can't thank you enough," said the girl. "for everything—your escort and your sympathy no less than your liberal donation. Will we not meet again before I go?"

Warmly, Arnold hoped so. For the second time that night, he felt the quick, hot clasp of fingers that were unbelievably strong, and, for the second time a sensation of insubstantiality possessed him. Hester was speaking low, hurried words and her voice was like the melody of a song. Abruptly, he raised his hat and walked away.

At first, he seemed to float, to drift past buildings that were composed of vapour. His mind, usually so well-disciplined and orderly, played hide-and-seek with him when he would have commanded it. Physically, he felt exhilarated, as though he had been for a swim in cold, salt water.

His eyes were held by a soft light in an upper window. Suddenly, it went out, and a figure in white was framed against the darkness. A woman's hand stretched forth and pushed the shutters into place.

Arnold began to wonder about Hester... He pictured her in a filmy night robe, moving softly about a darkened room. How ivory-white was her skin... how satin-smooth! He could still feel the curve of her breast beneath his hand. His fingers tingled with the clasp of her strong, clinging grip. Hester Ashburn in his room... How delicious to lie in bed and watch her adjust the shutter in the moonlight...

He caught himself up with a jerk. Not from shame of reflections such as these. They were all right, so long as they did not merge into deeds or even definite longings. They were natural to men. But he had done something that provoked his discomfort. He had promised this girl one hundred dollars... one hundred dollars... when Naomi needed extra money for her precious servant!

A very awkward situation, especially since this was a lean month. He couldn't very well tell Naomi that he preferred to give one hundred dollars to a girl with red-gold hair and long, white hands and a siren's voice; and he certainly could not repudiate his promise to Hester Ashburn... It would serve Naomi right if her told her he could not raise the money. She had no business to behave in this high-handed fashion...

The rage he would like to have summoned, refused to answer his call. One hundred dollars! Why in heaven's name, had he said one hundred dollars? It was an unheard of sum to contribute to anything. Naomi would hear of it, of course; and Uncle Toby. Naturally, they would wonder, even if they said nothing. And on top of her taunting him with insufficient providing for the house...

Light flared in the window of the fruit shop at the corner. "Oranges, 75 cents a dozen," he read as he passed.

Oranges, seventy-five cents? Outrageous! And they ate three each morning, unless Uncle Toby felt like having the juice squeezed into a tumbler, when he took more than his share. Why, they probably used two dozen oranges a week—a dollar and a half, six dollars a month, seventy-two dollars a year!

He rarely thought about the price of food. He rarely did any shopping. But it occurred to him that if oranges were seventy-five cents a dozen, and other provisions proportionately high, Naomi must have added a considerable amount to that which he and Uncle Toby gave her.

Then a wave of self-pity blotted out resentment against the economic situation.

"Here I am," he thought, "struggling against every known handicap—strong competitors, too little capital and lack of appreciation. Not a word of encouragement from anybody! My wife engrossed in her own affairs, and grudging me the personal care a man of my temperament requires. She takes no interest in her home. I believe she would like me to live in a sort of editorial office, at the mercy of some ill-trained servant."

At the mention of servant, his discomfort increased. He crept upstairs more quietly than usual, undressed by the light from the hall, and went to bed in the spare room.

Naomi must be made aware of his displeasure!

CHAPTER 11

HE CAME down to breakfast convinced that he was exceedingly ill. Life seemed to be turned inside out. All the pleasing sensations of the evening previous were reversed. A cruel depression weighed upon his spirit.

"I am not at all well," he announced, hoping that Naomi would chide him—contritely—for having slept in the spare room. She knew that he was always upset after sleeping in a strange bed, and the spare room had an eastern exposure.

"Is there anything particular the matter?" She asked, pouring his coffee, "or do you just feel as though the world had turned sour?"

"I have a cruel headache," he retorted, really thinking this was true.

Naomi was sorry. Perhaps he'd better not go to the office. If there was anything she could do...

"Nothing, thank you," he said, implying, as was his custom, that no woman—indeed, few men—could cope with the vast problems that crowded his days. "As a matter of fact, my responsibilities are more than ordinarily heavy just now. Life insurance this month, fire insurance next month—" he paused, hoping that his wife would be smitten with her inconsideration in foisting a new and unexpected burden upon him, and also in an endeavour to make a fortuitous opening for his next announcement.

He had not anticipated such difficulty in mentioning his gift to Hester Ashburn. He was not in the habit of apologising to his wife. Rarely did he make an explanation. He stated facts. That was sufficient. "I have planned to do thus and so," he would say. "Next week, we will arrange..." To have convinced him that this was tyranny would have been utterly impossible.

"Then this business of the servant," he said. "It isn't as if I had expected it—or—prepared for it."

Again he paused. Nothing had been further from his intention than saying this. He had not meant to refer to the circumstance in so many words at all. He was only weakening the effect he wished to create—the part of the injured husband.

His irritation against Naomi increased. To her, he attributed this unprecedented embarrassment and constraint. If she had shown any interest, if she had asked questions, if she had admitted her wrong-doing, everything would have been pleasant. After all, why should he find it difficult to tell her? Wasn't the money his? Hadn't he worked for it slavishly? Did he indulge in any of the extravagances that other men pretended to consider necessities? He was the very embodiment of frugality and self-denial. Even Naomi would not argue that. Wasn't she eternally bothering him about buying new clothes?

At the moment, Arnold overlooked the fact that he liked to see her sitting by the table, mending his clothing. There was an aspect of wifely submissiveness in the picture that mightily pleased him. Naomi performed her disagreeable task well, and never were his garments unsightly or uncomfortable. But he gave her no credit for that. He didn't consider her, at all. It was his own self-denial that dominated his thinking. Other men didn't wear patched and darned clothing. He knew, for he'd asked them!

If Naomi was the woman she ought to be—the woman he hoped she was—she would approve his generosity. She would realise, with penitence, that but for her headlong lunge, there would have been no pinch. They could, between them, have regulated the expenditure. It really was her fault, Arnold told himself—not that he liked openly to blame a woman.

"Are you looking for anything?" she asked, surprised to see him hovering around the door.

"No, thank you. But I was forgetting to mention—er—it just occurred to me to say that last night I attended a meeting at the Parish Hall. There will probably be a notice of it in this morning's paper. To say it was interesting is not enough. It was inspiring—a fact which will be ably concealed, no doubt, in the garbled account provided for the public. I—er—promised one hundred dollars towards the furtherance of a certain form of missionary endeavour that is being carried on by a—er—Miss—er—Ashburn. She is a very unusual woman and is doing a very unusual work. I believe it would interest and appeal to you."

He couldn't resist the temptation to linger and witness the effect of this announcement. To himself, he said it would be cowardly, undignified, to bolt.

Naomi's manner was not quite what he had anticipated. In fact, he could not divine precisely what thoughts were passing in her mind. There was a brief pause before she asked—

"Did you say one h-hundred dollars, Arnold?"

He repeated the figures, adding, "The appeal was quite irresistible. One felt that too much could not be done to ameliorate the condition of those unfortunate Indian women and children."

Naomi stared after him. One hundred dollars to ameliorate the condition of Indian women and children... She wanted to laugh. Or was it to cry?

Uncle Toby's bell rang, and she did neither. She hurried into the kitchen to get his tray. Then the daily round of household duties claimed her. An impression of pleasant orderliness must be created upon the maid.

A telegram arrived, asking her to rush out an article for Easter. "Depending on you," it read. "Go to press next week. Don't fail us." She strained against her obligations until their shackles bit deep into her sensitive spirit. Plan as she would, work as she did, there was always *one more job* between her and a sense of freedom. Had a different temperament been hers, or a different husband, perhaps she could have left the beds unmade and the dishes unwashed while the urge to write was strong. As matters stood, she was enslaved by the habits of other people, by the conquest of the trifle, by an absurd routine and fictitious importance placed upon regularity. For, although regularity is to be highly commended in the running of a clock, it must be recognised as an obstruction to the working of a creative mind.

A thin trickle of water met her eyes as she took what she had thought was a last look into the kitchen. It had its rise under the refrigerator, and purled across the linoleum to a spot behind the gas stove. There it formed a shallow pool.

"To-day, of all days!" thought Naomi. "Why not last week, or next? And yet, it's a wonder that it has held out so long... Cheap, even when we were married... and I remember Arnold was convinced—when he heard the price—that we should get along without one. He said his mother kept her provisions in the cellar! A new refrigerator... and I've engaged a maid... and Arnold has promised one hundred dollars to ameliorate the condition of Indian women..."

The ice and provisions had to come out before she telephoned the tinsmith. The kitchen, with its bright blue woodwork and blue and white enamel-ware, presented a very disordered appearance, in the meantime. Naomi began to hope that the girl would be late, that she wouldn't come at all... And yet, some one must take charge of the house, after Tuesday.

Jennie McQuaig appeared at the front door in good time to hamper Naomi's preparations for lunch. She was a neat-looking girl who seemed to strike a balance between the palpably untrained applicants who wished to be one of the family, and those whose manner suggested noble lineage, and whose years of service had bred a superiority that bordered closely upon insolence. She listened to the multitude of instructions with artless affability and managed to convey the impression that domestic work, in her opinion, was not life's gravest consideration. Naomi's anxiety that things should go smoothly, awoke but feeble response. A leak in the refrigerator? Why, that was nothing! It took more than that to worry her!

"Now, about lunch," said Naomi. "I've made a beginning, as you see. We have simple meals, very simple indeed. But we like them well cooked and daintily served."

"Sure," approved Jennie.

"You are in charge, now," said Naomi, smiling. "Just look about and get your bearings; and do remember that the meals *must* be punctual."

Jennie consulted a gold wrist watch, held it to her ear, shook it and attacked the stem-winder reproachfully. "Took it into its head to stop," she said. "What time do you have breakfast?"

Naomi told her. "I like to get to my desk early in the mornings," she added, wondering if that was, in effect, what Shireen would have said.

"Get where?"

"To my desk. I am a writer, you know—er—stories and books and things."

She had meant to say more, to point out her need for quiet, to enjoin upon this girl from the start the necessity of uninterrupted periods for work. But she didn't. She couldn't.

Native shyness and Arnold's unsympathetic judgements made her deprecate her writing. She simply could not bring herself to invest it with the importance that it was due. Just as Arnold found it difficult to admit his weakness, so Naomi found it difficult to parade her strength, to demand consideration for her power of achievement.

"I want you to be happy here," she said, pausing in the doorway, "to look upon our house as your home."

Jennie offered no objection to this sentiment. Indeed, she seemed to enter into the spirit of it, right heartily. Sitting in her bed room, trying to arrange "Easter thoughts" with some degree of coherency, Naomi was unpleasantly conscious of boisterous merriment in the kitchen; and when she descended thither, to urge a little haste in the matter of luncheon, she discovered her assistant in agreeable converse with the tinsmith—both seated on the table enjoying the expensive and succulent apples that were Uncle Toby's especial delight.

Luncheon was fifteen minutes late.

A dreadful constraint lay like a blight upon the meal. All three of them were depressed by the alien presence of the maid. At moments, Arnold and Uncle Toby showed towards her an exaggerated courtesy that was both ridiculous and embarrassing and, in the next, they adopted an attitude that was almost hostile. Naomi rose from the table thankfully. The experience had been thoroughly exhausting.

"I might have known there would be difficulties at first," she told herself, endeavouring to capture a happier frame of mind. "We are all absurdly set in our ways—how set, I never realised. The girl is not stupid... It won't take her long to learn..." And once more the word Tuesday flamed across the background of her deliberate thinking.

As the hours wore on, and she found herself confronted by the seemingly illimitable task of instructing Jennie in what that gay young person described as their "funny little ways," a wave of fiery revolt caught her on its rising tide. Consciously or not, Arnold and Uncle Toby had made matters unnecessarily trying, instead of being encouraging and helpful.

"Tyranny!" she cried. "Another illustration of that will-to-rule which is so firmly entrenched behind the personality of Man! To them, Jennie is the embodiment of my rebellion, and they seek, through her, to punish me. It isn't fair! It isn't fair!"

She didn't want to tyrannise. In striving for certain measures that were opposed to her husband's viewpoint, she felt that no progressive intelligence could accuse her of tyranny. Tyranny was government, harsh administration, the asserting of authority, the imposition of one will upon another.

Nothing was farther from Naomi's intention than taking precedence over the men of her household. She had no greater desire to be a master than a slave. She knew that the highest ideal for married people is equality—a state where love has suspended authority—where each seeks the happiness of the other, where neither commands and neither obeys. Ingersoll, that noble Apostle of Unbelief, said that there will never be a generation of great men until there has been a generation of free women, "free in thought," she reflected, "free of that sense of dominance, of the obligation to please and pacify; free to fail and learn from failure, and free to strive again."

She sat at her desk, motionless, while these thoughts surged into her mind. They could not, she feared, be correlated to an Easter article, and they were too personal to appear in *The Book of the Hour*. She could not deliberately hurt Arnold.

Shireen telephoned to ask her to drive and hear a new chapter. "It's absolutely the best thing I've done yet," she cried. "Doolydear is as proud as if I'd presented him with twins. I worked most of last night, and am just getting up. We'll pick up Hugo and somebody else," she added by way of offering a further attraction.

Naomi felt she could not leave Jennie alone on her first afternoon. She said so guardedly, fearing lest she should hurt the girl by an implication of distrust. Shireen found her attitude utterly incomprehensible. "I thought the idea of getting a servant," she said, petulantly, "was to allow you to go out more, to give you greater freedom..."

Hugo telephoned. Carrying on a conversation with him was unsatisfactory and mutually disappointing. Jennie did not miss a word of Naomi's share.

"That gentleman has a nice voice," she observed, "the kind of voice that sounds grand in the dark. I set a good deal of store by men's voices, don't you?"

She certainly did not concentrate on any one type, and spent most of the afternoon communicating to her friends how easily she had found a place and how amiable were the members of the household.

"Sure, I like it first rate," she asserted, with flattering monotony. "Come and see me. There ain't much to do."

"Young fella from my home," she explained, several times. "I told his mother I'd look after him."

"Are you engaged to any of these men?" Naomi mustered courage to ask.

With a sharp scream, Jennie disclaimed such a suggestion.

"I ain't the marryin' kind," she averred. "Men change just as soon as they get to be your husband. There's some difference in 'em before... but all husbands is the same. If God meant us to marry men, I allus wonder why he made such a poor job of 'em!"

Despite which unflattering opinion, all her efforts were devoted to their comfort and convenience. This was evident in such foolish little things...

She was careful to fill Arnold's glass and Uncle Toby's, although the water-bottle stood between them. Against the pangs of Naomi's thirst, however, she made no provision. When Uncle Toby dropped his napkin, she was quick to pick it up and return it to him; but when, through her own clumsiness, she swept Naomi's fork from the table, she retired precipitously to stifle a giggle that bid fair to overcome her, allowing the mistress of the house to retrieve her own property. And Naomi suffered the incident to pass without remonstrance. All day she had tutored, explained and supervised. Never had she realised the number and absurdity of their individual habits. She despaired of ever training anyone else to remember them.

"No, Jennie, don't give Mr. St. John a small amount of milk in a large glass," she interrupted. "He likes a small glass, full to the brim. This is the particular cup Mr. Lennox uses; and he does not eat fruit sugar. You must put this little bowl beside his plate. The brown bread is especially for Mr. St. John. Always keep ahead with it. He wants it a day old. No, don't give Mr. Lennox that piece! He prefers the end— the heel, some people call it, Wait a moment—this is not salt, it's soda. Put it here, where Mr. St. John can reach it. He takes a pinch in water after dinner... No, we don't have soup every night, but when we do, try to remember that Mr. Lennox won't use this round soup spoon... Get another one out of the drawer..."

It had been like that all day.

Jennie McQuaig came through the ordeal without loss of energy or temper. She sang lusty ballads while removing the traces of dinner, punctuating certain phrases with a crashing of china and granite-ware, that suggested the introduction of cymbals in the midst of a barbaric hymn.

Arnold frowned and closed the living-room door. He was explaining to Uncle Toby how far-reaching was the effect of his gift to Hester Ashburn. Nearly everyone he met discussed it.

"I was astonished," he said, "to discover the degree of interest that has been stimulated. After all, the public is very easily swayed! Because a poor man gives cheerfully of his slender resources, the townsfolk are touched and hasten to follow his example. With that absurd lack of accuracy that characterises most affairs of this sort, people are referring to the work as 'my cause.'"

Naomi listened without comment. It was obvious to her that any pricking of conscience he may have suffered, any fugitive regret, had been dissipated by the warmth of public sentiment. A quaint thought came to her as she went to her desk, and she wondered if it might not be possible to arouse some enthusiasm over his promised assistance towards the amelioration of the condition of Mrs. Arnold Lennox? How gratified he would be if friends applauded his conduct! How happily he would watch the experiment!

But the romance of the commonplace held no corner in Arnold's imagination. He was profoundly stirred by a dew-washed rose in a park, or a well-kept garden, but he never could see that rose in relation to the table in his kitchen. Its presence there would not have altered the atmosphere for him one jot or tittle. He worshipped Beauty as he worshipped God. Both, to him, were sacred. But both must be kept apart from intimate contact, divorced from all reality, otherwise they would not remain pure and unsullied. And love... Love, also, must have a hallowed casket of its own, shut away from the contamination of too familiar usage. It was there to be apostrophised, looked at in secret, associated with a buried past, and laid away again. That it could in any way be related to making beds, respect for his wife's working hours, or palliation of the awkwardness of an untrained servant, was a conception that was profoundly repugnant to him. He could not see that as sunlight flings showers of gold into the hovels of the slums, so love illumines the humblest task. He was enslaved by a rigid sense of propriety, and carrying love about in a scuttle of coal, or finding it in the vacuum cleaner, offered, in his judgement, an insult to the finest impulses in life. Arnold inevitably laid the best things away—clothes, trinkets, table linen, silver, religion. His gift to Hester Ashburn was remote from immediate surroundings. It was an act of devotion. His promise to Naomi was a vastly different matter; it was an enforced and virtueless domestic measure.

The house shivered as a door slammed, and Jennie McQuaig set out to redeem her promise to some boy's mother. Naomi was not surprised to find that she had not turned down the beds; neither had she filled Uncle Toby's thermos bottle, nor switched off the light in her bed room. These important details arranged, she returned to her desk and assembled, by sheer force of will, a few thoughts that seemed suitable for Easter. There was nothing original in them. In fact, they were the platitudes which the Editor himself, had expressed and, therefore they appeared to him inspired and illuminating. He wrote a most complimentary letter of acknowledgement and enclosed a liberal cheque.

Naomi lay awake that night, following, simultaneously, two distinct lines of thought. At least, she tried to follow both. One carried her away with Hugo, and the other left her at home with Arnold. But the future—after Tuesday—was dark and impenetrable. She simply could not visualise her life with Hugo. She was going... she had given him her word... she had promised herself an end to this state of bondage. But it was so much easier to see herself struggling with Jennie McQuaig, to hear her remonstrance when some attention to the men had been neglected. If was even less difficult to imagine an imitation of Shireen's household... although she was forced to confess that, as a step towards fuller freedom, Jennie's first day had not been a conspicuous success.

CHAPTER 12

NAOMI awoke on Tuesday morning, expecting to glow with intense elation. But she was disappointed. She was conscious only of utter weariness, of a desire to lie quietly in bed for days, for years, forever.

Last night, Arnold had declared that he could, without loss of dignity, mitigate the harshness of his discipline. He could forgive. For driving home his displeasure at the situation that had been forced upon him, a certain constraint throughout the day would serve.

Naomi had been given little opportunity to protest. Under the influence of a merciful sedative she had fallen asleep, unaware of her husband's restlessness, of his struggle to find a potent reason to do what he wished to do. When, at last, he was convinced that the act he anticipated was an expression of forgiveness and that forgiveness was required of those who profess the doctrines of Christianity, he went quickly to her. But his gratification in attaining to so spiritual a frame of mind was tempered by his wife's unresponsiveness. To do him justice, he did not know that he violated a half-drugged woman. "Sullen," he said to himself. "Her old fault. She makes no effort to conquer it." And, this conviction being firmly established, his own triumph shone the brighter, and he fell comfortably to sleep.

———

Panting a little as a result of the exercises with which nothing ever interfered, Arnold came back into the room. He always looked fresh and rosy after his bath, like a healthy baby.

"Hadn't you better get up?" he said. "That girl never has a meal on time, and I dislike to be hurried over breakfast."

"Yes," returned Naomi. "I must get up. Somehow, it seems a great effort this morning."

"That's disappointing. Now that you are relieved of all household duties, I expected you would be practically immune to physical distress."

A stinging retort rose to Naomi's lips. But she crushed it. He was absolutely sincere. He would not—could not—see that a housekeeper, a homemaker, had anything to do. He honestly believed that since Jennie McQuaig came, Naomi was as free of the trivial round of common tasks as he was, himself.

"What a shock he will suffer when I am gone!" she thought. "Poor Arnold!"

She got into a negligée (Arnold did not like to see her in a negligée at breakfast. *He* was fully dressed and equipped for the day's work, why not she?) and hurried downstairs to help the helper. If this could only be different from other mornings, she said to herself; if she could only come upon some evidence of pleasing magic, performed during the night! For example, the electrolier, chipped accidentally by Arnold healed of its wound; the film of dust that rose from the flue and settled on the console table might have chosen some other place to rest; the morning paper might have been brought inside and laid at Arnold's plate, and breakfast might have been already spread temptingly before her. Flowers, she thought... if she could, for once, have dozens and dozens of roses! And nothing to do... just for a little while... a sense of relaxation, leisure... If she could only feel that the forecast of great happiness marked this day!

The kitchen presented an aspect of hideous confusion. Apparently, every pan, dish and spoon had been requisitioned in the preparation of a simple meal. Jennie was sawing cheerfully at a fresh loaf of bread while two half-cut loaves languished in the box beside her. The coffee pot was weeping stealthy brown tears over its fat belly. A partially-gnawed apple lay upon the table.

"It's one grand day," cried Jennie gaily. "Everything's got to go right to-day! I think we'll get along fine, don't you? I was telling my boy-friend last night—"

"What about the bacon?" interrupted Naomi. "I want to show you exactly how Mr. Lennox likes it cooked. He is just a little particular about his bacon."

Three very small slices were brought to light. Naomi exclaimed in surprise.

"Maybe hadn't ought to have et it," suggested Jennie McQuaig. "I don't care over-much for veal, and last night I cooked a couple of pieces for my supper. But there's enough for Mr. Lennox," she announced, comfortingly. "It won't matter about us. For once, we can do without."

Inwardly, Naomi smiled. We can do without! How significant—that "we!" How admirably it demonstrated the girl's attitude towards Man! How ineradicable was the instinct to sacrifice, to serve!

Already, Jennie McQuaig had betrayed her position in regard to the members of the household. Already, she had assigned them the relationship they should hold towards her. In less than twenty-four hours, she had tacitly agreed to enter into a compact with a sister-woman to provide material comfort for two mere men. That any peculiar effort should be directed towards relieving the mistress of the house, obviously did not offer itself for serious consideration. It was evident that she expected to work with Naomi, not for her.

"Here's a nice big orange," said the girl. "I'll put it on Mr. —er—on the old gentleman's tray. I gave him the best of the toast... old people, you know..."

Naomi drank a little coffee while Arnold glanced at the news. He had his own paper at the office, but always appropriated during breakfast the one to which she subscribed. Usually, Uncle Toby took it next, so that, by the time her turn came round, she was engrossed either with household routine, or had seized the opportunity to do a little writing.

"Miss Ashburn's fund is growing," commented Arnold. "I see the Bishop has made an appeal. You had better ask her here, I think, before too many others decide to entertain her. I don't know how long she intends to stay in town."

Naomi murmured something that Arnold understood as a matter of course, to be acquiescence. He said he would discuss the arrangements more fully at noon. At the door he turned.

"Good-bye."

"Good-bye, Arnold," said Naomi, half tempted to kiss him.

This was the last time. She would never come to the door with him again. She would never feel that cruel sense of imprisonment as he shut her in to perform a round of thankless tasks when she longed passionately to be doing something else. To-morrow morning, she would ... What *would* she be doing to-morrow morning?

Naomi found it impossible to picture herself encompassed by the ambit of Hugo's life. She could recite her intentions. She could repeat the schedule of arrangements as they had been made. But she could not link them up with her inner consciousness. They were like a set of revolving wheels, which, operating perfectly in themselves, missed the particular cog that bound them to the rest of the machine and enabled them to function as a whole.

"If I could only feel happier," she thought, following the tuneful Jennie to the kitchen. "It isn't fair to Hugo to go to him like this... I can't seem to burst the husk that's imprisoning me. I'm numb... Maybe I'm ill... But if that's the trouble, I should go to a hospital."

Suppose, by this time to-morrow, she should be sorry! How scarifying would be the recollection that no emotional urge prompted her to take the step. She was cheated of the dizzying madness that drives women joyously into a lover's arms. There came to her the horrible suspicion that she loved not Hugo more, but Arnold less. The thought tormented her until she did not know what were her sensations. She couldn't be so calculating... she couldn't go to Hugo merely as a means towards freedom... If it was only freedom that she sought, why not go away alone? Blankness followed. Alone... no, never! It was inconceivable that she should sever every human tie in exchange for a problematic literary success. Besides, Hugo would never allow her to stay alone...

"Suppose we make out a menu for the week," she suggested. In less than two hours, Hugo would be waiting for her at the station.

"Sure," agreed the girl. "That'll be a good thing. We don't have to follow it."

Ordering progressed exactly as usual. Arnold's clothes were sent to be pressed. The man came to read the meter. Half a load of kindling was delivered. Uncle Toby sent down his new waist-coat to have a spot removed.

Naomi gathered up what was written of *The Book of the Hour*, stuffed a sheaf of notes into an envelope and laid them in the top of her suitcase. It was the one she had used when she went away with Arnold.

"*Why* does it matter?" she cried. "Why can't I be concerned with fundamentals rather than these irritating and absurd externalities? Every moment should be a burning moment... I am going to be free... free... This is my spiritual regeneration... and I am emotionally numb, thinking of trifles that bind me to a miserable past."

A faint flicker of emotion touched her as she placed in the bag a nightdress she had never worn. That mattered, but she would allow herself no time to dwell upon the sensations it provoked. Handkerchiefs... there were not many. The rest were in the laundry... Thursday...Yes, it would come home Thursday, and Thursday would be Jennie's afternoon out. Who would receive and pay for it, she wondered? Uncle Toby? If the man carried it away again, there would be unthinkable confusion.

Her little sewing case. She had taken that, also, on her honeymoon, and Arnold had given her several opportunities to use it. It was then that she had first mended a garment for him without asking him to take it off.

"Your dear hands," he had said. "I love to feel them fluttering about me. You must never allow them to grow red and coarse, Naomi. I could not bear that!"

She wondered if Hugo would discover buttons that were loose, or a rip in the lining of his overcoat.

"This sort of thing always happens in books," she thought, "the sort of thing that touches the nobler instincts of the erring wife and drives her back to the song of the vacuum cleaner when her soul would have winged its way to the melody of the nightingale. Thank God, I am spared the discovery of a baby's first shoe, or the Bible that my mother gave me on my wedding day!" She searched through the strange assortment of merchandise that constitutes the confusion of a woman's top drawer, and found a quotation from Ingersoll—

"What light is to the eyes, what love is to the heart, Liberty is to the soul of man. Without it, there comes suffocation, degradation and death.

"Liberty is the condition of progress. Without Liberty there remains only barbarism. Without Liberty there can be no civilization...

"Liberty, thou art the god of my idolatry!... Thou askest naught from man except the things that good men hate—the whip, the chain, the dungeon key... At thy sacred shrine, hypocrisy does not bow, virtue does not tremble, superstition's feeble tapers do not burn but Reason holds aloft her inextinguishable torch whose holy light will one day flood the world."

As she sorted hair nets, gloves, a trinket or two, boxes of pins, powder, the circumstances in which she had laid that clipping away flashed across her mind. She had cut it out, intending to show it to Arnold after he had forbidden her to hold any further intercourse with Shireen Dey.

How vividly the scene recurred to her! How clearly their conversation echoed in her memory, how furious Arnold had been!

Shireen had driven over to spend the afternoon. She had brought an armful of roses. In the bright fire-glow, they nodded drowsily, breathing an exotic perfume. Uncle Toby was in the South; Arnold was at the office. The house was still and seemed to be deliciously her own.

Then, unexpectedly early, Arnold had come home.

He accepted the cup of tea Shireen had thrust upon him in his most disagreeably faultless manner. His attentions and well-modulated banalities had been beyond criticism. At first, he even responded to Shireen's gay jibes with heavily frosted witticisms. But Naomi could feel the tension, the cold anger that underlay his words, and she knew that when, like a rubber band, his self-control gave way, he would arrange to stand sufficiently near for one end to whip against her spirit.

161

"I've been hearing part of the new book," said Shireen. "I think it's immense."

"Really?" murmured Arnold. "You are very kind."

"Nothing of the sort," contradicted the visitor. "Discriminating, if you like, but not kind. As a matter of fact, Mr. Lennox, you do insufficient justice to Naomi's genius—for the woman is a genius, and no mistake. You don't appreciate her, by half. I speak, now, as a critic, rather than a friend. But I think that with you, the relation should be reversed. You should be the friend, rather than the critic. Why, I actually suffer for her, realising the few moments she is free to spend at her desk every day."

"Let me take your cup," urged Arnold, with careful courtesy. "No more? Er—does my wife give you the impression of a prisoner shut away from light and air?"

"She doesn't, but her work does, and she accomplishes too little in the volume of it. Art, Mr. Lennox, is a far more jealous god than most people seem to think, and the hours for devotion are not fixed at regular periods, like early Mass or Evening Prayer. One must hold oneself in readiness at all times to respond to the call. It's a case of 'Lord, here am I,' at any hour of the day or night. To say, 'I'll be there in a moment, when I've finished what I'm doing,' is fatal. Believe me, I've tried, and I know."

"If Art requires its disciples to be monsters of egotism and selfishness, then I think we should close the temples, so to say," observed Arnold. "Women have certain functions— sacred functions—to perform, and, because of this, they have been held in reverence by men. When a woman repudiates her debt to mankind, when she deliberately creates for herself another sphere, then she ceases to be a woman worthy of chivalrous consideration."

"But see here," cried Shireen, "why should she be less a

woman because she is a creator of something other than red and squirming babies? For in its last analysis, that's what you really mean. What of Hypatia, Joan of Arc, Florence Nightengale, Anne Hutchinson—to mention only a few whose names pop into my mind at the moment? Could they have performed their very definite service to civilisation from within the narrow confines of the sphere apportioned them by man? Of course not!" she answered herself, vigorously. "In every age, the woman who wants to create—a poem, a picture, a vocation, a 'new' social code, must first struggle clear of the ancient tradition that a man is not a man unless his wife is wholly dependent upon him. This is one of the countless methods by which she pomades his vanity. Why can't man be content to see that he is only *half* of the human species? Why must he want to hold dominion over all?"

"Well, I don't believe I quite follow you," returned Arnold, with icy politeness. "Man's sphere throughout the ages seems to me to have been one of protection, provision. My simple philosophy is expressed in the idea of service. So far as I can see it, men have served their women faithfully—even to paying the supreme sacrifice in times of war. Is it too much to expect—say fifty per cent service in return?"

"I admit," Shireen answered, "that there are too many women in whom the commutual sense, the reciprocal sense, is lacking. They want to eat their cake and have it, too. Like the slaves in the South, they achieved freedom too suddenly. They don't know how to use it. Mentally, physically, economically, they are parasites. They will not last. Think of the others, however; of the women whose mental development and chosen sphere of endeavour—whose creative ability—justifies them in demanding the identical type of freedom that is accorded men. What of the woman artist, musician, decorator, physician, lawyer? Suppose, to drive home my argument more clearly, you were a novelist, would you not claim the independence necessary to pursue your vocation?"

Arnold observed that unless he were one of the great masters of literature, he could not imagine himself engrossed with the business of writing, at all. Comparatively few men, he ventured, devoted themselves exclusively to literature of that sort.

"In other words," Shireen cut in, "you mean to imply that they do something useful as a regular profession and scribble as a hobby or a pastime?"

"That expresses pretty closely what I mean. Moreover, I think you will grant that a large percentage of the women who write are not actuated by the promptings of genius or the need to make a living. Most of them, I think you will find, are adequately provided for by some man. They have gone mad over this idea of independence. They have lost the sense of service. It is they, not we, who reject a fifty-fifty basis for our relationship. Because a story or a picture, or a song brings financial return, they assume that they have no further responsibilities, no other duties. Personally, I cannot believe that, in her heart, any true and upright woman wishes to be exempt from a life of Christian service to her fellow beings."

"The creative life is a Christian life," retorted Shireen. "The creative life is the only life that really matters."

Then she kissed Naomi impulsively and rushed from the house.

As the door closed, Arnold's temper reached its utmost limit. It snapped across Naomi's face, so to say, leaving an ugly scar. The things he said, the accusations he made, could never be wiped from Memory's slate. He assumed that his wife had criticised him to another woman. He was stung almost to madness by what he termed her disloyalty. It never occurred to him that Shireen Dey could perceive in his conduct the attitude with which she had charged him.

"Henceforth," he cried, "I forbid that woman to enter my house!"

"But isn't part of the house mine?" Naomi had asked. "I will admit her to that, in future, for I can't obey you in this matter, Arnold, and it would not be honest to pretend that I can. Please don't look so grievously hurt. Can't you imagine how you would feel had I taken a similar stand in regard to one of your friends? If you could *only* open your eyes to the fact that my feelings are identical with yours... that, just as you would be stung if I forbade one of your friends the house, so I am smarting at the present moment. If you would try to see that, I think we would both be happier."

"If you derive any satisfaction from disregarding my wishes," said Arnold, stiffly, "then of course, I have nothing more to say, except that the influence of that woman upon you is simply poisonous. In the circumstances, I think I will have my dinner down town."

Naomi glanced at the clipping which she knew by heart, and recalled that she had never shown it to Arnold. While his resentment against her was bitter, Ingersoll's message would have been wasted. When his anger cooled, it seemed foolish to revive the affair. And now, she could not bring herself to leave the cutting, lest it appear like a taunt, lest it inflict an unnecessary wound. She thrust it into her bag.

Eleven o'clock! Uncle Toby was stirring upstairs. Suppose he should come into her room for a little chat! How could she get out of the house, undiscovered, with a suitcase? A disquieting sense of failure took possession of her. Something was sure to happen. She could think of no plausible story that would cover her escape. Perhaps it would bet better, after all, to blurt out the truth. But that was out of the question. Uncle Toby would get in touch with Arnold, and there would be a scene at the station...

Hairpins! Had she forgotten them? Soon, she would have her hair cut off anyway. Unlike Arnold and Uncle Toby, Hugo approved of women with short hair. She wondered where he was going, what would be their first stopping place, whether he had made any ultimate plans. She hadn't. She had begged him to spare her that part. Her intention was to slip from the house, telephone Jennie from the station that she would not be home for lunch, and send Arnold a wire some time during the afternoon. After that... a blank.

She closed the bag and took it downstairs, hiding it beneath the Chesterfield. Oh, this sneaking off was loathsome! If she only dared send for a taxi, risk Uncle Toby's discovery, and set forth upon her new life with honesty and high courage! But it was too late to think of that now. The minutes were passing with incredible rapidity. She returned to her room, put on her hat and coat, and crept down stairs. On the bottom step, she paused, listening. Uncle Toby had nearly discovered her as he descended to his bath.

"Over it, he'll spend his usual hour," she thought, remembering that this need not annoy her again. Did Hugo take possession of the bath room, she wondered, using it not only as a place for cleansing his person, but as a barber shop, gymnasium, dressing room and library?

In the living room, habit asserted itself. She glanced rapidly about, as was her custom before leaving the house. An irritating insistence of domesticity made her wonder whether she had forgotten anything. With an effort, she shook herself mentally free.

It would be awkward to meet anyone—Mrs. Allyn, for

instance. It would be difficult to explain the suitcase. Oh, if she only dared tell the truth!

An utterly grotesque conversation whirled through her mind.

Mrs. Allyn—Oh, I see you are going away.

Herself—Yes, I am leaving my husband.

Mrs. Allyn—Indeed? How interesting! Some other man, I suppose?

Herself—Incidentally, but the primary reason is my work. I must work!

Mrs. Allyn—Well, my dear, I hope the arrangement will be successful. I do, indeed. Men are exacting though. In one way, or—in several. Let me hear from you. As an experiment, it's worth trying. I've often thought of it myself… Perhaps, some day…

Panting a little, Naomi opened the door. The bridge was nearly crossed. She was about to pass out of her old life into…

"Oh, my God!"

Her muscles stiffened. Her eyes grew wide. There, at the gate, like the angel with a flaming sword, stood a shining black ambulance. She knew intuitively that something had happened to Arnold.

CHAPTER 13

NAOMI preceded the stretcher-bearers upstairs. Time seemed to stand still; or, if not that, to accommodate itself to their slow and measured tread. Some sort of curious spell had fallen on the world.

She had ample opportunity to fling the incriminating suitcase into a cupboard, remove her hat and coat and arrange the bed before they reached her room. All the while, she kept thinking, "There may have been some mistake... some other Lennox... I'll say, That is not my husband!" Then regardless of everything, of Uncle Toby, Jennie McQuaig, *everything*, she would rush to the station.

But no... there wasn't any mistake. It was Arnold that they carried; Arnold who neither moved nor spoke, whose face was covered with a striped gray blanket. She didn't know whether he was hurt or dead.

A sound broke in upon her consciousness. Uncle Toby was splashing about in the bath-room; and Jennie McQuaig's voice rose in raucous gaiety from the kitchen. How could this be possible? Centuries had passed since she left this room, left them making those identical sounds. She was young, then, five hundred years ago... The clock? It must have stopped... A vague thought of Pompeii and its arrested life, floated through her mind.

One of the stretcher-bearers was speaking. He was a very brisk young man; thin, swarthy, with black lacquered hair and a manner of resolute professionalism. His eyes flashed at Naomi and away again, as if he feared that the sight of her might arouse some slumbering weakness in him. "No room for emotions in my business," he seemed to say. "If you are lovely, I'd better not see it; if you are suffering, I don't want to know it. And there's no use screaming, for I'm as deaf as I am blind."

He laid hold of the blanket, and paused.

"Unconscious, now," Naomi heard him say. "No cause for alarm. Got off rather better than the others. He'll come round, presently. Doctor ought to be here, any minute."

Dispassionately, she watched him hover over Arnold, undress him, put him into bed. She saw the ugly blue marks that spread from his face down one side of his body, unmoved. She knew that his arm was broken.

Dear God, how that clock raced along! Perhaps it was fast. There might still be time... A taxi could do it...

What madness! She had taken off her hat and coat. It would be impossible to put them on while these two men were watching.

Why had she stayed at all? Why had she not braved Jennie's amazement and walked out of the back door as they came in the front? Now she was trapped... trapped... and Hugo was waiting!

As though, speaking through some medium other than her own throat, she asked:

"What happened?"

"Elevator," was the succinct reply. The brisk young man was at work with restoratives. He talked with a fine economy of words, as one who has been trained to regard any form of waste as inefficiency. "Operator killed. Two women pretty badly crushed. Telegraph boy, too." He was encouraged to proceed by the impassivity of Naomi's face, and plunged into details as though speaking to a trained nurse.

Naomi listened with the calmness of despair. She heard what he said, she could even visualise the dreadful scene, but she could feel nothing, neither revulsion, distress nor horror. She was numb.

Her head was filled with cloudy voices, distinguishable above the staccato flow of the young man's story. She struggled to silence them, and failed.

"This is the end!" How curiously clear were the words. "The end has come before the beginning. I might have known it would happen like this... Any other way would have left me a loophole. If I had only started five minutes sooner! If Arnold had only been taken to a hospital!"

A flood of confused impressions drowned definite words and phrases. Suppose she *had* left the house before they arrived... suppose she had gone, all unknowing to the station... A horrid picture formed in her mind: Jennie screaming at the door... Uncle Toby emerging in a panic from the bath-room... the frantic search for her... the doctor's dismay... public sympathy for Arnold! Oh, yes, she saw clearly enough that, in the circumstances, every door and every heart would be closed against her... and then, too, she thought of her own shock when she saw the papers...

Dear God, what an escape! In another minute, she would have been beyond recall!

The brisk young man put an electric pad at Arnold's feet. His rapid movements bewildered Naomi, made her head swim. She picked up a few words of his conversation and tried to correlate them to what was going on. Somehow, she seemed to be no part of the scene.

"He'll come round, all right. Pretty sound constitution, I should say. Pays to keep fit, doesn't it? Never lost consciousness until we were on our way here. Insisted that the others be attended to first. Plenty of grit, I'll say. Didn't like to hear the kid cry—the little telegraph chap I was telling you about... had to move him away. Ah, that's better... Here, Jim, hold this bottle..."

Naomi's attention drifted away, and she thought of Hugo pacing about the station, holding desperately to his faith in her word. She had promised. She had assured him that her mind was fixed; no matter what happened, she would be there. He had trusted her. She had persuaded him to put away his doubt. "Oh, my dear," he had cried in the telephone, "don't fail me this time. Think what you are saying, and, if you are going to weaken, for God's sake, do it now—don't wait until the last minute!"

She had waited until the last minute. No explanation was possible. He would not call her up, she knew, lest he should miss her. There was no way by which she could reach him.

A spasm of agony shot through her, shattering the merciful numbness that over her had lain like a shield. She was burned, she was crushed, she was strangled, she was torn in that eternity of exquisite pain. A moan, low and terrible, escaped from her lips.

The brisk young man looked up in surprise. He rushed at her, pushed her into a chair, and commanded her to drink.

"*Everything's* all right," he insisted. "No earthly reason for you to worry. Nasty blow on the head, of course, but nothing serious, and a broken arm's only a little inconvenient."

She nodded, finding it difficult to swallow. If she could only lose consciousness, drop dead. It must be in moments like these that people cut their throats, shot themselves, drank carbolic acid—employed any means whereby they might gain release from such unendurable anguish.

The brisk young man became almost pompously paternal. Comforting phrases rolled from him like a relentless sea. He knelt beside her and chafed her hands; he seized a magazine and fanned her. Under cover of his profession, he took harmless little liberties—touched her forehead, patted her knee, pressed her against his shoulder for support.

"Don't resist me," he seemed to say. "You are to me, just so much saw-dust. I am quite unaffected by all this—it is part of my job. My only sensation is one of impatience. Women are such a nuisance. They always need fussing over at the most inconvenient times! You appeared to be different, but I suppose none of you are different. You are all the same. We have to put up with you, that's all."

And all the while, Naomi saw, as a clairvoyant might have seen, that he did not regard her as so much saw-dust, nor was her unaffected by the more intimate contact with her. Although he had admired her coolness and self-control, he was infinitely more touched by this demonstration of her weakness. He was gratified. There lurked in it a subtle relation to himself. Immediately, he became the masterful male, the arbiter, the Man. He was warmed to perceive how moving and profound was her attachment to the inert lump of clay upon the bed. Lennox was an estimable fellow, no doubt; pleasing in his own way, but... An agreeable vision of himself drifted across his mind, and he dwelt upon the ease with which he could stir the hearts of women to devastating devotion.

Naomi wished that he would hold her in the chair, that he would weight her with enormous chains against which she could struggle impotently. It seemed that, without some form of physical detention, she *must* rush from the room, and to Hugo. He would be standing by the iron gate now, comparing his watch with the big clock overhead. He had almost given up hope. People streamed past him, walking jerkily, as they do in motion pictures. Here was a thin-lipped woman flinging angry sentences at her pertinent and panting husband; there, a man, hard-eyed and stern-jawed, snarled at his wife, who had just dashed in. Would

Hugo's face have glowed with joyous relief at her approach, or would he have glowered at her, pushed her along the platform, eased the cruel tension he had suffered by means of sharp reproofs?

She closed her hands convulsively. One of the young man's fingers was imprisoned in her clasp. What a sense of power it gave him—that clinging hold! How splendidly he reacted to the realisation of her dependence! He began to promise her—and himself—noble and extravagant achievements.

"You just trust me," he commanded. "I'll—"

Naomi did not listen. She must not scream, nor cry aloud. She must choke back Hugo's name when it rose to her lips. Think... think... how could she reach him in the shortest possible time? How soon could she send him an explanation?

What a fool she had been about their journey! How childish! If she only knew where he was going, at what place he intended to stop! A telegram addressed to his office would be cruelly delayed. Meanwhile, he would be enduring inexpressible torment, even though he despised her.

"Depend on me," said the brisk young man, "I'll—"

Hugo... Hugo! She nearly spoke the words aloud. With a last despairing look, he would be running towards the gateman with two tickets in his hand. Two tickets! Cramped for years by financial restrictions, Naomi found time to regret that extra ticket. A refund, of course... but, if he had bought it through to the West... Money! Her mind flashed back to Arnold. Did one pay these ambulance men, or did they send an account? Should one recognise their kindness by a personal honorarium? She had a little of her own money in the house. How ironical that it should be put to this use. She had intended to spend it with Hugo; not for Arnold.

Insurance... Arnold had spoken of insurance... Did he, by any chance, carry an accident policy? Here was another expense... He would suffer economically, she knew. There would be no thought of a trained nurse. *Her* services would be deemed adequate. But even should the accident prove slight, even if they were spared a lengthy period of invalidism, there would be a perceptible drain upon their resources. Her earning capacity would be submerged. The writer would surrender to the wife—the wife whose physical and mental endurance would be taxed to their utmost; whose solicitous ministrations would encourage such exactions as a salaried attendant would not have tolerated for an hour. Arnold scarcely knew the meaning of the word "illness," but Naomi recalled several instances when he had been indisposed.

A bell rang sharply. A door opened. "Here's the doctor, now," said the brisk young man, and rose from his unprofessional position.

Dr. Darrell dominated the room. Even Arnold responded to his compelling personality.

"He's coming round," announced the brisk young man, cold and unemotional again.

Naomi moved so that she could see the clock. Hugo had passed through the gate. It had clanged after him, leaving her on this side. Forever... No, no! She would *not* be fatalistic, superstitious. Some day, they would be able to recall this hour with a smile...

What was the doctor saying? "...possibility of internal injury... X-ray... In the meantime, you will do this... you must do that..."

Naomi felt driven to speak. Her spirit rose in revolt. She hated the doctor and his manner of a supreme dictator.

She resented his implication of her inferior intelligence. She rebelled against the performance of the thankless tasks he imposed upon her. "...hot fomentations every half hour... keep him quiet, free from worry... no excitement..."

She ceased to listen. What impossible things men required of women! How could she do all that and superintend the management of the house and care for Uncle Toby's comfort and get on with her writing? Why should it be expected of her? She pictured herself in Arnold's place, and imagined the doctor's advice to him. How it would differ from the commands he had just laid down. How lightly Arnold would escape the results of her misfortune. Would he stay home from the office to read her proof, keep her correspondence up to date, write to her dictation? Would he oversee the daily routine and keep *her* from worrying?

And there was not a word—even perfunctory—appreciating the task he had imposed.

"Don't you think," asked Naomi, "that considering everything, my husband would be well advised to go to a hospital?"

"I do," returned the doctor.

"We tried to persuade him," broke in the brisk young man, "but he wouldn't hear of it. Insisted upon being brought home. Said he knew—" the speaker regarded Naomi with cautious admiration "—that his wife would wish to look after him—that she would not deliver him up to the questionable ministrations of an unsympathetic stranger."

A clamant note followed the last words. Naomi stood rigid until its echo died away. It was the whistle of the train she had missed.

CHAPTER 14

ARNOLD's injuries proved to be very slight, but, such as they were, he made the most of them.

Never before had he felt justified in the exercising of deliberate tyranny, but now it seemed to Naomi that, from the moment he regained consciousness, his greatest pleasure lay in devising means whereby she might be kept busy. And she couldn't protest. Knowing his irrational habit of mind, she understood how sincere was his belief that every moment barren of service must be for her a miserable one; that her happiness lay in continuous attention, and that only by unremitting devotion could she hope to assuage the anxiety that possessed her. Assuming that her tasks were performed eagerly, he found it easy to conclude that her body was inured to physical strain.

"The true woman," she had often heard him say, "is in her element when ministering to the sick and ailing. It is her supreme pleasure to mitigate pain."

Naomi could never bring herself to confess that she was anything but a "true" woman who, besides her passion for nursing, enjoyed the routine work of her home, and who had not realised herself until she held her new-born babe to her breast! She couldn't bear to destroy Arnold's pretty fancies any more than she could have stripped the mask from the face of Santa Claus before a trusting child. It seemed unsportsmanlike to deliver an unnecessary blow when he was down, and, under normal conditions, there never arose a convenient opportunity. But, time after time, she offered a wordless prayer to Heaven that his eyes might be opened, or that someone would warn him against a too-literal practice of his theories. If Uncle Toby would only speak on her behalf, or the doctor—or even Jennie McQuaig! If only someone would remark, "Naomi looks like a ghost, herself. We must try to relieve the strain upon her." No one, however, had ever concerned themselves to discover the measure of her endurance, and she supposed no one ever would.

Proceeding from task to task, she marvelled that anybody could be so insensitive as Arnold, so completely self-centred that the eye failed to see and the ear failed to hear the deadly weariness that marked her every movement. Even her voice sank to a feeble tone.

As a matter of fact, both Arnold and the doctor *were* aware of Naomi's distress. But the former regarded it with secret gratification, and the latter with impatience. To Arnold, it was proof of her unsuspected intensity of affection for him. Obviously, she was unnerved by the haunting thought of what might have happened! He found her ghastly appearance almost pleasing.

The doctor, on the other hand, could see no excuse for a woman of Naomi's intelligence deliberately inviting a nervous collapse. Had he not assured her that there was no cause for worry? Could she not discriminate between truth and the soothing lies he was so frequently obliged to tell?

"If you don't behave like a rational being," he remonstrated, the day following the accident, "*you* will be *really* ill. And then who will look after you? Can't you believe me when I tell you that—"

He emphasised the trifling character of Arnold's injuries and explained again that he was suffering chiefly from nervous shock. A matter of temperament... and opportunity! Some people struggled against it, and some—he indicated the sick-room—surrendered. Why, if Arnold had been a labourer without insurance of any kind, he would have been back at work within twenty-four hours!

And yet, in the next instant, he would strengthen his patient's belief in the seriousness of his case, and encourage him to exact unnecessary attendance from her.

"Don't exert yourself in any way," he advised. "Just relax. Lie here and be happy. Rest and don't worry."

"Ah, but that's so difficult," Arnold sighed. "It's virtually impossible for one who has carried heavy responsibilities to let go and lean on the strength—or, more properly, the weakness—of a woman. However," he continued, addressing Naomi, "I'm afraid the doctor is right, my dear. I'm a pretty sick man, and *you'll* have to take care of *me*, for a change. I promise to give you as little trouble as possible."

What would happen if she attempted to shatter these agreeable illusions? What would happen to any wife who refused to feed her husband's vanity, to suggest by deed, if not by word—in silence, if not in speech—that he is everything but what he thinks he is. To demolish the particular niche in which he has placed himself would be to invite domestic chaos. Man can find no contentment with a woman who is not a good housekeeper for his spirit as well as his body. His Ego must move in an atmosphere that is swept clear of the dust of discouragement; it needs the coolness of patience and the warmth of blind faith; it delights in feminine weakness as a contrast to masculine prowess. The wise woman shades it from the glare of truth that will reveal worn and shabby spots, at the same time she lets in sufficient air and sunshine to keep it vital and strong.

"You are right, my dear," are the words a husband craves to hear most frequently on his wife's lips, and "You are wonderful" is the expression he seeks tirelessly in her eyes.

But doctors, thought Naomi—why could they not be honest enough to help women? Was it the persistence of tradition that influenced their treatment of men, or was it consideration for their own pocket-book? Courage would be required to deprive a patient of the enjoyment of painless individualism. Where was the physician who would say:

"Why, there's nothing the matter with you, old chap! Your only ailment is Man's natural desire to be petted and fussed over! Just go ahead as usual, and forget your troubles. After all, the only serious ones are those that never happen!"

Certainly, she could not imagine such word's on Darrell's lips, but, if he ever uttered them, she knew they would be addressed to a woman. Women—generally speaking—do not expect a *comfortable* illness. No physician of penetration harasses a housekeeper by advising her to achieve the impossible. "Do as little as you *can*," he says. "You are not improving your condition by standing so much. However, if you must—" He knows full well that her house cannot take care of itself, and that her husband will not take her to his office and combine his work with that of a trained nurse! Therefore, he does not expect her to resign herself literally to his pleasant commands. Only a man obeys a doctor's orders with unswerving fidelity. Fundamentally, women seek excuses to make work; men, to avoid it.

———

The telephone rang. Naomi's hand, halfway on its journey to Arnold's mouth, quivered. Perhaps this was word from Hugo!

"Be careful," cried Arnold. "You're spilling it! I wonder who that is... Listen!"

She listened. Downstairs, Jennie McQuaig spoke with the cheery responsiveness of a telephone girl in a hospital.

"Oh, he's just fine and dandy!" she declared. "It wasn't near so bad as they expected... Yes, his arm was broke', but not in the worst place... Sure! Oh, he'll be around again soon... He ain't rully sick, you know... Awright, I'll tell him you called."

Arnold's face was white with anger.

"I wish you would answer the telephone, in future," he said. "That girl's manner is simply abominable! If you could realise how unhappy I am in the mere knowledge that she is in the house, I think you would get rid of her."

"Can you take the rest of this beef tea?"

The patient shook his head. His appetite was gone. Naomi took the cup away.

She understood his hostility toward Jennie. He resented her disposal of his accident in so buoyant a fashion. He liked to hear reference made to it with the gravity, the anxiety, he felt it deserved. Surely, a man forbidden to think of business, or, indeed, anything at all, save a complete recovery—surely, such a case should not be discussed without a *semblance* of apprehension!

"If you will be all right for a little while," said Naomi, "I'll leave you. I should like to lie down."

"Lie down?" echoed Arnold. "Oh!"

Arnold did not approve of lying down. He looked upon it as a slothful habit. A nap in a chair after dinner was quite a different matter. By this means, great minds refreshed themselves after the exhausting labours of the day. There was nothing slothful in that.

"Is there anything I can do for you before I go?"

"No, thank you! Well—er—yes. You might open the window. The room seems very close. And—just a moment, please—I would like another pillow. I may be able to glance over those illustrated papers that Allyn sent me. It will be difficult with one hand, but I can't lie here doing nothing... Thank you! The magazines, please. You must remember the doctor said I was not to stretch out my arm..."

Naomi reached the door of the spare room, when he called her. "I don't like to trouble you, but fear that you won't be satisfied with the temperature of the hot-water bottle." He made a weak movement with his foot. "By the time you wake up, it will probably be stone cold."

———

She dropped on the bed feeling that sleep had already overtaken her, that she was virtually unconscious. But contact with the pillow brought about a curious change, and she became wide awake again. Her head was filled with the confusion of sharp noises. When she closed her eyes, great balls of fire rolled before her, and each time that sleep crept near, they collided with a thunderous report that threatened to tear her head asunder. No actual bombardment could have frayed her nerves more thoroughly.

Broken thoughts, like spiders on a quiet pool, darted through her mind. She didn't want to think. She wanted to sleep—to sleep in silent darkness for hours and hours... Three days, and not a line from Hugo! But, then, why should he write? He had finished with her, forever. No amount of explaining could convert him to her understanding of her duty. Naked facts were eloquent. She had forsaken him for Arnold!

Her thoughts took another turn. Perhaps he hadn't heard of the accident. That would make a difference. He would find he had been accusing her unjustly. He had probably left the city too heartsick to take any interest in the press, and, when he did look over a paper, in all likelihood he had passed the zone in which reference to the "elevator disaster" had been continuous.

Of course, there was the darker side... It was quite possible that he *had* read the papers and found it impossible to forgive her this latest act of self-abnegating sentimentalism.

"Another evidence of woman's inherited sense of bondage," she could imagine hearing him say. "Your *husband*! Any excuse to put on the shackles, rather than shake them off! Go your own way, my dear. I can fight the world for you—with you—but not against you. You were called upon to make a choice between us, and you chose Arnold. The deed proclaims its governing impulse. Impossible to get away from that!"

Clearly, she saw that even though she might make him forgive her, she could never make him understand.

Her wire may never have reached him. She had no address other than the office, and forwarding telegrams is not always a successful means of communication. If only she hadn't been such a fool about the trip! If only she had allowed him to discuss it with her and explain where he was going! What did her wilful ignorance really signify, she demanded, to the thunder of those flaming balls? A pathetic attempt to capture a sense of helplessness in the hands of Fate, for one thing; a puerile effort to feel that she was borne away by a power stronger than herself—that she was innocent of any part in the abduction. She was endeavouring to keep her moral skirts clean, to escape responsibility, to hoodwink her own conscience!

Naomi buried her face in the pillow. What a despicable creature she was... how cowardly... how weak! No wonder life hurt her at every turn. She dragged it about like a ball and chain. Why could she not wear it like Shireen, as a rose upon her bosom? Or even as a crown of thorns, like Arnold, who rejoiced in his martyrdom through an assurance of a heavenly reward?

Downstairs, the telephone rang.

Naomi started up, listening. Perhaps it was a long distance call from Hugo, or a wire! Her heart swelled until it seemed to crowd the breath from her body. Her ears were filled with a loud bubbling. There was just a chance—oh, a chance in a million—that Hugo had come back!

Arnold's voice roused her to action.

"I asked you to answer the telephone," he called. "Please don't allow that girl to take any messages for me."

She hurried down, conscious that her husband was listening. She hoped it was Hugo; she couldn't talk to him now, and there were such myriads of things she wanted to say. A wire would not be so embarrassing. She would invent some kind of a lie... pretend it was the butche ... "Oh, yes, the lean meat for beef tea..." That would do. Of course, if the operator heard her, she would think she was crazy...

The bell rang furiously. It seemed to tear at Naomi's head with claws of steel. She put her hand on the metal discs and quivered as they vibrated beneath her palm. Oh, if it should be Hugo!

"Hello!" she managed to say.

"...nox... there?"

For an instant, she thought some one was singing at the other end of the line; singing in a low, monotonous contralto. Then, out of the musical indistinctness, she picked out a sentence or two. "...enquire for Mr. Lennox... If Mrs. Lennox could speak to me..."

"She is speaking."

"Oh!" A pause. "Mrs. Lennox, my name is Ashburn—Hester Ashburn. You don't know me—"

"My husband has spoken of you," interrupted Naomi. "He was planning that we should meet."

"How charming of him! Will you tell me how he is? I've been out of town for several days, too engrossed with my own affairs to read the papers. Only this moment, I heard of the accident from Mr. Allyn. I am inexpressibly shocked."

"Everyone was."

"And Mr. Lennox?"

Naomi rallied her wits, concerned more with satisfying Arnold than giving the girl any accurate information. She painted a dark picture of his condition, and emphasised his patience. When she paused, lacking further invention, Hester asked—

"Did I understand you to say his arm was broken?"

"Yes—the left."

"And I suppose he was dreadfully bruised?"

"Oh, yes! Dreadfully..."

"If I could only *do* something!" cried Hester. "Isn't there *anything* you can suggest? Would he allow me to see him— not as a visitor, you know, but an extra nurse? I am quite at home in a sick-room, Mrs. Lennox. If you would only let me help you!"

Naomi thanked her. She was grateful for the thought, and caught eagerly at this opportunity for relaxation, or even a brief period for work.

She called up to Arnold. His enthusiasm was almost torrid. In another mood, it would have amused her. With a redundance of polite and appreciative phrases, he hoped Miss Ashburn was free to come to him this afternoon.

"Free?" she echoed. "Of course I am free. After all he did for my poor little mission... I'll jump into a taxi and come at once. And you are not to consider me, at all. I am going to relieve you!"

She came before the preparations that Arnold required were complete. He demanded his velvet smoking jacket and blue silk pyjamas. His hair needed brushing and his chin a coat of talcum powder. He must have the comfortable chair from the spare room for his guest, and the dressing table ought to be rearranged. Where were the flowers sent to him by the Curling Club? Down stairs? Well, he wanted them... placed there, if you please... No, *there*! He couldn't point; the doctor had warned him against stretching his arm, but surely, *that* was the obvious place! And turn the card around so that she could see it... Now, what about a little sprinkle of toilet water—"that stuff of yours? Can't you freshen up the room a bit?" His voice was sharp with excitement.

"There she is!" he cried before the bell had stilled its whirring. "Go down at once! Never mind the window. Hurry! I don't know what that vulgar girl may do. One's first impression..."

Naomi could not have said exactly what manner of woman she expected to find in Hester Ashburn, but the vision that confronted her at the foot of the stairs was a distinct surprise. Like Arnold, her ideas of missionaries were conventional.

The girl held out impulsive hands.

"It was too good of you to let me come," she cried, and her voice set some pulse in Naomi's being a-quiver. "If you could only know how I have longed for an opportunity to show Mr. Lennox my gratitude! It was he who carried my meeting to undreamed success, who stimulated the people—" She broke off rather self-consciously. "But how stupid of me! As if you didn't know his splendid qualities!"

Mechanically, Naomi's lips uttered correct phrases. She simply couldn't think any more. A haze blurred her vision and gave to the whole situation that aspect of unreality one associates with a dream. It would be more restful, she decided, to sleep without dreaming, without standing about and talking... talking...

She led the way upstairs, wondering why she was there, at all. She should have been off somewhere with Hugo, leaving this flaming creature to find her way alone to Arnold's room. There was something quite humorous in a girl's going into Arnold's room. The reason was not very clear, but Naomi felt an impulse to laugh.

She talked over her shoulder, trying to grasp the details of Hester's costume. It illustrated the expensive simplicity that defies imitation and baffles the envious. It was distinctive by its very inconspicuousness. Brown, thought Naomi, an exquisite rich brown, suggestive of cocoa and whipped cream. Blue fox furs. A restrained note of colour about the small hat, and a flash of sun-gold hair... No, Hester Ashburn was not one's idea of a missionary.

At the door, Naomi stood aside for her guest to pass. "Go right in," she said. "Arnold is expecting you."

Hester hesitated an instant on the threshold, betraying—and conquering—a maidenly embarrassment that would have been charming fifty years ago. Then she subdued herself to the tenor of the sickroom, and approached the bed.

Arnold made a gallant attempt to take her hand. With a pretty gesture of authority, she forbade him to exert himself and, sighing, he obeyed her. Naomi noticed that he had become very much the invalid since she left the room. Just as he curled better before a gallery, as he prayed more zealously in a well-filled, well-dressed church, so now, his suffering grew more acute under the stimulation of Hester's sympathy. He threatened to collapse altogether.

"Take Miss Ashburn's coat, my dear," he commanded, feebly, "and draw the blind so the sun won't shine directly in her eyes. There! That's better, isn't it?" He moved cautiously, and addressed his guest. "The hardest feature of this accident is the continuous hurt to my pride... my sense of dependence. I would rather do without something I want, than feel myself a burden to others. And yet, it is almost impossible to lie here, helpless, hour after hour, without requiring a little attention."

Naomi felt Hester Ashburn's eyes upon her, and flushed. She could scarcely explain that Arnold intended this heroic pronouncement to less as a complaint of negligence on her part, than an illustration of his considerateness. Seeing himself exclusively in the foreground of existence, it never occurred to him that an observer could see on either side and beyond his imposing figure, and that his shadow was apt to distort everything on which it rested. On the rare occasions when she had tried to point out the effect of his attitude on other people, he had been genuinely amazed at the misinterpretation she had placed upon his words; irritated by what he termed her super-egotism. Therefore, she had learned to hold her tongue. Arnold would not be criticised.

"What about tea, my dear?" he asked. "I'm sure Miss Ashburn would enjoy it."

Miss Ashburn protested that she came to help, that she did not wish to give any trouble.

"Oh, but tea is not trouble," Arnold assured her. "Is it, my dear?"

Naomi echoed this hospitable prevarication and distrusting the result of her handmaiden's unsupervised efforts, went herself to the kitchen.

A bell rang.

"Somebody else is a-comin'," said Jennie, darting past her to the door. "You watch the toast and I'll let him in."

After a moment's absence she returned, observing: "I thought it might be more visitors, but it was a shoffer with a basket for Mr. Lennox. He said it was for you, but I knew he'd made a mistake, and carried it right upstairs. Them shoffers is so busy thinkin' well of themselves, they don't waste no time on common sense. Gee, Mrs. Lennox, ain't that lady a dream? I could set and look at her all day!"

Naomi suggested that a more profitable occupation would be carrying the tray upstairs. "I'll go ahead and get the little table ready."

On the top step, she paused. Above the rustle of tissue paper, and the faint tinkle of china, Arnold's voice rose distinctly.

"Really, I'm overwhelmed! But, then, everyone has been so kind! Thank you... Just put it there, on the table. Please don't wait upon me! It hurts. My wife will attend to everything... I suppose that, even in India, you must have heard of the novelist, Shireen Dey?"

"Indeed, yes!"

"This beautiful hamper is from her. She is a great friend of ours, our most intimate friend, I think I may say. A charming woman, for all her success... My dear," he broke off as Naomi entered the room, "see this basket from Shireen Dey? Isn't that a tempting array of food? I almost believe I could enjoy a little..."

Hester urged him to take advantage of the slightest desire to eat. She was not in favour of regular meals for an invalid. "I always give my patients nourishment when they want it," she said, "and I never force them to take it against their inclination."

Arnold was much impressed with this system, and Naomi visualised herself preparing meals at extraordinarily inconvenient hours.

"Do I hear Uncle Toby?" he enquired. "My wife's uncle," he explained. "For several years he has shared my home."

Naomi marvelled that Arnold could convey so flattering a picture of himself in a single sentence. Without seeming to boast, without deliberate exaggeration, he presented an example of Christian excellence that compelled her admiration.

The old man came jauntily upstairs and into the room. He wore an air of buoyancy and general well-being that made Naomi appear by contrast something like a weather-beaten tombstone. Arnold performed the necessary introduction and invited Uncle Toby to have tea. Meanwhile, Hester handed Naomi a letter which had accompanied the hamper and insisted that she should read it then and there.

"Let me pour the tea," she begged. "I want to feel that I have been of some real service to you."

So Naomi moved away from the group, broke the huge gold seal and read—

> *You precious thing!*
>
> *I don't telephone because I know you have too much to do as matters stand... Oh, I know! Do not think, however, that you are absent from my thoughts. On the contrary. This morning, in the middle of my strongest chapter—and really, darling, this one is immense! Like blows on some deep-sounding metal instrument!—Well, in the middle of it, you just popped into my head, and would not be dislodged. I can't say I was entirely pleased, but surrendered at last, dismissed Miss Heathecote, and sent for Cook. Together, we planned this hamper, which is all for you—you—you!*
>
> *I am praying that it falls directly into your hands; that the ebullient rustic does not exhibit it before those two he-vampires of yours. I want the invalid—THE REAL INVALID—to have it, and*

if you can enjoy food once removed, so to say, I'll send you a basket every morning... plus violets. Seriously, my ewe lamb, I beg you to put this stuff into your own little tummy. I know only too well how much—or how little opportunity you have to think about yourself. And you need nourishment! The broth is made from four well concentrated crate-fed birds, the mushrooms are all ready to serve, save for a little heating. Try the port just before going to bed. It's wonderfully soothing. And do enjoy the guava jelly! You always make such a fuss over it at my house. This is part of a new lot that has just come, from my ardent and unknown admirer in the south. I charge you, as you value our friendship, to share it with nobody."

She had no time to taste the flavour of the situation, for Arnold's voice signified that he needed her help. He was very awkward and self-conscious.

"Don't eat the toast," he urged, hospitable. "One can have toast any time. Do try some of this delicious short-bread. Mrs. Dey's cook is famous for it. Miss Ashburn, you must take a bit of this guava jelly. Give me a taste, my dear... and Uncle Toby. Really, this is the first time I have enjoyed my food since the accident."

Uncle Toby demonstrated the beneficial effect of daily exercise. "I am ravenous," he said.

"You must share these squab with me to-night, sir," said Arnold.

Uncle Toby demurred. It would never do to deprive the invalid of the delicacies designed for him. A robust man like himself could eat anything! They engaged in friendly argument over the merits of their respective constitutions.

"And now the port," commanded Arnold. "We must drink to the success of Mrs. Dey's next book."

Naomi said she would go down for a cork-screw.

"Can't I go, my love? asked Uncle Toby, charmingly courteous—and sitting perfectly still.

Naomi murmured something about glasses and escaped from the room. She struggled against a burst of hysterical laughter. Heaven knew she didn't begrudge them the food! She couldn't imagine herself interested in anything to eat, and, in any event, she could no more have carried out Shireen's injunctions literally, than she could have walked across the Black Sea. But the royal manner in which her basket had been appropriated was funny! It was a joke that anyone would appreciate, with the possible exception of Arnold—and Shireen.

CHAPTER 15

HESTER ASHBURN came to the house every day. She came "because she loved to help dear Naomi, and because she was so supremely happy in a sick-room."

To what extent she enjoyed the comfortable gift of self-deception, Naomi could not determine, but certainly her sphere of practical assistance was extremely small.

Nor was this entirely her fault. Arnold was to blame. A rigid sense of courtesy made it impossible for him to relieve his wife at the expense of a guest. Besides, he did not wish to associate Hester Ashburn with the grosser aspects of existence. She was so beautiful! And he worshipped Beauty. But, like God, it must be kept apart from every-day realities, else it would become a commonplace, itself. In a long-past incarnation, Arnold Lennox, for all his religious fervour—which was genuine—had not followed the simple Nazarene. The attributes of divinity were not apparent to him in a familiar. He liked to meditate on the Son of God, but the Son of Man was a very dim-clad figure. The Saviour of the World must not suffer contact with the World. He must appear in splendour, guarded by cohorts glittering in mail. He must call down thunder and lightning upon his enemies and use the powers of Heaven to inspire fear in his terrible judgments. The appearance of any qualities that were human would, for him, obliterate those that were divine.

So with Beauty. It was not written that he should see a mud-puddle glorified by the reflection of the moon. Rather must he deplore the befoulment of something so radiant, so pure. And for him, no woman could retain her charm once he had discovered her preparing a chicken for his dinner.

But he loved to have Hester, this brilliant ornament, in his room. He loved to feign sleep in order that he might watch her at a time when she was unconscious of his scrutiny. What a picture she made, framed by the open window, her hair like living flame, her face pale and cold by contrast, her eyes glowing with the light of spiritual visions!

He invented a dozen pretty little ceremonies that it was her exclusive privilege to perform. And she undertook them with all the gravity of an operating surgeon. He consulted her about his diet and accepted her suggestions with childlike trust. But it was Naomi who carried them out. Seemingly by tacit consent, Arnold and Hester Ashburn left all the homelier tasks for her to execute.

Hester was inventive, too, cosseting Arnold in a way that he adored, and achieving, meanwhile, a semblance of professionalism. She instituted a type of massage for the fingers of his injured hand, and she had a way of arranging the pillows that was wonderfully restful. It required him to sit up within the circle of her arm while she pulled and pushed and thumped them gently into place behind him.

Arnold's sensations were very agreeable, but he did not dwell upon this aspect of his convalescence. He preferred to think that weakness *forced* him to lean against her small, firm breasts, to bury his face in the scented valley between them; that exertion quickened his breathing and enabled him to draw deep into his being the delicate perfume that her warm, slim body gave forth. He believed that he suffered acutely, lying in one position for any length of time.

A week raced by.

"I'm wondering if I shall ever be strong again," he sighed, one morning, slipping reluctantly from her clasp.

An expression of fierce possessiveness flared in her eyes. He did not see it, nor could he be quite certain that her clasp tightened.

"Of course you will! Only—"

"Only what?"

"I am wicked enough to hope—that you won't recover—too soon."

He sunned himself in the implication of these words, playing with his pleasure, teasing and worrying it, extracting from it the last drop of sweetness it contained. He achieved a cunning surprise in the question—

"Why?"

"Because—because I have been—I am so happy taking care of you."

The answer struck deeper than he had anticipated. He was a little startled at his own response. Perhaps it was her voice. It frequently produced an answering vibration. Extravagant expressions rose to his lips, but he crushed them. "Noble nurse!" Or "Wonder woman!" would sound perfervid, and somewhat ridiculous.

He compromised.

"It's like you to say a kindly thing, otherwise I must be tormented by remorse at having imposed on you so long, and kept you from your work."

"But this *is* my work."

"In a broad sense, yes; but it's not the work you came to this country to accomplish."

"I really came for a holiday," said Hester. "It was my own idea—quite voluntary—to speak in a few churches and try to raise money for my Mission."

"Instead of which, you undertake the nursing of a stranger," said Arnold, in a solemn tone.

"That is serving God."

"Through one of the least worthy of his creatures."

Her smile was a tender contradiction, and Arnold, who could think of no points in support of his statement, allowed her to triumph in the argument.

St. Margaret's chimes shook their call to worship out upon the morning.

"Isn't it a dear church?" Hester murmured. "I can imagine what it means for you to miss the service."

"There are compensations," returned Arnold. Then, uneasy at hearing the start truth fall so glibly from his lips, "I've been given strength to bear my pain, and—and—everyone has been so exceedingly kind."

She showed her disappointment at the last part of this bleak utterance and, for some unaccountable reason, Arnold felt pleased.

"Yes, it's a dear church," he repeated, "and has given me much spiritual refreshment."

"I shall always associate it with you," said Hester.

"And I, with you," he rejoined.

A silence followed the last note of the hymn. Conversational themes seemed to have deserted Arnold, and he wished Hester would say something. Chatter of any sort was more acceptable to him than silence, for he was incapable of feeling that sweeter companionship, that communion of spirit, that is possible only when the wagging of tongues is stilled.

"Does there seem to be a large congregation?" he managed to say.

"Very! And that adorable Airedale dog—"

"Ah, yes—Allyn's Scotchie. A great friend of mine. Is he offering a paw of welcome to certain people as they pass?"

"Yes."

"I taught him the trick. He is a most zealous member of the reception committee. We couldn't get along without him. It was actually Scotchie who was responsible for my going in to hear you speak, that night."

"Why, the blessed animal!" cried Hester. "I wish I could give him something."

Arnold mentioned maple buds and instantly regretted it. Upon the heels of his regret came self-castigation. What a cad he was to feel jealous of Hester Ashburn! Suppose Scotchie did transfer his affection to her!

"Speaking of one's friends," he said, "what are your plans after discharging this troublesome patient? Of course, you will proceed with your lectures?"

They had discussed many topics during these days of un-usual intimacy—their childhood, their thwarted ambitions, the necessity for discipline, the glory of the sacrifice. Arnold recalled that, as a young man, he had hoped to fit himself for the Ministry, but the pressure of temporal affairs had prevented. Renunciation seemed to be a finer course in the sight of God, and so he had tried to do his duty in that sphere of business life to which he had been called. All things worked out for the best, he supposed, for if he might say so without a thought of disloyalty, he found very little spiritual congeniality in his home.

"I don't know how Naomi would have regarded me in Holy Orders," he sighed.

Hester spoke again in great detail of the searing circum-stance which had thrown her into the arms of the Church, until Arnold was conscious of active dislike for this un-known man. What a bounder he must have been!

The one subject they had not touched upon was her im-mediate future. Upon this, Arnold had devoted some time in speculation.

Hester, it seemed, had made no plans. The Bishop with whom she had lately conferred, was distinctly opposed to her settling down to routine work. He suggested that, for a few months, she forget the Mission—as if she could!—and build herself up for the labours that awaited her return.

"Sound advice," commented Arnold.

"In the event of following it," said the girl, "I don't know what to do with my summer. Having no family, and no friends, I feel rather lost over here."

"Why not stay on where you are?" asked the bold Arnold. "Our little town offers few excitements, but the climate is pleasant and you have made friends."

A short pause.

"Mr. Allyn was good enough to make the same suggestion," said Hester.

Oh, Allyn had suggested this, had he? Arnold was acutely conscious of anger. It seemed that everyone had been consulted except himself! He opened his lips to make known his annoyance when a distinctly soothing thought crossed his fretted mind. Hester's consultation with Allyn had been prompted, in all likelihood, by her tender solicitude for him. He was ill. Patently, she hesitated to worry him.

"Do you think you would like to stay?" The query was very quietly put.

"I should love to spend the summer here."

"Then," cried Arnold, "let's consider the matter settled, and fret no more about it!"

They laughed, as though a doubtful moment had passed off more agreeably than had expected. And they stopped abruptly as Naomi came in with a pineapple frappé, which Hester had suggested and which Arnold demanded every morning.

"What is Miss Ashburn going to have?" asked the hospitable host. Naomi apologised. She had been very stupid when giving her order, yesterday, and had quite forgotten to mention pineapple. There was only enough for one.

An embarrassing moment followed. A sense of domestic decency prevented Arnold's attacking her in the presence of a guest. But she knew that his outbreak was only delayed, and that it would lose no fervour by the postponement. She also felt Hester's conviction that the action was deliberate, that it was an expression of rebellion against this small service.

"But you must have something!" Arnold insisted. "Why not some of my nice port?"

Hester allowed herself to be persuaded to accept the wine, and Naomi went downstairs to arrange it on a tray.

"I thought Mrs. Lennox—er—Naomi—had gone to church," said Hester, when they were once more alone.

"She doesn't go very often," sighed Arnold. "I've become almost accustomed to attending Service without her." A little pause. "It's inexplicable to me that one should be insensible to spiritual hunger, that one should feel content to fill life with material considerations."

"Oh, well, Naomi is such a busy little soul," remarked Hester, sweetly, "no doubt she feels she hasn't time to go to Church. It is hard for some women to see above domestic obligations and make opportunities for higher things." Then, as though fearing that further criticism would be an infringement of good taste, she asked, "Would you care to have me read the Morning Prayer?"

"It would give me inexpressible pleasure."

The girl read well. Some persons might have considered her a shade theatrical, but none could have accused her of being either mechanical or dull. The beautiful cadences of her voice enriched the words, making them sound like some ancient incantation. They hypnotised Arnold as he lay very still, watching her.

He listened in his own peculiar way; with his outward ear, as he might have listened to her reading Tamil or Choctaw. He felt the words pass over him like the caress of a soft, white hand. His emotions were stirred, and this stood for him in lieu of spiritual devotion.

His thoughts ran their own course, while his lips framed the correct responses. What a picture she would have made in a pulpit! How exquisite that face above the flowing vestments! Why shouldn't women enter the Ministry, he asked himself, boldly? Who exerted the true spiritual influences of the world? What a sensation she would create, healing bodies and saving souls!

Saving souls! How gloriously she would have fulfilled this mission, charged idolators to turn from sin, brought pagans to repentance, even in the days when the price for so doing would have been martyrdom! Arnold closed his eyes and gave himself over to the picture of Hester yielding to martyrdom—God's finest destiny! Oh, he thought, superb!

He saw her as *Hypatia—Theon's* daughter, with gleaming hair that Athene might have envied. He looked into her uplifted eyes, dimmed by some inward awe, as if her soul were far away, and face to face with God. Vividly he saw her rising to her full height on the steps of the church, naked, snow-white, her golden hair drawn round a body that quivered with shame and indignation, as the hoarse, brutal clamour of the mob threatened, and drowned out her speech. He thrilled to the depths of his being when they dragged her down, and trampled her and tore her tender flesh apart. Oh, glorious woman! Superb!

Hester led forth to meet the onslaught of snarling beasts... Hester at the stake! He had no realisation of the savage joy that caught him at the idea of her exultant pain.

He thought of himself joined by the bonds of holy wedlock to Naomi—a woman who had no conception of the finer things of life. Never in all the years of their marriage had she suggested reading the Service with him. He didn't want to be unkind, but, really, it seemed as though her thoughts never rose above the kitchen... except when she betook herself to her desk for the gratification of selfish ambition.

No companionship, no sympathy for his spiritual needs, whatever! A lingering death of the soul, that was what he suffered. How different everything would have been, had he met Hester... His wife... his wife... He closed his eyes, but, even so, they were filled with the vision of lovely women, all wearing Hester's form and kneeling at his feet.

Penetrating and exquisite sensations possessed him, and a gentle moisture bathed his skin. The ineffable purity of such a union... For the sake of his soul's refinement, Arnold permitted himself the indescribable torment of imagining that glorious, unsullied body, innocent of clothing, clasped close against his heart...

The whirr of the telephone startled both of them. Hester paused.

"Would you like me to take the message?" she asked.

"Certainly not! I wouldn't dream of allowing you to wear yourself out by running up and down stairs. But if you don't mind closing the door, we can proceed with the Service without interruption."

Naomi left her work in Uncle Toby's room, wondering who could be calling at this hour. Some of Arnold's curling friends, most likely; some one who would suggest dropping in during the afternoon. That would mean tea. She had done more "entertaining" since the accident than during the whole year, previous.

And lunch... probably Hester Ashburn would be asked again, to-day. And she didn't care for spinach. Was there enough asparagus, she wondered?

It was annoying about that pineapple... the sort of thing one could never explain...

"Hello," she called, trying not to gasp into the telephone.

"Naomi, is that you?"

"*Hugo!*"

"I'm just this instant off the train. Picked up your wire yesterday on my way home... I must see you!"

"Yes, of course," she answered, thinking of the two upstairs.

"Was Arnold really hurt?"

"Oh, yes. The elevator dropped from the seventh floor."

"My God. Is it serious?"

"N-no!"

"Hm! Is he still laid up?"

"Yes."

"Have you a nurse?"

"No."

"Damn!" said Hugo. "I say, can you possibly see me now?"

"I think so—for a few minutes anyway."

She went upstairs as rapidly as her heavy limbs would bear her. Rouge, powder and lipstick were in Arnold's room. Her heart sank as she passed the mirror. Why did weariness distort her face into something not pathetic, but repulsive?

She watched for him and opened the door herself, turning from him as she did so.

"Don't look at me," she cried. "I don't want to see the reflection of my ugliness in your eyes."

"You poor darling! Never mind your looks. We'll pull down the blinds, if you say so. I want to hear what has happened."

He was determined not to betray the shock he felt at the sight of her. Equally was he resolved to conquer his rising temper at the thought that all this sacrifice had been made for Arnold. At the same time, there was no doubting the genuineness of her suffering on his account. Profoundly touched, he tried to soothe her, when she cried again and again—

"If only I had been able to let you know, I could have endured everything! It was thinking of you, and what *you* must think, that has tormented me. Nothing to do but wait—wait—"

"—wait upon Arnold," he suddenly flared.

He was more sympathetic, however than Naomi had expected. No reproaches came. No agonising on his own account. For once, she was allowed to luxuriate in her own misery, while he played the role of the comforter.

But not for long. Immolation on the altar of man's selfishness had become too fixed a habit to be broken, and presently she set aside her distress and sought to comfort him. She caressed his forehead with delicate fingers, and her eyes, behind their tears were deep with tenderness.

"I know you must have suffered cruelly," she said. "I will try to make it all up to you, my love."

"Kiss me," he begged softly.

"Be careful," she warned. "The house seems very full of people, these days."

"I suppose common decency demands that I speak to Arnold," he said. "May I go up for a second?"

Naomi did not like to refuse, although a cordial reception of Hugo Main was extremely problematical.

The closed door was a surprise. She had never known it shut before.

"Here's another visitor, Arnold," she cried, as gaily as she could.

Main advanced a step or two. A sharp exclamation checked him.

"Why, Hugo!" cried Hester.

"Well, but the gods!" he retorted. "You—of all people!"

CHAPTER 16

HESTER did not stay for lunch. She rose as Hugo made his adieux and left the house with him.

"What an extraordinary thing," she began, her voice higher-pitched than usual, "meeting you—like this—after all these years... and in the Lennox home, of all places."

Hugo regarded her out of the corner of his eye.

"Why 'of all places?'"

Hester flushed. Hugo made her feel silly, childish, not worth while. He seemed to find in her every utterance some cause for tolerant amusement—an old habit of his.

"Because—because—well, bluntly, because I can't imagine you and Mr. Lennox being very congenial friends."

Said Hugo—

"You are kinder to me than I deserve."

Hester was not insensitive to the colour of irony in his words, but over-excited as she was, she could not see it in relation to Arnold. Her mind was in a turmoil. Sensations she had believed to be utterly extinct, tore at her with once-familiar insistence, and produced at one and the same time, a surge of ecstatic joy and exquisite, penetrating pain.

She looked sharply at Hugo, wondering if he divined the tumult that raged beneath her surface calm, if he suspected the unconquered weakness that robbed her of self-control and reduced her to a mass of quivering emotions.

How she hated this man! She hated his assurance, his indifference, his acceptance of her presence as though they had parted but yesterday! She knew that when their shoulders touched, she, for him, was just a shoulder. Always, he had made of her sense of power, an absurdity, an illusion.

"Kinder than you deserve?" she repeated, looking at him with pretty, if ill-feigned puzzlement. "Oh! Don't go back to that, please! I've forgotten it. Long ago, I admitted the wisdom of your course. It... it would have been... disastrous, wouldn't it? Now, Hugo, truly?"

"There's no pretending that I'm an easy chap to get on with."

"But, I too, was difficult... stupid. I was so tiresomely young, Hugo, so lacking in understanding of men. On the whole, I think you were very patient with me."

To himself, Main cried, "Oh, dear heaven, hear her!" Aloud, he mumbled words that sounded like unworthiness and generosity. Then he enquired whether Hester still enjoyed her life in the East.

"You might as well ask me if enjoy life," she told him, in her platform voice.

"All right. I will. Do you?"

"Do I what?" He bewildered her.

"Enjoy life. Isn't that what we were discussing? Do you find it full of dazzling colour? Melodious with song? Soft and fragrant with well-earned ease? In a word, are you so happy, so intensely alive that there is nearly as much joy in your tears as in your smile?"

"Oh, Hugo, you were always so extravagant!"

"That's because I was born under two stars—one wasn't enough. You see, I have no choice. Are you happy?"

Hester avowed that she found intense joy in carrying God's word to the hungry heathen, and Hugo fore-bore to comment upon the delicacy of such refreshment. She continued.

"I wish you had come to my meeting. I think you would have gained a better idea of the work given my poor hands to perform."

"Well, it hasn't hurt them any. I noticed that they were as beautiful as ever, while you were talking to Arnold."

The stain on Hester's cheeks deepened. How vividly she remembered Hugo's reluctant compliments. With what intensity they moved her!

"You're aware," she said, more gently," that I'm speaking in a figurative sense. At the Mission, one does no actual work... there are swarms of servants. When I speak of work, of course, I mean spiritual endeavour."

"Oh!"

"I have quite a corps of assistants, both native and white, and am therefore free to devote myself to—"

"The more congenial problems of existence."

She shot a suspicious glance at him, but his mien was grave and disarming. "If you like to put it that way," she said.

Hugo asked how she was supported.

"I am the chief supporter of the Mission. It's mine! I didn't want to be dependent upon any church or restricted by any episcopal rulings. But we co-operate with everyone who is doing a similar work, and the plan has worked very well. You see, I call it the Richard Alney Mission, and regard it as a memorial to father!"

"An original idea to maintain it with his money."

"A monument much better than one built of stone," she defended. "I want to enlarge my hospital. That's why I'm begging."

From Hester, Hugo learned of the part Arnold played in her campaign; how he had stimulated public interest, how he had subscribed her first hundred dollars.

"He's been so good to me," she said. "I'm sure I don't know why."

"He would be," murmured Hugo.

Unaware of Arnold's exact financial resources, Hugo knew enough to realise where the result of such monstrously selfish generosity would fall. Inwardly, he cursed the condition which gave one man power to create so much distress, and denied another the privilege of relieving it. If only Naomi weren't such a proud little creature; so obstinate in her pride! If only she would let him help!

He made no attempt to follow Hester's enthusiastic exposition of human kindness—the kindness of Mr. Allyn, of Dr. Darrell, of Lawyer Bosworth, of Banker Hewitt, of Broker Dutton, of Bishop Bradley. At the time, he was not even conscious that all these kindnesses had been revealed in persons of the sterner sex; she didn't mention the name of a woman. He was wondering by what argument, or trickery he could guard Naomi from the effect of her husband's kindness, until the day when she would be released from it forever.

Naomi had such definite ideas about accepting his assistance. He had tried to thrust it upon her before. Very fixed and discomforting ideas. Virtue, he thought, is so unyielding. It's so much harder to cope with than vice. It gives the other fellow so small an advantage—if any. All things considered, Naomi was ungenerous to refuse his help. Hester didn't mind taking money—nor, in the same circumstances, would Shireen...

He moved his shoulders with impatience, and blurted—

"You get a good 'kick' from this thing, don't you?"

For an instant, Hester was blindly angry. Never had anyone offered such an insult to her idealistic pretensions! She could have struck him down for his hateful words and manner, for his mercilessly just estimate of her secret sensations!

But the moment passed, leaving her bitter retort unspoken. Hugo's rancour appeared suddenly to her in a new light. The flame of anger cooled, giving way to an agreeable glow of gratification.

"He's jealous," thought Hester, "jealous because I've accepted help from Arnold! Amazing Hugo! It's almost incredible!"

Visibly she softened.

"*Everyone* has been interested and kind. But I feel particularly grateful to Mr. Lennox for starting the campaign. That's all."

"How long shall you stay around here?" asked her companion.

"This morning, discussing my plans with—er—discussing my plans, I almost decided to stay here throughout the summer. Why?"

Hugo chose to accept the decision as final, and approved it. He thought she would like the place, the climate, the Club House, the Golf Links, the people. Obviously, he was eager to have her stay.

She sheered off from him, invented reasons for proceeding elsewhere, leaving the west, altogether. Then, capriciously, she began to discuss her apartment—the advisability of taking a year's lease, the possibility of subletting, when she gave it up. And, as though this flavour of domesticity reminded her of the matter for the first time, she turned to her companion and asked, "By the way... are you married, Hugo?"

"No. Are you?"

"No... Oh, no!"

"Why not? Don't you believe with Butler that to live is like to love—all reason is against it, and all healthy instinct for it?"

"I believe that one can be purged of the kind of love he means. I love my work—that is enough. But you, Hugo, you should think of marrying."

"I do. I'm always thinking of it... seldom think of anything else."

She bit her lip. He was laughing at her. Or was that the mask he wore to hide his pain? Did he, perchance, repent of his impetuous conduct and wish to re-establish the old relation?

"I wish I could see you happily married," she said, "to some good woman who would understand how superficial and harmless are your cynicisms, and with whom you would not be reluctant to disclose your better, higher self."

"That's the most vindictive thing you've said yet," he protested. "Why don't *you* marry—one of those milk-veined missionaries, with whom—I forget the exact quotation, but with whom you could suffer all those terrible inflictions you wished for me?"

Hester's reasons were not quite clear. To avoid admitting that marrying a good man would be an infliction, she rather stressed the rarity of unmarried men who came within her purlieu. Then, to obliterate the unfavourable impression created by this statement, she fell into a deeper trap by complaining that men who seemed to care for her were not good men.

"Contrast is too great," suggested Hugo. "That's what's the matter with virtue; it's always putting you in a class different from other men. It throws up a barrier between you and the common herd. Your virtuous person is forever trying to force his doses on somebody, make one see the sinfulness of some other person. Consider this case—You can't find a man good enough for you! Look at me... there are dozens... yes, hundreds of women I could marry; plenty good enough for me; too good. Why? I'm full of sin. I haven't got a virtue in my system."

Hester shook her head and sighed.

"Ah, Hugo," she said, "you haven't changed."

"Neither have you!" He looked down at her, tolerantly, as a fond uncle might have done.

"Oh, but I have—immeasurably! I'm not at all the same silly girl you knew. As for all the nonsense you've been talking, I shan't argue. I shan't even take you seriously."

They had reached the door of her apartment, and she asked if he would come in.

"Some other time, if I may," He took her un-gloved hand, moving his thumb over its smooth skin. "And you'll stay through the summer?"

"Do you—do you want me to?"

"Why, yes."

"For old times' sake... or just why?" His tone was too matter-of-fact to please her. "Because," she went on, "because you mustn't think—I mean, you ought to know—that a revival of those days is quite out of the question. But I'm eager to be your friend."

"Oh," said Hugo. "So that's the way you feel?"

"Positively," lied Hester, clumsily. "But you'll come to see me soon, won't you?"

"Of course!"

"Good-bye."

CHAPTER 17

HUGO contended that Hester Ashburn was the solution to their problem.

"I'm not much on this sign-from-heaven stuff," he declared, "but if there ever was one, she is it! I see her not only as the hand of Providence, but the whole body—quite an appealing body, too, in a *maigre* sort of way."

"But Arnold may not want to marry her," objected Naomi. "If he doesn't, she won't be a solution, at all."

"God save us!" cried Hugo. "What next? There was a time when finding him a servant was your chief concern. Must you now hold me on a leash until he is also provided with a wife?"

"Don't joke," begged Naomi. "I am serious!"

"As if I didn't know it! Seriousness, my fondest girl, is you most oppressive vice."

"But don't you see that my chance for happiness is greater if *he* is happy—if," she added, hurriedly, "I haven' t left a trail of bitterness and hatred behind me?"

"No." Hugo was definite. There was altogether too much consideration for Arnold in this affair. There always had been. "No! I can't see that it matters a damn. You know as well as I do that nothing will make Arnold happy. He has a misery-complex, highly developed."

"Granted; but there are degrees of misery, and Hester might make him less unhappy than he would be alone. They are better mated than he and I ever were."

Main agreed that if it were possible to suit either of them, they were suited to one another. "And as for marrying," he added, "leave it to her... Unless I misjudge the damsel, she'll get him."

"How can you be so sure?"

"I hesitate to boast of my conquests, but accept my word for it—Hester Ashburn is a determined stalker. It takes a strong and courageous man to escape her."

"Hugo!"

"That's God's truth!"

Naomi asked why, then, she had never married.

"Fastidious, for one thing, and lack of opportunity for another. How many irresistible unmarried men do you think she has met since she knew me?"

"None, I suppose."

"Precisely. She admitted as much, yesterday, when I took her home. Therefore, she put men out of her life and concentrated upon a spiritual romance."

Naomi protested that he was not fair to the girl. "You can't sneer at one who has proven her religious zeal by work so admirable as hers."

"Religious bunkum!" he retorted. "She's religious, if you call a fanatic religious. She has no idea whatever of selfless service. She does what she wants to do, and does it hard, trusting that God's desires may coincide. No exalted love of the heathen Hindu took her out to the Mission, my dear. She went to heal her own silly pride, exactly as one would go hunting big game in Abyssinia. Incidentally, she sacrificed her parents... Why look here," he broke off, impatiently, "she actually *told* them they must endure torture for her sake! When I bolted and she flounced off to India, her father promptly went to pieces. The comfort the old man received on his death-bed was a letter from her explaining that she had given herself to God, and that earthly ties were but a drag upon her soul. She could not serve two masters. In expiation for her sins, she must suffer, and her cruellest pain came from a knowledge that her loved ones were unhappy... Both of them died of broken hearts. She's got their lives to answer for... Religious nothing!" he repeated. "She's a sensualist, and her sensuality, lacking normal expression, had bulged over, out of the physical into the spiritual. You've seen a weed, defying the flagstone of a garden path, and sneaking up through the crevice? That's Hester! She's a voluptuary, clutching at gratification wherever she can find it. Believe me, I know!"

Naomi argued the point no further, but carried the discussion back to Arnold.

"My anxiety for his happiness," she began, "is not inspired—"

"I should say not! Motivated, is a better word."

"Well, motivated, then... it's not motivated by fine or noble impulses. On the contrary! I want him to be happy, because if he finds happiness by taking the same questionable path I travelled in my quest for it, perhaps he will feel a measure of sympathy; perhaps he'll understand. At least, he will be shorn of his superiority, and unable to sit in judgement upon me."

"The pot and the kettle," commented Hugo, nodding. "I see," Then he laughed. "You're an honest creature, Naomi! Fancy your telling me that. Woman, I love you to distraction!"

"If I could only make Arnold feel as I feel—or make him realise that his sensations are not in the nature of a particular and private endowment, utterly unlike mine."

"How do you mean?"

Naomi said she would like to answer in the form of a crisp epigram, but that being out of the question, she would give him a practical example.

"Arnold expects me to interest myself in all the things he likes—to read the books he recommends, to sit through

interminable curling matches, to find refreshment in ex-
hibitions that are stodgy and dull, to prefer a walk in the
country to a dance at the Club—all that sort of thing. But,
he also expects me to find pleasure in all the things he dis-
likes and doesn't want to do; for instance, getting up first. I
do that, because I'm not supposed to mind. In the matter of
work his outlook is similarly cramped. He can't understand
that I, too, have ambitions and discouragements, hopes
and anxieties, triumphs and failures, and that for them, as
well as for physical conditions, I would respond to the same
treatment I apply to him. In a word, he expects me to be
like him, and at the same time, to be quite different."

"I'd see him in—" began Hugo.

"No, you wouldn't... not if you understood, as I do, how
innocently he makes his demands. He wouldn't require a sacrifice of me. But it never occurs to him that anything he could
ask, would be a sacrifice. Don't you see? I should like to carry
out his wishes, if I were cast in the mould of a good woman!"

"Rot," protested Hugo.

"Not at all! Arnold is no different from hundreds of men
who insist that the wife holding views divergent from their
own, *does not love her husband*!"

Vehemently, Hugo denied this. He accused Arnold of
being an insufferable ass and egoist, and asked heaven to
spare him an attribute in common.

"For months," Naomi continued, "he has objected to our
friendship, not only because he disapproves of you, but because he thinks that a wife should need no companionship
other than her husband's. He argues that it should not be a
sacrifice to me to meet his wishes and give you up. To admit
the contrary is to confess that I no longer love him."

"Well he's right there, anyhow," said Hugo, with some
malice.

"That's not the point. I'm curious to see whether he'll apply all this to himself upon realising that he is entering an identical relationship with Hester. Oh, I want him to love her, to yearn for her... so that he can understand my love for you. I want him to marry her, and be so happy that he'll have no time or inclination to hurl criticism at me. There, you see how cowardly and petty I am?"

Hugo remarked that this was very interesting. He hoped, however, that the passion of the psychological student would not overcome that of the normal woman for her mate. "Naomi," he said, "I can't be patient forever! This situation is now grotesque. We are living an anticlimax. Don't you feel it to be so, yourself?"

She made no answer.

"Can you forget that engagement with me which was broken? Do you think we can ignore it and go back to the first stages of our friendship? Moreover, don't you understand that, to me, there is no less joyful occupation than sitting around while you study Arnold's mental convolutions?"

"My dear one!" Naomi was suddenly soft and tender. "To forget that Tuesday morning would be to forget you. I love you, Hugo, but—"

Exactly... but! You love me, *but* you can't leave Arnold."

"I can! I will!"

"Then prove it! Come away with me, now—to-night!"

"Ah, Hugo, you are not kind!"

He laughed. "Are you?"

"I don't know, but I can't go to-night."

"Well, then—when?"

"Soon."

"What are you waiting for?"

"It's almost impossible for me to make you understand... a feeling, a longing, to do the thing decently, somehow.

Rushing off in the middle of the night looks like the act of a lust-mad pair who are controlled by the moment, rather than the considered step of rational people who are offering a challenge to one of the most unsuccessful institutions in life. Be patient just a little while longer."

He said he would try, but he became very much a tyrant. His fondling grew ungoverned and coarse.

She could not respond, and yet pity for him—a desire to compensate for all that he had suffered—prompted her to feign enjoyment in his violence. And all the while she was asking herself—

"Why should I submit! Why should he not feel *my* mood and adapt himself to me? When will women learn not to do this thing?"

"Love me!" he commanded, again and again, and Naomi shrank from the brute quality in his voice, even though she realised that, to him, it was the note of wooing.

He left, overwrought and miserable, and she crept up to bed feeling that he had drained her of every ounce of strength.

Arnold's recovery was very slow, but, when even the doctor could suggest no further excuse for invalidism, he took up the threads of his normal existence. That is to say, he went each day to the office.

Naomi dressed and fed him, for he still wore his sling, as proudly as he had worn his first long pants. He appropriated her paper as usual, and equipped himself with world news, before setting forth to resume Scotchie's ration of exactly two and a half maple buds and receive the enquiries of friends and acquaintances—enquiries which he never wearied of answering in detail.

He saw Hester frequently. She deferred to him in a variety of matters, personal as well as those pertaining to the

Mission. They met at Service, at church gatherings, at the Allyns', in her apartment, and in his home. But, tempering his pleasure in their association, Arnold became aware of a growing uneasiness. At first, this seemed like nothing more significant than the natural desire of a cautious and conventional man to avoid criticism. He foresaw not menace to his comfort, his peace of mind. He was insensible to the faint tremors that threatened shipwreck. He did not even compare his conduct with Naomi's, and find it—similar. No! He simply realised that gossip must arise from even the most innocent friendship between a married man and a girl so young and beautiful as Hester Ashburn; and from the sting of poisoned tongues, chivalry demanded that he protect her.

But, gradually, restraint chafed him. He was not broken to the curb of discipline, to the practice of self-denial where an acute desire was involved. He endured patched underwear, and bought an overcoat only every third winter, but he never missed a trip with the Curling Club, although he was one of half a dozen spares. Curling was productive of physical fitness, and the crushing responsibilities he carried made it essential for him to keep physically fit. A duty, indeed! No easy-going for him. He had to stick right on the job, working at work, not playing at it.

When uneasiness crystallised, and Arnold saw his conduct in the light of indiscretion, he girded on his moral armour and prepared to engage the enemy to his contentment. It was impossible to deny that indiscretions frequently expanded into definite wrongs, and, consciously, Arnold Lennox would do no wrong. A triumph over temptation did not mean, however, the sacrifice of some agreeable pursuit. Rather was it the result of his ability to argue that the desired course was right.

In this immediate struggle, Hester was a powerful ally.

They were strolling through the Park one amber afternoon when the Misses Thurlow passed. The salutation of these ladies gave Arnold a shock. In it, he read the thought—

"Why, we met them here only day before yesterday! And Mrs. Claxton said she observed them walking together the day before that! One can't think ill of Mr. Lennox, but—"

Mentally, Arnold squirmed. Why? He was going to be absolutely honest with himself, an achievement of which precious few people were capable. His conscience was troubled, and conscience, he reflected, is a fair barometer to conduct. On Friday, he had been uncomfortably aware that, although his meeting with Hester the day before was accidental, they had seen one another by appointment on Wednesday, while Monday... Could it be that he was doing wrong?

No! He stoutly denied it. There was nothing wrong in giving of his judgement and experience for the advancement of such a cause as hers. One might as well argue that conferences with the Reverend Haddington Allyn were suggestive of evil! And yet, eyes that were focussed within suspicions' narrow range, ears that were attuned to the voice of scandal, would, he admitted, find ample evidence upon which to build. Besides, there was the danger—oh, sweet thought!— that the girl would grow too dependent on him. He recalled the clinging touch of her hands—hands that never failed to stir him with the most fantastic desire; he thought of her eyes, opening to his glance as a flower to the sun. He remembered the contact with her body as she held him to her breast... Resolutely, Arnold snapped off the thought. He was not a conceited man, he hoped, but never had he discovered any signs of his unattractiveness for women.

No, there was nothing *wrong* in this friendship, but the Misses Thurlow had warned him that speculation had already arisen, and that danger lay ahead. Conventions were at times inapplicable and galling, but one could not flout them. He and Hester must see less of one another.

Tactfully, in his opinion, he laid his views before her.

"Perhaps you are right," she said, after an uncomfortable silence. "You have such sound judgement and fine perceptions. For myself, I am exceedingly stupid. You see, I have been accustomed to associate with men in a work that—out there, at least—does not lend itself to this sort of cruel misunderstanding."

"Western civilisation suffers from a multiplicity of narrow judgements," floundered Arnold, conscious that he had slipped downward in her estimation.

"I ask God to be my judge," Hester continued, "and if my mind and heart are clean, then He approves, and I have nothing to fear. Long ago, when my father was dying and I was put to a terrible test, I came to see that it is a form of cowardice to do always what others think one should do. But," she added hastily, "I understand exactly what you mean, and will act accordingly. I would cut off my right hand, rather than be an embarrassment to you."

Arnold declared that it was of her he thought—a chivalrous untruth he soon succeeded in believing. "A man's position is different," he said.

"I don't admit that, but, even if I did, the 'difference' is not applicable in your case. If one of us needs protection more than the other, it is you. I am free; whatever I may do, concerns myself only, reacts upon no other person. Were you free—" the tone in which she spoke the words fell over him like an enchantment "—the circle which convention draws around you would be perceptibly enlarged. As matters stand, it is not of me, but your wife, that you must think. She deserves that you should not place her in an equivocal position before the world. I see that, clearly now, and realise that we had better cancel our engagement for to-morrow. You can write out the list of books for our little library and mail it to me."

But Arnold would not agree to so drastic a measure. He wished to appear a coward in Hester's eyes as little as a libertine in the eyes of his neighbours. And, by heaven, Hester was right! Only a poltroon would conform to the standards set by narrow-minded guardians of the world's morality. He had many faults, he knew, but none would say of him that he lacked courage to stand behind a principle! Anyone could follow the dictates of the mob, but the spirit of the martyrs was required to advance the profession of a different faith. For this very defiance of prescribed thinking, the Christ was crucified!

Arnold tread on air. He was inexpressibly exalted. Hester was right. The difficult course was the one approved of God. Let the world misjudge him. He was no weakling. He could suffer!

"I would regret more than I can say," he told her, "any change in our plans—any restriction to our friendship. I only felt it my duty to show you the situation as I see it. For my part, I have always considered over-emphasis on innocence as a fair indication that guilt inspired it. I have no right to assume, however, that you are of the same opinion."

"Oh, but I am!" Hester cried. "If you haven't understood *that*, it is because I am denied your splendid gift of expression. I tried to say the same thing when speaking of a clear conscience. Why should we behave as though we were guilty?"

"We must not!"

"I wonder if you know what your friendship means to me," the girl went on, singing monotonously into the soft spring air. "I'm so proud of it; I'm so jealous of it; I prize it as I would a holy thing!"

Arnold was simply transported. He quivered with gratification. No one had ever spoken like that to him, before. She was proud of his friendship; jealous of it; prized it as she would a holy thing! God, what a royal creature she was, with her fearlessness, her frankness, her capacity for devotion! A woman in a million! How different from the sly, avaricious female, eager for life's greatest moments, but unwilling to pay their price. How superbly honest she was, innocent of coquetry and curvetting; how scornful of duplicity, evasion! If Hester Ashburn loved a man, he reasoned; she would stand like a goddess and declare herself before the world!

"Any true friendship is a holy thing," he heard himself say, "rare and beautiful."

"To me, it is the Spirit of the Holy Ghost," Hester added. "Rejecting it would be like rejecting Christ."

Yes, yes! He possessed himself of that thought, built upon it and pointed to it as his own.

"Rejection culminated in Calvary, you know."

How wonderful, she murmured, that he should think that too! Then, "Has it ever occurred to you, we may be less charitable towards our neighbours than is compatible with the Christian faith? For example, would you regard people with suspicion and impute to them motives that are less noble than your own?"

"Indeed, no!"

"Well, why, then, should one suspect that others are less generous?"

Arnold was abashed. Perhaps he had done the Misses Thurlow an injustice. He was sure he had. Hester was right. He had never realised his pietist habit of expecting meanness from the world.

"I am not worthy to kiss the hem of your garment," he declared.

"Oh!" She drew in her breath as though his words had caused her pain, but he gave her no time to reply. A new aspect of the discussion had occurred to him.

"Elbert Hubbard used to contend," he observed, "that the world was falling upward. At the time, I was unprepared to accept the new order of things, and took issue with the statement. But to-day, its truth is particularly clear to me. Contrast the freedom you enjoy with the restrictions imposed upon women two hundred years ago. Imagine our friend, Shireen Dey, in an eighteenth-century New England town... why she would have been burned at the stake!"

Hester caught the thought, added an ornamental touch or two and handed it back. Nature, she suggested, takes every opportunity to reveal the Beauty of Life. A flower will blossom in what seems to be an impossible environment; a dog will remain faithful to the most unworthy master. A criminal in solitary confinement, she went on, is denied any expression of Beauty, but give him a measure of freedom, place him on parole, and the good that is in him triumphs. Similarly, in the association of men and women—segregate them, assume that any intercourse between them will be evil, and their best impulses will be stifled. But grant them liberty of action and the result will be an exquisite communion that is beyond reproach.

"And, speaking from the more practical standpoint," supplemented Arnold, "it would be ridiculous to apply antiquated standards of propriety to our present course of conduct."

"That's a good summary." Hester drew out her latch-key. "Will you come in?"

Arnold's punctual soul demurred. He knew that dinner would be waiting, but a confession of his new faith was of greater importance. Hester's sitting-room stirred some slumbering consciousness, some dim memory of Oriental splendour. He could not have described it in total nor in part, but he yielded to its influence as he yielded to the music of an organ.

"I can only stay a moment," he said.

"Hasn't this been a wonderful afternoon?" She closed the door and stood close before him.

He made ready to answer the question. But no words came. A curious faintness seized him. He groped forward with his unbandaged arm, spun round and round high above the clouds and came to earth to find Hester crushed against his breast, her warm lips quivering under his own.

"My master! My king!" she whispered. "Ah, Arnold, if you could know how I love you!"

"But I have no right to your love." He was still bemused, wondering how this thing had happened. "I am a cad to accept so royal a gift—when I can offer you nothing comparable in return."

"Do you hold your friendship so cheap a gift?"

"Is it really of any use to you?" he questioned in reply.

"I have told you it is like the blessing of the Holy Ghost. Do not take it from me."

Her long, pale, perfumed hands caressed his face, passed back of his head, drew it downwards to her breast, and held it there. He was conscious of a fantastic wish to become an infant, to close his lips upon the firm, red buds that rose and fell so tumultuously beneath the thin fabric of her gown. Instead, he lifted his head, asking for her mouth again.

"Poor wounded arm," she crooned, kissing the black silk sling. "Poor aching, lonely heart!"

"Not now... never, while I hold your love."

"And you are not sorry—you won't go home and re-proach yourself because—this—this—has happened?"

He protested. Extravagant phrases gushed from him, and all the while he was not unaware that he was playing this unfamiliar role with finesse and mutual satisfaction.

"I must leave you," he said, at last. "I long to be alone with my ecstasy—and my pain."

Outside, he looked at his watch. Half an hour late. He thought uncomfortably of Naomi's mute disapproval. Poor Naomi! He didn't love her. Never had. Never could. Some-how, he pictured her languishing because she was denied the radiance of his devotion.

He was suddenly very sorry for her, which was the reason he gave himself for hurrying to a bookshop and buying her a new volume of verse.

Vaguely, he realised she would have preferred prose.

For the first time, he made a direct comparison between his wife and Hester Ashburn. For the first time, he cried, "I love her! I love her!" And he was not ashamed. He was uplifted. She was a beautiful star, beyond his reach, beyond his hope of attainment... His adoration for her was a God-given thing, a new Cross to bear, along the steep and rugged path that led to the place of his soul's crucifixion.

CHAPTER 18

SHIREEN had always sniffed at Arnold's lofty pretensions, and now she warned Naomi against his growing intimacy with Hester Ashburn.

"George Moore remarked that excessive idealism is dangerous," she said, "and unless my perceptions have suddenly become dulled, these two exalted spirits are steering directly for the shoals."

Naomi felt no anxiety, but granting such might be the case, asked what she could do about it.

"What does the lawful and abused wife generally do?" laughed Shireen.

"I'm not sure I know what you imply. There is of course, the Divorce Court, and there are lesser and more ineffective measures. Are you thinking of divorce?"

"But certainly!"

"It would be a filthy job—spying on them in search of 'evidence,'" said Naomi. "And if there should be nothing actionable in their association—" she shuddered. "No, my dear, I don't think I could do it."

"Ninny!"

"You're right."

Shireen became very serious. "Oh, Naomi, you blessed martyr," she cried, "*do* be sensible! I am a successful woman, and therefore a selfish beast, but, next to myself and Doolydear, I love you, and I want you to be happy! May I be utterly and brutally frank?"

Naomi nodded.

"Well, then, do you imagine, even in your fondness for dreams, that you can ever be happy with Arnold?"

"Not exactly happy—no!"

"Nothing less than happiness is worth living for," asserted Shireen. "Why don't you leave him?"

"Any answer I make will sound to you feeble and irrational."

"I'm prepared for that from you," laughed Shireen. "Make it!"

Naomi sighed. "Call it weakness of character, then. I can't stand by my professions, my beliefs. I must do what I am expected to do!"

"Dear heaven," murmured the other.

"I know! Don't think I'm not bitterly aware of the trouble. Don't imagine I lie down without fighting. I'm always fighting—intelligence against instinct. And instinct wins—wins—wins! It's that damnable old woman-thing... the desire for respectability as it is translated by the masses, the dread of censure, the shrinking from disagreeable prominence. It's reluctance to inflict pain and buy my pleasure at that price; perhaps it's superstitious fear of the consequences. It's an echo—absurd, if you like, but vivid—of the tradition that woman must be true to one man, regardless of how polygamous he may be. It's—it's all these things and many more that make me efface myself and travel with the mob."

"You'll have a large group of friends who travel against the mob, too," commented Shireen. "I don't know that they are quite a 'mob' as yet, but their numbers command respect."

Naomi nodded, but made no direct answer. "In me, there seems to be concentrated all the inhibitions that have enslaved women throughout the ages. I *can't* break free! I'm like a dog," she continued, "chained for so long to its kennel that the habit of bondage is stronger than the sense of freedom, and the wretched creature sits all day in the shadow of its home, even when the chains are broken and lie loose upon the ground. If only Arnold ill-treated me—"

"But he does!"

"Not as the world is accustomed to regard ill-treatment. Oh, I can't make you understand, Shireen, but I seem to wear my spirit on the outside of my body; I feel people's thoughts too much, and moving in an atmosphere of reproach and disapproval, would have practically the same effect as stoning me to death."

Shireen considered this last. "I can imagine a person being sensitive to that degree," she said, "but I can't imagine not trying to overcome it. It retards development."

Naomi did try! Eternally, she was at war with her environment. She told Shireen of the night she sent Arnold to bed without her. "I didn't gain anything," she cried. "His irritation pounded against my consciousness exactly as if he had been pounding on the door. I had to put my work away."

"But if you left him, wouldn't you get beyond the zone of his influence?"

"Perhaps."

Shireen darted a look at her companion and asked—

"Would you be happy alone?"

"I don't know. Probably not, for, although I feel a thousand years old and tired to the point of disintegration, there is some curious yearning for emotional adventure."

"Then, the idea of a love—or lovers—is not repugnant to you?"

Naomi wondered how much Shireen suspected.

"Lovers? Well there's something about promiscuity—" she began.

"Who said anything about promiscuity?" flared the other. "Or about depriving the masses of the institution of Holy Matrimony—which, I divine, will be your next objection?

The goose's sauce is by no means sauce for the gander. But you can't be so archaic as to believe that some especial virtue attaches to the One-Man woman! You do feel, don't you, that a certain discriminating minority is justified in-forming congenial associations whenever they may occur?"

"Ye-es," admitted Naomi, "always with the reservation that there would be some sort of limit to the number of their attachments."

"The word 'discriminating' disposes of that. However, in your case, why not consider another marriage?"

Naomi smiled.

"You are travelling rapidly," she answered. "Remember, I am not yet divorced."

"You will be! I'm sure of it... unless you weaken..."

"...and ignore my opportunity, I suppose you mean."

"Precisely."

The argument was getting beyond Naomi's control. She couldn't concentrate. Her thoughts, which she tried to marshal like good soldiers, broke rank the instant she turned away, and lay down in scattered groups upon the field of her mind. The beginning of a sentence would form, and the end of it would trail away in mistiness. What did it amount to—all this talking about it and about? One came out by the same door where in one went.

Her wandering attention was caught by the fluttering of three birds on the window-ledge. Two males were contend-ing for the favour of a spirited little lady. While they hopped and pecked and beat their wings, she twittered in shrill ex-citement, circling round the contestants and urging them to greater deeds of valour.

The right of might soon made itself evident. The weaker bird was driven to the wall by his rival, whose attack in-creased in ferocity. Breathlessly, Naomi watched. Surely, thought she, the little coquette is enjoying the weakling's defeat! Oh, the cruelty of her!

There was no doubt about it. Watching her opportunity, she flew at the battered bird and added her strength to that of the swaggering victor. With a choked cry, a curious little squeak, the smaller suitor spread his wings and escaped, leaving the lovers laughing at his discomfiture.

Shireen had been watching, too. "There you are," she said. "Take your example from nature. The human being, the civilised human being, is the only creature that concerns himself with the weak and inefficient. Get up, little Naomi, when you see the exalted Arnold weakening, get up, give him an extra peck and send him flying."

"That is the very time I couldn't do it," said Naomi.

"Oh, you are impossible! Why? Don't, I beg of you, plead the maternal instinct! I could not bear it from you!"

"All right! Call it inherited instinct, then. Who has cared for the wounded since the beginning of time? To whom do men turn when sick or hurt? Who is the healer of the world? I can't help it, Shireen! Of course, surrender to heredity is weakness. Consider the drunkard. But when one is free of taint, it is easy to be hard on those who are not. All your life, you've been encouraged, in self-expression. Your parents, your brothers, spoiled you. It was 'Give Shireen the first choice, boys!' Or 'You mustn't make any plans yet. Shireen is the one to be considered!'"

"Well?"

"The opposite applies to me. All my life I have been trained to suppress my natural self, to adjust and adapt myself to some one else—a man. I had no brothers. My father was a tyrant in his way. And when Uncle Toby came to visit us, we were slaves to his slightest whim. With Arnold, it was the same, and even you, who have achieved this splendid emancipation, would find it difficult to enjoy your freedom in my environment, for, unlike Julius, Arnold does not *want* to help a woman towards spiritual, mental and economic equality. He seizes every opportunity to remind her of her bondage."

"All the more reason that you should assist in the culmination of this little romance, and get rid of him."

"You don't know the torment of carrying on an eternal warfare between your reason and your instinct."

"Oh, there were certain things I had to overcome," Shireen protested. "It wasn't so easy as you seem to think. And like all other women, I shrank from hurting the man who loved me. But if we were to have peace, it had to be done, so I shut my eyes and waded in. Look here," she broke off, suddenly, "is it in you to assert yourself with *any* man?"

"I wonder!"

She fancied herself married to Hugo and surrendering to the Woman-instinct in uncountable little ways. She saw herself constantly on the alert to please him, to hold his affection, to make herself desirable in his eyes. For she loved him. There was no doubt about that, now. She loved him and, therefore—amazing female—she wanted to wear the shackles of his forging and serve him!

Naturally, she argued with herself, there was greater happiness to be found in serving the man you loved, than one towards whom you merely discharged a conjugal duty. But she should not want to serve, at all! She should want to be free! Would Hugo be proof against her instinct to surrender? Would he protect her from herself? Or would she presently find that the tyranny of love was almost as devastating as the tyranny of selfishness?

"I love you!" answered Hugo's every argument.

"I thought you loved me!" answered Arnold's.

Shireen's voice recalled her.

"Time enough to discuss that later," she was saying. "But speaking again of Arnold, can't you see that he's no different from other men?"

"There's where you are wrong," Naomi cried. "He *is*!" He's in a class by himself... Oh, yes, certainly he thinks he's in love with Hester Ashburn. That's apparent to anyone who troubles to translate the oafish expression in his eyes. But I tell you, my dear, his enjoyment will lie in denying himself all save the most innocuous gratifications. He will be perfectly content believing himself a martyr to morality and an inscrutable Fate."

Shireen pursed her lips. Could he not suffer just as acutely, she suggested, through a little self-indulgence and resentment against the necessity for secret possessiveness?

"That's just the point. His suffering would be *too* acute. There would be too much danger—danger of discovery, and danger of remorse. Arnold could not endure the realisation that he had done wrong. No, my dear, I know him. He will be a perfect lover—in theory. But in practice..."

"He's an aesthetic moron," commented Shireen, making a note of the phrase. "Some day, I'll put him in a book. But don't imagine that he isn't human, or be surprised when your baronial husband confesses that he has surrendered to an overmastering passion—only he will call it 'holy.' Because my dear, when all's said and done, the magnetic missionary must not be underrated as a factor—or, should I say, an actor?—in this little *comédie romantique*."

Naomi didn't want to underrate Hester. With rather a shock, she realised how desperately anxious she was to find evidence of Arnold's defection, to know that love had triumphed over egotism and that he wished to enter into a permanent relationship that would leave her free. Oh, if they could only part in friendliness, in mutual sympathy and understanding!

But she couldn't imagine it. Arnold was steeped, saturated in classic convention, and never, she knew, would he grant her—or any other woman—mental and emotional enfranchisement. Never would he comprehend that Masculine and Feminine are but two aspects of the same manifestation, actuated by identical impulses and governed by identical limitations. To him, men and women would always remain dissimilar and distantly-related beings, with sharply defined capabilities, obligations and latitudes. There was Man's life and Woman's life, Man's work and Woman's work, Man's God and Woman's, although, of this latter conviction, he was not entirely conscious. Men and women were attracted and held by their differences. To conceive of their being alike was tantamount to assuming that *a certain man* was effeminate.

No! Arnold would never grant her the same longings, the same temptation that stirred him.

"Have you ever watched the guilty pair?" Shireen questioned.

"Never. When they are together, I don't watch them."

"What delicacy! However, you shall have an opportunity to observe them this evening. You are all coming here to dine."

"What? Who is coming?"

"Oh, all the dramatis personae of the play. Even the admirable ancient, Uncle Toby. I had just finished telephoning when you came in."

"But—but—what for?"

"To amuse me, and convince you. Just wait and see. I've been planning it for days. We'll have a war of glittering wits. Great fun!"

"I don't feel like glittering," said Naomi, vaguely uneasy. In Shireen's present mood, any dreadful thing might happen.

How had she won Arnold's consent? By some shrewd trick, most likely. He had accepted her hampers and made much of her attention during his illness, but Naomi was astonished at his acceptance of this invitation, especially if he knew that Hugo was also included. Arnold had never liked Hugo, but since Hester's revelation, dislike had developed into open enmity. "The man is a cad, a scoundrel," he exclaimed, at every mention of his name. "Knowing his record, I can't understand how decent people can tolerate him. For myself, I shall never speak to him again."

He regarded Hugo as the betrayer of an innocent girl's faith. Moreover, he was preposterously jealous of him—not on Naomi's account, but on Hester's. It was evident to any one save Arnold, that Hester's attitude of Christian forgiveness was slightly overdone. She smiled gently at Hugo, but there was acquisitiveness in the smile. And the more she smiled, the fiercer did Arnold's jealousy flame. He could not attain to such spiritual altitudes. He could not forgive. On the contrary. He damned Main to eternal hell, and stood ready to snatch Hester from the burning.

Shireen knew all this, thought Naomi. So why was she bringing these inharmonious elements together? Why precipitate a break? What was her object? Was she trying to help, by doing what Naomi wouldn't do for herself? Was she laying a trap for Arnold and Hester Ashburn?

No, no! That wasn't cricket. So offensive was the very idea, that Naomi felt an impulse to warn them. Then she saw Shireen smiling at her.

"Banish painful thoughts from your mind," she said. "I know the rules of the game. Whatever else may have been said to blacken my character, no one has ever accused me

of cheating. Now, run along and change. The car is waiting.
I'll send it back to your house at half-past seven."

CHAPTER 19

HESTER was very late.

"She's done it purposely," whispered Shireen to Naomi. "But just wait... and watch... and pray! She can't get away with this sort of thing, here!"

Arnold was unhappy. He kept looking at his watch and fidgeting, convinced, as the minutes wore on, that illness or accident had overtaken the girl. He could imagine no other reason for keeping a dinner party waiting. Conversation became a dialogue between Shireen and her husband.

"We'll allow her one more minute," cried the hostess, with too gay a smile. "Then, if she isn't here, we'll have our cocktails."

Fifteen minutes late, thought Arnold, consulting his watch once more. What dreadful thing could have happened? He felt that he must telephone and learn the worst. Why didn't someone think of the telephone? Just sitting and waiting...

The cocktails and Hester arrived at the same instant. Shireen cut short her pretty excuses with a counter apology.

"Knowing that you don't drink, I thought you'd forgive us if we had ours," she said.

"Of course, I'll forgive you," returned Hester, sweetly. "But why do you assume I don't drink?"

"Good Heavens!" cried the hostess. "*Do* you? I'm crushed with shame! Doolydear, bring a glass for Miss Ashburn... quickly!" Then in the awkward silence that followed, "Whatever could have given me such an idea? Aren't you a leading spirit in the Temperance Movement...

didn't I read somewhere that you are strong for prohibition and that sort of thing?"

"If 'that sort of thing' means the Purity League," replied Hester, "I'm on the Executive of *that*."

"Then I wasn't so far wrong, after all," sighed Shireen. "I knew there was something you wouldn't do!"

Julius gravely offered her a cocktail.

———

Naomi found herself seated between the tenor—Edouard La Gloire—with whom Shireen's name was being associated, and Hugo. Opposite were Uncle Toby, Hester and Arnold. How frankly Shireen arranged these affairs. How naturally she threw interested couples together (of course, Uncle Toby and Julius would play chess, after dinner), and how blandly she pursued the pleasant course, indifferent alike to praise and criticism!

Arnold's irritation had almost vanished.

"Please don't scold me," murmured Hester, and under cover of the table, she had timidly caressed his knee. "There was no one to help, and I am not accustomed to dressing alone."

Uncle Toby was responding to the bold flattery of his hostess; LaGloire to the excellence of her cuisine. Hugo's lips were set in a faint, sardonic smile. Julius appeared, as usual, insensitive to any unpleasant undercurrents. Shireen's eyes gleamed with a hard brilliance. True to her promise, she was determined to make the party glitter.

The conversation turned to happiness.

"It takes courage to be happy," she cried, looking around the table in a way that suggested to Naomi the flicking of a whip. "The average person leads a life of quiet desperation."

"Resignation," amended Hugo.

"Resignation is confirmed desperation," Naomi surprised herself by adding.

Arnold shot at her a glance of cold displeasure. He would have objected to the sentiment, in any case. He opposed it now because he was opposed to anything which might be said in support of Hugo.

"I think Mrs. Dey is right," he observed. "It takes courage to be happy, for happiness is dependent upon the consciousness of fidelity to duty..."

"...which often necessitates the enduring of great pain," supplemented Hester, eager to range herself on the side of righteousness. "It takes courage to endure pain in a proper Christian spirit." She looked at her plate, determined not to accuse Hugo by so much as a glance of the eye.

"The collection this morning will be devoted to—" began Shireen, when a pleading look from Naomi checked her.

"I'm afraid I wasn't thinking of anything quite so serious and spiritual," she explained. "I meant just the ordinary light and gaiety everyone could put into life if they would; if they weren't impregnated with the fallacy that there is virtue in being miserable."

"Isn't that frothy kind of happiness too often identical with selfishness?" asked Hester.

"No more that the life-is-real-life-is-earnest-and-the-grave-is-not-its-goal kind of seriousness is identical with spirituality."

"Spiritual fat," suggested Hugo.

"Exactly," agreed Shireen, "and there's nothing worse than fat—physical, mental, or spiritual."

"Yes," contradicted Naomi, "there's one thing worse— marrow-fat," and she laughed a little hysterically.

LaGloire lifted his eyes from his plate and spoke gloomily.

"I am of the opinion that scarcely one of us in every hundred knows the rapture that should be ours."

"The spiritual rapture?" insisted Arnold.

"Certainly, spiritual... but not the travestied spirituality of the churches."

Hester and Arnold openly joined forces. Uncle Toby, feeling unequal to actual conflict, stood ready to administer First Aid and strengthen the combatants.

"It is the deplorable fashion of the day to deride religion," said Arnold, after a sharp outbreak of hostilities.

"I do not deride religion," cried the tenor. "My quarrel is with the translation of it by the churches. Can't you see that the beautiful instincts of religion have been smothered under a shroud of religious vested interests?"

"Absolutely," said Hugo.

"That is the sort of cant used to support a dangerous revival of paganism," Hester acclaimed. "It is the excuse men offer or taking the primrose path and avoiding—or evading—the sacrifices required of every Christian."

"But Christianity is not *religion*," argued LaGloire. "It is only one interpretation of it—and most inadequate, at that! Beauty is religion. Martyrdom is not beautiful. Suffering is not beautiful. The distorted mind that conceives pain to be an expression of spirituality is, in my opinion, denying God."

An excited chorus answered him. When the clamour dropped to an indignant murmur, Hugo spoke.

"Dogmatism has paralysed religion until it has become a mockery of spiritual concepts," he said. "Why should we base our hope of salvation upon documents that are three hundred years out of alignment with the time they claim to mirror? I prefer to base my religious philosophy upon living, modern, vital experience."

"Creative evolution is the religion of the twentieth century," said LaGloire, before anyone else could speak. "It is interesting to watch it emerge from the ashes of pseudo-Christianity."

Naomi looked with secret alarm at her husband. Rarely had she seen him in the grip of such violent fury. He was not accustomed to argument, to having his pronouncements assailed. He did not like to have the comfortable structure upon which he based his thoughts and conduct rocked and shaken. "Sacrilege" covered any divergence from his religious opinions. He half rose from his chair, intending to take Naomi home. He wouldn't stay in a hostile atmosphere to receive insults and to hear these men blaspheme!

And Shireen sat there enjoying it all. She made no move to establish peace. She loved a row, and precipitated one as often as she could. She looked at Hester's flaming cheeks and blazing eyes, delighted with the turn the argument had taken. Her only regret was the fact that she hadn't seated the party differently. She knew that Arnold and the missionary person were clinging to one another's hands underneath the table.

"We'll have coffee in the drawing room," she said, "and continue the discussion there." Then, by way of explanation to Hester, who had not heard this speech before, "I never leave the men in the dining room. That custom, like so many other traditions, has outlived its usefulness. There are drinks and smokes in every corner, and there is freedom all over the house. Come along, everybody!"

The party separated into couples. Hester and Arnold disappeared; Julius and Uncle Toby settled to their game of chess; from the music-room came the languid strains of a love song that Shireen was playing to LaGloire. Hugo led Naomi into the Workshop.

"Didn't you think dinner very amusing?" asked the former. "Who but Shireen would have dreamed of throwing such an antipathetic group together?"

"Arnold will never recover from it," said Naomi.

"Does it matter?" demanded Hugo, peevishly.

"Not very much." She nearly added, "Nothing does."

Many a time, she had prayed for callousness, for a healing of the raw spots that every smallest unpleasantness seemed to inflame. But now that a curious casing seemed to envelop her body and spirit, she was anything but happy. A cold and dreadful drowsiness lay upon her.

Hugo possessed himself of her hand. She was scarcely conscious of the contact.

"Sometimes," he said, "I wonder if it is possible for two people to understand one another, utterly. Consider our case... it seems to me that, were I in your place, I would leave Arnold this very night. Nothing would matter save getting away from him. Why don't you feel that way, my dear?"

She shrugged. She had strength neither to enter into an argument nor to direct the course of conversation into a less contentious groove. Hugo gathered her to him and covered her eyes, her neck, her lips, with kisses. They burned, but in an unreal sort of way.

"This habit of getting outside myself and looking on, is taking hold of me," thought Naomi. "I must try to—"

"Woman!" cried Hugo. "Are you really such a cold little devil, or do you detach yourself because it throws me into a frenzy! By God, Naomi, sometimes when you are in this mood, I'm afraid I'll forget to be delicate and gentle!"

Hugo saw the age-old Woman-fear leap into Naomi's eyes, and cursed himself for his hot words. "What I really mean," he went on hurriedly, "is, that it startles me, at times, to see how little my love *touches* you—to see how placid you are when—when—I am not."

Naomi lashed herself into a defense.

"Do you expect me to want exercise when you want it, rest when you are tired, food when you feel hungry?"

"The points are not analogous," he declared. "The flare of passion is like the contact of two electric wires. Both should respond. If one does not, there is something very much the matter. Why, your lightest touch," he told her, "burns me like a divine fire."

"Which is just another way of saying that, like Arnold (though unconsciously, perhaps), you expect *me* to respond to *your* moods, whatever they may be."

"No, no! That's not true!"

"You have just proven its truth by confessing disappointment when *I* don't meet *you* on your emotional plane."

"But see here," cried Hugo, "love is different from exercise, from rest, and physical hunger and thirst—all that rot."

"Granted. The implication behind your remarks, however, is simply this—you will always be disappointed when I don't adapt myself to you... Oh, you won't want to know I'm doing it, but you'll not quite be happy if I don't."

Hurt, Hugo accused her of injustice, unreasonableness.

"But look at you now!" exclaimed Naomi. "You expect me to agree with you! In the matter of your love for me, why, instead of asking me to respond, why don't you attune yourself to my mood?"

He thought an instant.

"Because loving is a delight, because the fact—and the act—of loving is the very thing that brings us together. That is what we mean to one another—the embodiment and demonstration of Love."

"Love should mean fifty-fifty," said Naomi, more gently. "Can you not understand that just as my unresponsiveness is a trial to you, your *demand* for love is a strain upon me? Can you not see that it is identical with forcing myself to eat when I am not hungry, or to walk when I would rather rest?"

"No. If love is a strain, then of course, you don't love me."

"Loving you is no strain, Hugo. But expressing it according to your formula is sometimes difficult."

"Formula! My God! When I think of the exquisite thrill the touch of your body gives me and remember that you call it a formula..."

"Dear, I'm sorry. It was not a happy word. I was trying to convince you that you have expressed the masculine principle, the fundamental Man-thought shared by most other men. Arnold is not conscious of imposing upon me any strain. He thinks, as you do—that I am a sort of mirror, reflecting his moods and desires."

"Oh, well," cried Hugo, jumping up and pacing about the room, "if you are going to make that kind of comparison, there's no use arguing any further. The two cases haven't a point in common."

"They have a principle," said Naomi holding her ground.

"You certainly take a very distorted view."

"Perhaps." Seeing his distress, she weakened. "Perhaps I am feeling the reaction of the last few weeks. As a matter of fact, I don't seem to *feel*, at all. There is a crust folded over me."

Hugo returned to his seat beside her.

"Knock it off, darling," he begged. "Come to me, and together we'll get rid of the cocoon. You are damnably tired. That's the trouble. It isn't credible that you should lose your sensitiveness, you contact with life... you, who have always been so warm and vivid!"

Naomi shook her head. There was a sense of relief, she told him, in being numb. It made pain so much less acute.

"Ah," he objected, "but so it makes pleasure."

"Yes, that's true. It's life, I suppose. Everything's polarised. In order to enjoy, one must also be prepared to suffer."

And, five minutes later, she heard herself promising to go with him to New York the following day.

CHAPTER 20

ARNOLD followed the doctor downstairs.

"Exactly what happened?" asked the latter.

"No one seems to know. We were standing in the vestibule saying good night, when, without a sound, she just plunged forward down the steps. You don't think it's anything serious, I trust?"

Darrell recalled that he was speaking to a patient just recovering from a violent shock. It would be a pity to worry him.

"Oh, no, not serious," he said. "Nothing organic, you know. She's just drained herself of strength—that's all. A collapse. I warned her. I saw it coming."

Arnold sighed.

"If she would only leave that confounded writing alone! She's perfectly well and normal, so long as I can keep her away from her desk."

"Ah, well," the doctor temporised, "if everyone obeyed the laws of nature, we poor devils would have a pretty thin time of it. Keep her quiet—in bed, of course. Absolute rest is the treatment she requires."

"Then a nurse won't be necessary?"

"Er—" began the doctor. He was strongly tempted to say yes, not only for Naomi's sake, but because, like many others of his profession, he was generously inclined towards all those who profit by the disorders of men. It has become an established custom for a physician to pass his patients around like a joint at a barbaric feast, so that as many associates as possible get a picking from the spoils.

"If you don't insist," Arnold interrupted, "I think we

will be managing alone. It will be a little difficult for me, I know," he touched his arm, "but just at the moment, I am constrained to sacrifice personal comfort on the altar of economy, wherever possible."

"Well, there's no harm in trying. I know a nurse would be a great convenience, but that is for you to say." He forgot Arnold's nerves and remembered Naomi's drawn gray face. "The main thing is to make her feel that she can rest; that she has nothing to do."

"She hasn't," declared Arnold. "Since I prevailed upon her to install a servant, she is quite independent of domestic responsibilities."

"Good! Then we'll have her around in a few weeks. And don't worry. I'll drop in at noon to-morrow."

———

Naomi was aroused by Arnold's voice, polite, insistent.

"I hope I didn't wake you, my dear," he was saying. "But, I simply *can't* get into my clothes, alone."

He advanced to the bed and sat down close beside her. In his uninjured hand were two buttons.

"These dropped off my shirt when I'd got it half on," he said. "Really, I can't undertake the struggle of pulling it off again. Would you be so kind as to sew them into place?"

Naomi dragged herself to a sitting position. Her heart pumped as though she had been running. She felt sick and very cold.

"Give me my sewing-box," she said, in a strained voice.

Arnold looked at her in pained surprise. Her tone was resistant and sullen; her manner, ungracious in the extreme. One might have thought her had asked her to clear away the winter's accumulation of ashes from the cellar!

"Where is it?" he demanded, without moving.

Heaven knew he hadn't pulled the buttons off purposely. He had writhed and twisted and put himself to no end of trouble, getting that shirt on. It was a wonder he hadn't torn it to ribbons! And he had tried to be careful. At every grunt and groan, he had expected Naomi would call out and offer to help him. But she didn't. She just lay there in her bed, listening without sympathy to his straining. And now behaving like this! "Give me my sewing-box!" she said. Not even please!

"Where is it?" he repeated.

Naomi passed her hand over her brow. The room seemed to be full of mist.

"It's—er—"

"I don't want to hurry you, my dear," said Arnold, "but I am a little late now. If you could only bring yourself to see the value of a—ah—a *tighter system*! I can't imagine being asked for anything in my office and not knowing where it was. You remember the case of my dear mother's spoon, and how it disappeared literally from beneath your hand..."

"You'll find the box in the second drawer—there—the right-hand corner," said Naomi. "And will you please give me my kimono? The room feels very cold."

Arnold was not quick to follow her instructions. His dignified slowness was supposed to be a protest against her manner... lying in bed and ordering him about in this sulky fashion, when he had the use of only one arm!

He handed her the kimono upside down, and while she struggled into it, jerked with one hand at the drawer. When it was tightly jammed on one side, he called over his shoulder—

"I'm very sorry, my dear, but, disabled as I am, it's quite impossible to get the thing open."

Naomi left her bed and wrestled with the drawer until it yielded the sewing-box into her hand. Arnold, standing beside her, noticed that her face was scarlet, and an unbecoming moisture lay upon her skin.

"She can't be very cold," he thought. "And the way she demanded that kimono..."

When he left the room, she lay panting upon the pillow, and thought about ice water.

"Ice water... water ice, she repeated. It was silly, muttering like this, but somehow the words just seemed to come. "Ice water... Iceland... iceberg... ice-bound... ice cream... What a number there were beginning with ice! One more, now... Ah! Icicle... that was a good one... icicle..."

"Mrs. Lennox?"

Jennie McQuaig stood beside the bed.

"Ice-man," whispered Naomi. "Ice-plant..."

"Mrs. Lennox," Jennie raised her voice, "ain't you gettin' up this morning?"

Naomi quailed. Hyper-sensitiveness and that fact that she never *had* stayed in bed while others performed her tasks, made it easy to detect a threat in the girl's words. It was as though she had said, "Look, here, you can't lie there doing nothing while I slave myself to death single-handed! I'm not going to be put upon! No sir! I'll leave first!"

Tales of desertion told by distracted women leaped into her mind. She tried to summon phrases that would convince Jennie she would be no extra burden. She would lie there all day and ask for nothing—absolutely nothing, if only she could be left alone!

"I thought I would rest for a while," she said, "but you needn't bother about me." Oh, Jennie mustn't leave! The thought of Arnold's bewilderment in a disorganised house was intolerable. It would force her, she knew, to do, once again, the impossible, to get up and carry on. He would be sorry, but he would be helpless...

"Can you take up Mr. St. John's tray, and see that everything is dainty and appetising?" she asked.

"Sure," spoke the optimist. "I know how to handle old folks. Their funny little ways don't bother me, none."

She bounded downstairs and stumbled up again to the accompaniment of clinking china and soft explosives which Naomi assumed marked the overflow of whatever liquids she carried. Liquids... water... watermains... Waterbury... Watertown... watermelon... How silly to keep muttering these interminable words! Waterways... waterwings... Ah, swimming! She could imagine herself swimming... how heavenly!

Bells of brass jangled in her ears and dragged her back from merciful oblivion. Once more, Jennie McQuaig stood beside her bed.

"I wouldn'tuv woke you," said she, "but there's a poor fella at the door sellin' needles. He ain't got no arms, and only one leg. He's a holy sight, and that's no joke, Mrs. Lennox. Will you buy a book of um, please?"

Naomi found a quarter and told the girl to return after disposing of the cripple. Then, she undertook the difficult task of directing the household management from her bed; ordering the meals, making a list of the necessary supplies, reminding Jennie of a dozen duties that formed part of the daily routine. And, as she talked, despair fell upon her. This was horrible! She couldn't endure it. It would be far, far easier to get up and to die with her boots on!

"When you go upstairs for Mr. St. John's tray, be sure to leave his room tidy, and please don't forget to make Mr. Lennox's bed... Then, the bath-tub, Jennie... I'm going to ask you to wash it out this morning... You remembered to empty the pan under the refrigerator, didn't you? Oh, *don't* forget that! You'll have an awful mess in the kitchen. And the card for the ice-man..."

It was endless. Arnold's clothes must go to-day to the presser; Uncle Toby's stout was all gone. Somebody (other than Uncle Toby) had to order more. The laundry should come home, should be sorted and put away. The paper-boy would call for his money in the afternoon...

Hugo telephoned.

"He says can't you come just for a minute to the phone?" called Jennie. "He's got a partickler message for you."

Naomi compelled herself to refuse. Neither Hugo nor Jennie approved, especially the latter. No sooner had she reached the top of the house than a bell summoned her downstairs again. The front door... the back door... the telephone...

The work did not progress very well. Naomi gave up all idea of sleeping and listened to that frantic scurrying about the house. Luncheon was bound to be late. Arnold would be irritable and Jennie would be utterly worn out... Heavens, how she thundered up and down the stairs! Naomi lay with throbbing head and muscles tense trying to think how she could make the routine lighter and so spare the girl.

Hugo sent a box of pink roses. Ten minutes later, a radiant cyclamen came from Shireen. Standing in the window, its profuse blossoms looked like a flock of butterflies, tethered to a slender tree. Just before noon, a pale and spiritual hyacinth was left at the house. No card was attached, but Naomi knew that it had come from Hester Ashburn.

The doctor and Arnold arrived together.

"Well," cried the former, "how do you feel after a nice, restful morning?"

"Disgustingly weak," said Naomi.

"How much nourishment have you taken?"

A little pause.

"None."

"What? No breakfast?"

Naomi was silent.

Darrell was clearly annoyed. He looked at the bluish, limp hands lying on the coverlet and noted the short, gasping breaths with impatience rather than sympathy.

"I'm afraid you don't understand the treatment," he said. "Rest, quiet and good plain food—plenty of it. If you can't eat—drink! Egg-nogg, milk, broth—something every two hours."

Arnold and Uncle Toby did not linger over luncheon, and when Naomi attempted to eat what had been prepared for them, the reason was only too apparent. But what remedy could she suggest? In the midst of countless interruptions, Jennie had done her cheerful worst. The food was tasteless, and untemptingly set before them. The niceties of service would always remain for her an unnecessary complication of life's problems.

"That girl is taking advantage of you," said Arnold, tramping about the room and jingling the keys in his pocket. "The food to-day has been positively inedible. I'm sorry to complain, but really, you must speak to her."

"It's too bad, Arnold. You see, this is the first time she has ever prepared a meal without me. And this morning, there were many interruptions."

"First time... without you? I'm afraid I don't understand."

Naomi was sure that he did. "She doesn't pretend to be an experienced cook, you know."

"If you have taken the pains to instruct her," he argued, "I should think that no further experience is necessary." Like most men, he enjoyed the comfortable delusion that food cooks itself; or, perhaps, that good cooking and poor cook-ing are contingent upon willingness and laziness.

"If she has prepared sausages once under your supervi-sion, I should think she could repeat the performance. No," he cried emphatically, following a thought of his own, "if you have spoiled her, no wonder I am paying the penalty! Why put me to the expense of a servant's wages if you are going to do all the work?"

"You wouldn't expect a young boy to take charge of your office," suggested Naomi almost distracted by his musical roving. "He could only attend to a very small part of the work."

"I can't hear you." Arnold halted in a distant part of the room and cocked his head on one side. "You are talking into the bed clothes, and your words are completely muffled."

"Never mind, dear," replied Naomi. "It was nothing important," and she covered her face to hide the gush of weak tears.

———

Two weeks dragged by.

Vainly did Darrell look for improvement in her condition.

She was a source of considerable anxiety to him. He couldn't understand her strained, drawn lips, the driven look about her eyes. Like Arnold, he arrived at the conclu-sion that Naomi was stubborn, that she was fighting against a return to normality. All she had to do was to let go!

Meanwhile, he soothed Arnold with promises of a speedy recovery, inadvertently conveying the impression that a sort of aggravated indolence held his patient in thrall. She had no temperature, he declared; no cough, no organic trouble. There wasn't a sign or symptom of pneumonia, mumps, measles or chickenpox. Even headaches (the generic term man uses to cover all the subtle and mysterious complaints to which woman is subject) were rare. Arnold, with his need to classify, to give a name to everything, doubted the reality of this illness, dismissed it as an illusion. Women, he knew, were prone to evade responsibilities on the ground of physical disablement, and, while Naomi might not deliberately choose, he suspected that she did a good deal of writing in bed.

He endeavoured to maintain domestic morale by laying on her the burden of his grievances. When those relating to Jennie and the house were exhausted, he fell back upon finance and the office. Both he and Uncle Toby asked after her health with perceptible personal interest, as though to say, "How soon do you expect to get up and attend to our comfort, once more?"

But she kept hoping that her spirit would harden, that she would feel life's buffeting less acutely. Oh, to be able to hear Jennie McQuaig smashing china, Uncle Toby swish cleansing powder in the bath-tub, Arnold's endless complaints, with sweet and unfamiliar calm! Oh, to lie in bed and know that nothing mattered; that bills, and letters from editors, and the manuscript of *The Book of the Hour* need awaken no interest and no concern!

Her friends were very kind. They telephoned at the most inconvenient hours and insisted upon calling unannounced to chat with her. As a sentinel, Jennie was a complete failure.

This neighbourly "running in" was horrible. It precluded all possibility of relaxation. Naomi had to spend some time each morning making both her room and herself presentable. She couldn't sleep. Her nerves were racked by the imminence of some one coming into her presence. Several times she had been roused by a visitor standing in the doorway, saying—

"You poor darling! It's a shame to wake you, but I just had to come to see how you were!"

One afternoon, Hugo called.

"You shouldn't have done this," said Naomi, when Jennie McQuaig, with a look of sympathetic understanding, had left him in her room. She hated that look in Jennie's eyes.

"Please don't scold me," cried Hugo. "I had to see you... I had to come! There was no satisfaction to be gleaned from that imbecile downstairs, and Arnold insists that you are merely resting. What is the matter with you, Naomi? You're not—" misery clouded his eyes "—you're not..."

"No." A ghostly smile touched the corners of her lips. "I assure you I'm *not*, Hugo!"

"Thank God!" he exclaimed, dropping to his knees beside the bed. "Don't think that I'm jealous. It's not that! I'll never be unreasonable, I swear! If you love another man better than me, you shall go to him. I will do everything in my power to promote your happiness. But this is different. You can't know the torment I've endured for days, thinking that perhaps you were going to bear Arnold a child. That would have been utterly intolerable!"

"Utterly," echoed Naomi.

Hugo had come with another plan. The instant she was able to travel he wanted to carry her off to a southern mountain resort—a sort of glorified sanatorium.

"Presently," he told her, "you will feel so happy and strong you'll scarcely recognise yourself. Meanwhile, I want to be your host—that's all. I won't go with you, if you prefer to go alone. Surely, we can arrange it so that there will be no possibility of scandal."

A little tremor of excitement ran through Naomi's body.

She imagined herself lying on a sunny verandah, caressed by the strong air of the surrounding hills. A uniformed attendant approaches. "Your chicken broth, Mrs. Lennox," she says. "Are you quite comfortable? Isn't there anything you would like me to do for you?" Twilight. She is being put to bed in a room kept tidy by hands other than her own. Presently, a dainty tray will be brought to her, and, when she has eaten all she can, it will be taken away. Then she will sleep... sleep... undisturbed, until she rings her bell in the morning.

"I'll go this week," she said, breathlessly.

Hugo, unprepared for such an abrupt capitulation, felt the victory going to his head. He rose from his knees and sat in a distant part of the room.

"It's the best arrangement we've made so far," he said. "Darrell will be jolly glad you're going away. Tell Arnold anything you please. The break will have been made decently, you see. Then you need not come back. When you're quite ready, you will come to me."

There was a little pause. Naomi closed her eyes. She could almost smell the sunshine, hear the gentle clatter of crisp bass-wood leaves...

Hugo lifted her into his arms. She knew he meant to be tender. Actually, he was exceedingly rough.

"Don't!" she cried sharply. "Let me alone. I hate to be dragged about like this!"

"I'm sorry... forgive me! You can't understand..." He was quite incoherent. "The other times, I had a feeling, an instinct, that you wouldn't come. Now, it seems to be real... you're mine. You're mine!"

"Go away this instant," said Naomi. "Positively, you mustn't be here when Uncle Toby comes in."

"Why are you so much afraid of those two men?" demanded Hugo.

"Because I have to live with them."

"Will you be afraid of me? Will you surrender your will to mine rather than promote temporary unpleasantness?"

"Probably."

"But you mustn't!" he cried. "You encourage tyranny. That's weak."

"Yes, I know. Surrender to heredity is a weakness. But, believe me, Hugo, it will be many generations before women triumph over this instinctive submission."

"Heredity plays a smaller part than vanity," said Hugo.

"Vanity is part of that inherited sense of dependence," Naomi declared. "Women had to attract, otherwise men would not have wanted to provide for them. And there remains a sense of physical fear, too."

"Absurd!"

"True, nevertheless. To women, man's displeasure is reminiscent of bodily violence, brutality. She shrinks—all unconsciously, perhaps—from the descending club, in accordance with the instinct of self-protection."

"Isn't it time to outgrow that?"

"Of course. But there isn't time to argue. You really must go!"

"Oh, very well," he sighed. "But what of your reservation? When would you like to start?"

"Day after to-morrow or, at latest, the day following that. I'm eager to go. This is the moment I've been waiting for. As you say, something about it is different—easier, more natural. I'm happy..."

"That's a great point," said Hugo. "You've never been before."

"I know. But this time I feel that a dream is coming true. It was a wonderful idea of yours, my dearest... I don't feel a bit afraid."

He laughed to cover his elation. An unaccustomed self-consciousness made him a little ashamed of his desire to shout, to dance, to crush this thin-clad woman-thing until she cried in pain.

"Silly child," he said. "Don't you know better than to boast that way? Be careful, or you will provoke me to beat you every evening for the sheer delight of testing my brute strength."

"What a contradiction," smiled Naomi, holding him from her with a determined hand.

"Of course! That's love. Besides, you, who are always prating about instinct, should know that a man *must* feel his power to vanquish entire armies for the woman he adores, otherwise he does not love her hard enough."

"Sometimes he mistakes her for the army," sighed Naomi. "In fact, very often."

"Don't let me vanquish you, my darling," cried the man, burying his face in her soft hair. "Fight, Naomi. I love you when you struggle!"

CHAPTER 21

NAOMI felt strengthened by an agreeable excitement. She didn't understand exactly what had happened to her. Nor did she care. It was enough to be energised and happy.

She sorted the correspondence that had accumulated during the past month, deciding to take most of it with her. Clothes... A trunk, of course... and paper and carbons. She would lie in the open air and finish *The Book of the Hour*.

No sneaking off this time, thank God! No stifling sense of shame, or fear of discovery. No falsehoods and quibbling. Everything seemed to have shaped itself for her convenience and her peace of mind. She hadn't felt so happy for years. Even the thought of Arnold... She rehearsed her announcement to him—a few simple facts, unvarnished by extenuation and vague promises. That was enough. She mustn't talk too much.

"To-morrow, I am going away," she would say. "I'm going to a sanatorium."

"A sanatorium?" His echo would betray displeased amazement. "Is there any particular reason for this fantastic step?"

"Only that I'm not improving. I don't get much chance to recover, at home."

"I did!" he would assuredly say.

"There was some one to take care of you," she would answer. "That makes all the difference in the world."

He would hint at the inescapable expense. She would interrupt, explaining that all such arrangements had been made. He would receive the intelligence with ill-concealed annoyance. This was the result of women's economic independence! He never had approved of it; never would.

Women weren't capable of using freedom. They could not, or would not, see themselves in relation to other people. They were selfish, obsessed by the craving for pleasure, rebellious against responsibility of any kind, contemptuous of domestic decorum.

"Of course, if you have completed all your arrangements," he would conclude, drawing the cloak of dignity over his impotence, "I have nothing more to say. If you can find happiness in disregarding me, in excluding me from your considerations, I suppose there is no alternative save to endure it. If am not ashamed, however, to confess that your attitude lately, has given me great distress. Perhaps you will be kind enough to advise me as to the date of your return?"

"Yes, Arnold," she would say, "of course, I'll write."

———

Sunshine, wood-scented sunshine, and sharp, fresh wind from the hills; the soft clatter of leaves; space, light, air. She would forget the imprisonment of these last weeks. Already, her spirit was responding to the promise of liberty. She was wild to get away!

Her hands trembled as she wove a bodkin through a piece of lace. Only a few hours more of clanging bells, consideration of food, household anxiety, effort to reduce the volume of complaints. By this time tomorrow, she would be free. Instead of nerve strain, she could have rest. The sense of duty would be replaced by the fulfilment of desire. It would not be a case of what she must do, but what she wished. Oh, to be relieved of the continuous presence of Arnold's will!

And there would be no immediate scandal. That was the best part of all. For weeks she would be secure from the consciousness of obloquy. The far-reaching sting of slander would not poison her calm days. And even when Arnold learned the truth, when he confirmed the suspicions of the townsfolk, and announced that she was not coming back—the bomb which had been fizzling all along, could not explode with any violent shock. Besides, distance, gladness and restored health would all be in her favour, robbing private and public condemnation of its sting.

———

After dinner, Uncle Toby went for a walk. Something must have gone wrong. With a quiver of misgiving, Naomi noted Arnold's firm tread on the stairs.

"How do you feel this evening?" he asked, coming into her room.

"I feel a decided improvement, thank you."

Arnold was devoutly glad to hear it. He assumed that there was hope of her getting about as usual in the near future.

"Is anything the matter?" she asked, knowing, of course, that there was.

"Is anything *not* the matter?" he countered. "I don't wish to seem lacking in consideration, my dear, but really, this sort of thing can't go on! You have no idea of the conditions downstairs, otherwise you couldn't lie contentedly in bed while your household goes to pieces."

Her household? Ordinarily it was his!

Naomi asked what he expected her to do.

"I see that you resent my criticism," he returned, stiffly. "A most unfortunate attitude, on your part, my dear. If you were ill or suffering, no amount of discomfort would have induced me to speak. Darrell, however, assures me that you are neither. Such being the case, and with nothing to do all day, you can surely set aside your writing long enough to give some small attention to your home."

Naomi felt an inrush of unaccustomed courage. For the first time in her life, she knew no fear of Arnold. Supposed she did wound his vanity, his self-esteem? Supposed she did intensify the prevailing discord? These were matters of no consequence compared with her passionate desire to defend herself against the injustice of his accusation, defend not only herself, but all similarly-situated women. She said—

"Stop that prowling, please, and sit down." Astonished at her tone, at himself for obeying, he did so. "I'm not going to quibble over the word 'contentedly,' but I do object to your implication that I sham illness in order to get on with my work. It might not be indelicate to mention, however, under these conditions, that the fruits of this same work kept the house running while you were ill, and several small cheques there on the table will meet our expenses for the next few days. A house cannot be maintained without money, Arnold, and I don't seem to remember that since your accident, you have given me any."

"It pleases you to taunt me with this."

"No, not taunt. But if you persist in deprecating my writing, in making yourself believe that it is some low form of dissipation, surely I may be permitted to remind you what we all owe to it. Furthermore, I don't spend the money I earn on personal things. I don't even enjoy the gratification of subscribing to charities, and taking an option on my seat in heaven."

Arnold muttered.

"I see you resent *my* criticism," said Naomi, without anger. "That is unfortunate, for it will blind you to the self-evident truth—you had no excuse on earth to contribute one hundred dollars to Hester Ashburn's Mission. In ameliorating the condition of Hindu women and children, you have impaired the condition of a woman much nearer home. It is not possible for you to deny that I must make up the deficit occasioned by your generous gift. And, mark you, Arnold, I don't complain of *that*! I am glad to help. I love to write. I would ask nothing better than to go to my office each day and provide for both of us a living."

"As usual," Arnold cut in, "you indulge, when excited, in the most absurd exaggerations."

Naomi smiled. "No. I don't exaggerate—in this matter, at least. Given your opportunities to work, I could provide for you quite as well as you provide for me. There is no reason for you to underestimate my earning power. There is nothing derogatory to you in admitting it. However, let that pass for the moment. You have made a very grave charge against me. I can see that it does not lack foundation if Darrell has led you to believe that I am quite normal."

"I didn't make so broad a statement," contradicted Arnold. "He said—"

"I think I can imagine. He told you practically what he confided to me when you were ill—that you were quite able to go to your office as usual."

"Impossible," cried Arnold, and began to recite his recent disabilities.

"Nevertheless, I assure you that Darrell regarded your case with no anxiety—no concern. Now, the point I make is this—did I relax my attentiveness on that account? Did I assume towards you the attitude you have shown towards me ever since I went to bed?"

"But my arm," Arnold reminded her, with frigid dignity. She mustn't overlook a broken arm.

Naomi overlooked it.

"How readily would you have recovered in your office, harassed by the petty annoyances that thrust themselves into your working hours? Imagine lying in bed beside the desk at the mercy of the office boy, the telephone, visitors! 'Mr. Lennox, this... Mr. Lennox, that...' all day long. Imagine that I am ill in your office, and that you are trying to keep your business running and attend me at the same time. Does the picture appeal to you?"

Arnold observed that nothing could be gained by such extravagant comparisons. As usual, he closed his eyes to the particular point Naomi was endeavouring to emphasise, made a wide detour around her logic, and came to an aggrieved halt before a barricade of his own raising.

"You seemed to have had very little care of me," he said, "thanks to the kindness of Hester Ashburn."

Calmly, almost humorously, Naomi drew the cloak from the comfortable delusion. Blind before, Arnold now became deaf. The only evidence he gave of hearing was in the hard-set muscles of his jaw.

"Rest," Naomi continued, "isn't a state that comes; it has to be provided for you. Let us grant that I am not ill, not suffering, but that I do need rest, what have you done to provide it for me? Have you ever brought me a tray, or prepared my food? Have you taken my messages, entertained my guests, or turned them away when I wished to sleep? Have you written my letters or kept my business affairs from getting into a discouraging muddle? I did these things for you."

"What of your servant?"

"She is no more omnipotent than your office boy. She requires constant supervision... as you have just been telling me... that's why she is a servant. And, even if she could think out the routine for herself, she could not possibly accomplish all the work and give me a fraction of the attention I should have."

"Many women achieve twice as much without complaint," argued Arnold. "Look at the farms."

Naomi reminded him that farmers do not live by the same standard he required.

"Say no more, he commanded. "I am weary of this eternal argument. It is apparent that you are ranged against me on the side of a vulgar domestic, and, while I scarcely expected sympathy from you, I did hope for justice."

"If you don't get justice," returned Naomi, "it's because you refuse to give it. I am ranging myself on the side of all women whose subjugation to man's dominance is taken for granted, whose toil is unappreciated—unacknowledged, indeed!—and whose capabilities and ambitions are crushed under the burdens men like you place upon them. There you sit, self-absorbed, considering *your* ease, *your* rights, *your* wrongs! Aggrieved because I am not clearing the stones from your path! And carrying out that metaphor, you not only refuse to help me clear, but you actually bring unnecessary material and dump it in my way so that I have extra work to do! What possible justification can you offer for sitting here day after day and tormenting me with your grievances, especially when you do absolutely nothing to remove the cause? That's not good sportsmanship, Arnold. It proves that you lack a sense of team-work. Surely your curling club would not tolerate so obstructive a member."

Arnold maintained a pale and lofty silence, so Naomi continued—

"Instead of complaining, I should think you would want to help that child downstairs. She came back on her afternoon 'out' to serve you. She is just as much entitled to these hours as you are entitled to your Sundays and Bank holidays."

"I have never been in the habit of working with my dependents," pronounced the master of the house.

"That is only too true, but it's not a boast of which you should be proud. Mind I'm not suggesting that you get up at six o'clock and do the marketing while I lie lazily in bed. That is the other painful extreme. The woman who contributes nothing but housekeeping to the establishment should, in my judgment, keep house. Man is accustomed to regard himself as the provider, but it is Woman who actually produces, creates. All of us should create something—even if it is but an illusion. Most men are quite content with that—with the illusion of domestic happiness. If, however, woman is capable and desirous of doing her share of the earning, then, she should be relieved of a proportionate amount of her household care."

"In that case," cried Arnold, as though he had found a weakness in her argument, "most of the women in the world would be scrambling for money-making positions."

"Why?"

"That they might be relieved of their household tasks."

"You mean that they would find almost any other kind of work more agreeable, and home-makers would become an extinct race?"

"Precisely!"

"Then," said Naomi, "although you have just admitted that housekeeping and home-making are the least agreeable of all jobs, you blandly impose them upon women. Is that fair?"

Arnold got impatiently to his feet. He rattled his keys with vigour.

"You always overlook the very crux of the matter," he said. "Women are fitted by Nature, by physical laws, to remain in the home. Men are assigned other duties. You can't change Nature."

"Oh, yes, you can! Men have advanced that theory ever since women began to compete with them. The crux of the matter, as you call it, is this—married life should be a reciprocal arrangement, a partnership, where the pleasant and unpleasant jobs are shared on a basis of fifty-fifty. Try to realise that a woman with a wage-earning capacity finds the entire charge of a household—plus eternal criticism—just as irksome as you would, were the positions reversed. Grant your wife—" not until long afterward did Naomi recall that she had no intention of pleading for herself; she visualised Hester Ashburn as the head of Arnold's home "—the same feelings that you possess. Show her the same consideration that you would show another man, a pal..."

"But I did not think I was marrying a pal," interrupted Arnold. "I wanted the finer qualities supposedly existent in a true woman."

"That is the best point you have made yet," said Naomi. "But it resolves itself into this—you wanted to be the dominant factor in an intimate association; you wanted to live with an agreeable echo of yourself; you wanted the machinery of life kept running perfectly without giving adequate assistance, and without being made aware of the labour required for its operation. In other words—rather cruel words, I admit—you have always wanted to *enjoy* the fruits of sacrifice, which meant that I must keep you in ignorance of the extent of my self-denials."

Arnold cried out at this. One would think he took the bread from her mouth, he exclaimed.

"You do," she told him. "Not always literally, or with violence, but with equal effectiveness. If there is bacon enough for one, you get it. If there is some especial delicacy on the table you invite Uncle Toby to have it. If I am tired, or particularly rushed, you suggest that I take up his tray in the morning. When we are both hurrying to dress, you stand in front of the mirror. Why," she added, smiling, "since the three of us have lived together, I've become accustomed to bathing in five inches of water. The tub has to be filled to the brim for the men of my household. What delectable mental dishes you have taken from me, I couldn't tell you. You'd never understand."

Before Arnold could interrupt again, she concluded—

"I am a little fed up with the Christian interpretation of sacrifice. It seems to be one-sided, so inevitably a means whereby the thoughtless and selfish shall profit by the duteousness and denials of the deserving."

With an inarticulate cry, Arnold flung himself from the room, and slammed the door.

——

He didn't go to the office in the morning. Naomi listened to his uneasy prowling and wondered what could be the matter. Was it possible, she asked herself, that her words had fallen upon fertile ground, that he had stayed at home to share her burdens and assume partial management of the home?

She wanted to do him justice, but could not picture him engaged with domestic occupations. Then, what was he doing? Merely tramping about and nursing his anger?

Should she call him or wait until he came to her of his own accord? She rehearsed her announcement once more. Poor Arnold. It would give him a severe shock.

"I am going away," she would tell him, presently. "I am going to a san—"

Abruptly, he came into the room.

"May I have a few minutes of your time undisturbed?" he asked.

He wanted her time undisturbed! The request was amusing, until she saw that he was locking the door.

She stared at him, a gray, broken old man. Twenty years had laid their weight upon him over-night.

"Why, Arnold, my *dear*!" she exclaimed. "You are ill. What on earth has happened?"

He sank into a chair and moistened his lips.

"I spent most of last night with Hester Ashburn," he mumbled.

Naomi felt a hideous desire to laugh. What an irreclaimable egoist he was! How he loved to invest his slightest words and actions with implications of importance! Had he not spent most of every evening with Hester for the last two weeks? He *was* funny!

But she held fast to a becoming gravity.

"Well, what of it dear? Did you tell her of our argument and fail to enlist a sympathetic ear? Did she range herself, too, on the side of a vulgar domestic, deserting—"

"Please, I don't wonder that you fail to understand me, but I am confessing that—that I've been—unfaithful to you, Naomi."

"*Arnold*!"

For an instant, she was stunned; then mad thoughts raced through her mind. It couldn't be true... Not Arnold! No, never, never! Not unfaithful... not really unfaithful. Of course not! What a fool to think he meant it literally. And yet, if he did—if he had—Oh God, then she was free... free!

She looked at him again. It must be true. His appearance confirmed it. To think that release had come in this way! To think that the most unlikely of all the gates that barred her freedom should have been opened. And by Arnold, himself! With a deep sigh, she fell back on her pillows.

It must be true—literally true. Nothing less could explain his terrible suffering. She understood his problem, realised he must find extenuation for his wrong-doing, justify it not only to himself, but to Hester and to her.

She was conscious of his shame, of his fierce longing for absolution. She saw that, as ever, he would sacrifice the willing victim, that he expected her to persuade him that what he wished to do, was right.

"I find it hard to believe you," she said.

"Your disbelief is like the twisting of the rack," he groaned. "And I have no excuse... You must hear all. To you, I will lay my soul bare. And remember, I do not ask forgiveness..."

"Arnold," cried Naomi, "I don't want you to tell me what happened. It is enough for me to know that you love Hester. I am glad! Honestly glad! There's nothing to forgive—nothing to distress yourself about. Quietly, we will arrange everything. In a few months, you—and I—will be free."

"No, no! That's out of the question. In your divine charity, you are forgetting my punishment. I have committed a grievous sin against two women, against myself, against my God. It is meet and right that I should expiate that sin."

"But there's no reason for me to expiate it, too. I assure you, Arnold, I want to go away. I want to be free!"

"Don't think you can deceive me," he groaned. "I have enjoyed your self-sacrifices too long. No, no! Listen, while I describe the downfall of a soul, and then pronounce judgement."

Naomi wondered what he would have said, had she asked, as he had demanded recently of her, "Aren't you rather theatrical?"

Naomi couldn't listen. A deadly fear laid its hand upon her. What devilish trick of fate was this, she asked herself? For years she had suffered under the association of the ignoble motives that Arnold imputed to her; was she now called upon to make a supreme sacrifice because he invested her with attributes that were non-existent... and divine?

She recalled the birds on Shireen's window-sill. They were Arnold, Hugo and herself. She would not submit to the tyranny of the weak. She would join forces with the strong. Arnold had a perfect right to enjoy his punishment, but there was no reason for him to thrust his misery upon her.

"...attracted from the first... so good during my illness... profoundly religious side..." Broken sentences impinged themselves upon her own train of thought, like snowballs on the bark of a tree. She was reminded of a game she used to play with Uncle Toby; one wrote B-a-l-t-i-m-o-r-e and at the same time spelled aloud "Washington." Or one wrote C-h-i-c-a-g-o and spelled "Seattle," letter by letter. Here was Arnold talking about himself and Hester while she fixed her mind upon herself and Hugo.

"...one afternoon... kissed her. I didn't mean to. The thing just happened. Don't think I'm trying to exonerate myself. No! I just want you to understand that there was nothing deliberate, calculated... I had no intention of doing anything more than admire her in a pure and abstract way."

"There was nothing impure in kissing her," said Naomi.

"It was the beginning of the end. You—a woman—are not expected to know the terrible power of passion. But I became like a man whose will was undermined by some devastating drug, whose self-control was sapped by some foul poison."

Again, Naomi tried to ease his pain. "You are giving yourself unnecessary suffering," she said. "All this is but another way of explaining that you fell in love with Hester and became conscious—perhaps for the first time in your life—of an irresistible physical appeal."

"Yes, yes!" He snatched eagerly at her understanding. "I loved her profoundly—it is your right to know that. And she was so lonely, so dependent upon me! Her need of me was bewildering, piteous, disarming. I had never known a woman so frank, so innocent of reserve."

He gave himself up to some brief and cruel memory, and then burst forth.

"Oh, you must know the worst of me! I dare not try to conceal anything from you! My thoughts rose in rebellion, mutinied. I lost control completely. I used to visualise her lovely body-curves naked under my hand. I used to hunger for her day and night..." He covered his face and shook with dry, hard sobbing. "Day and night, I starved for the touch of her soft, white flesh."

A great pity welled up in Naomi's breast. His torment was terrible to see. She had never heard a man crying.

"My dear, my dear!" she murmured. "Try to understand what I say, and take comfort. All this is nothing that should distress you so. I don't feel wronged. Hester needn't. I am glad to give you your freedom. She shall be legally—and morally—yours. She is much better suited to you than I am. Don't sob that way!"

He caught her hand, and dropped it quickly.

"Your goodness only adds to my pain," he cried. "For it is you who will not understand... Last night, I left the house in an unforgivable frame of mind. I went right to her. The room was fragrant—you possibly recall the curious Oriental perfume that seems to be a part of her?—and lighted only with moonbeams. I began to tell her of our conversation... Oh, flay me with your scorn for such disloyalty. I deserve it."

"I don't want to flay you, but if you must tell me, go on."

"In justice to myself, you should know that I fought to the best of my poor ability. Oh, my dear, I did struggle! You believe me, do you not?"

She nodded.

"She sat close beside me... in the moonlight... very still. Suddenly, she made a little movement, and—I turned to discover that she—she had slipped out of her robe; that she had—nothing on!"

"Nothing?" cried Naomi. "Naked?"

"Naked as your hand. I wasn't responsible. Perhaps you recall one night, soon after our marriage—the only night, I think I may say, when bestiality triumphed over my delicacy towards you?"

Again she nodded.

"Imagine that deplorable condition intensified a thousand-fold... No," he repeated, "I was not responsible."

"Of course not. You weren't to blame. And you mustn't allow yourself to suffer so. We will all be happy, especially I. This gives me an excuse to leave you—makes everything much easier for me. I've already arranged to go to a sanatorium."

"I don't believe you," cried Arnold, lifting a face she scarcely recognised. "This is just a natural reaction following the shocking confession I have made. Your pride is hurt. Your finer sensibilities are outraged. Otherwise, you would not be a true woman. But I can't let you go. I must protect you from yourself. You shall not be driven from your home."

"But I want to go," Naomi insisted, wildly. "I have longed to leave you—for months!"

"That cannot be possible. I have not known Hester for months. You won't deny that everything was all right till she came."

"I will deny it! Nothing has been right between us for years! I have been desperately unhappy. Last night, I tried to tell you why, and you wouldn't listen. I don't want to go on living with you, Arnold. I want to choose my own life."

The birds, she reminded herself, the birds! She must fight for her very existence, now. This was the time to strike. Never, in all her life, might she have another chance. She mustn't weaken.

"You see, Arnold," she went on breathlessly, "we can't pretend to love one another, any more." She had intended to say, "I don't love you," but couldn't. "Our interests are as wide apart as the poles. Our very principles, ideals, have changed. No longer can I submit to your judgments, and I fear you will never be converted to mine. Between us there is no sympathy... no understanding. *I want to leave you...* please get that idea into your mind. I want to go where I am free to work without other responsibilities and interruptions. Call it selfish, if you like, but there you are. Let us, then, in all friendliness arrange to separate."

"Willingly," Arnold replied, "*if* such a step would further your interests or your happiness. But it cannot! You are speaking on impulse... your suggestion is not the outcome of leisured deliberation. Oh, my poor little bruised wife, I know that you are crying out in your pain, like a wounded animal that seeks a corner in which to hide... God forgive me..."

Naomi began to beat about rather wildly. Everything was going wrong. Arnold's compassion was deadlier than his inconsideration. It was closing in upon her; crushing her down.

"I'm like an animal that is trapped," she cried. "I tell you, it has been the dream of my life to get away! I have thought of it day and night for weeks! I want liberty of thought and action."

"Yes, dear," he interrupted, soothingly. "You shall have it—right here in your own home. I have forfeited all claim upon your consideration, your regard. You won't have to complain of me again. Just put all thought of me away from you and follow your inclinations as though I did not exist. That is the course for us. No punishment dealt by your hands will be too severe for me to accept in the humblest spirit."

"But I don't want to punish you—if I have to stay here to do it," she cried. A dreadful numbness was creeping over her. The room had grown very cold. She began to tremble. "What you have done is no concern of mine, save that it provides me the right to leave you. *I want to go*! Besides," a ray of hope shone across the descending darkness, "what of Hester? Do you acknowledge no responsibility towards her?"

Arnold twisted in evident pain.

"Two wrongs can never make a right," he said thickly. "I will recover from this madness when she is gone. She has her work... Out there, I would not be necessary to her. Moreover, although I do not blame her—the fault was equally mine—there came to me, simultaneously with her surrender, a sense of revulsion. I tell you this, my dear, to prove that I am not wholly depraved. There must be a spark of decency alive, when I could feel revolted by her voluntary degradation. We are all alike, we men," he said. "To hold us, our women must be pure. I offer her my pity, my profound penitence, but never again my respect and love. The remembrance of last night would ever stand between us. I could not hope to be happy."

Naomi felt the walls of the room closing in about her. Life seemed to ebb away, leaving a stone image sitting there in her place, staring at the gray ghost that had been her husband. "I'll go, to-morrow, of course," she told herself. "This can't make any difference in the end."

But it did in the beginning! That was the trouble. If only Arnold's suffering were less acute! If only she could beat him to earth, now, while he was fluttering, and close her ears to the echo of his cries! "Be strong," she kept commanding herself. "This is only sentimental maternalism, an emotional outbreak of thwarted motherhood. You can't take all humanity to your breast and give it comfort."

Of course not! But she did so ardently want to leave him happy. The memory of his anguish, his helplessness would haunt her. Besides... there was his confessed revulsion. If *only* he had not mentioned that, and insisted that all men require their women to be pure!

Dear God, would Hugo turn from her like this? Would he offer her his penitence and profound pity? She fought against the thought. Hugo was different. He regarded this attitude of mind as "superstitious." And yet, suppose...

No, no, she wouldn't look at the other side. Anything was better than immolating herself on the altar of Arnold's sacrifice. She held no illusion as to their changed relations; she foresaw the result of his self-imposed punishment. His exaggerated deference and humility would presently become intolerable. It would impose on her a sense of vindictiveness, as though she vengefully kicked a dog that was down. Added to her other tasks, would be that of re-establishing his self-esteem, thrusting the sceptre again into his hand.

This was the sort of liberty he so gravely offered her!

She must fight free of him. Remember the birds! Another day's delay would not matter, but, at all costs, she must go... go! To stay would mean suicide of the mind and of the soul.

Her voice was strangely harsh as she spoke.

"You are asking a good deal of me, Arnold. I am not prepared to go on as before..."

"Naturally," he interrupted. "It is for you to make conditions, and for me to obey. I will live like a pauper upon your bounty, and every breath shall be a prayer for the expiation of my sin. Only through serving you, can I hope for peace."

"Could you do what you expect of me?" she demanded. "Could you?"

"No, I don't think I could."

"Then how can you ask me to go through with so difficult an undertaking?"

"Because," he answered simply, "you are more excellent than I!"

He had voiced man's excuse for sacrificing woman throughout the ages!

———

Naomi bent over *The Book of the Hour* trying to find forgetfulness in its pages. She had written to Hugo. She had burned her bridges. She sat among the ashes of her dreams.

"Complete emancipation for women," she had written in an unfinished chapter, "is a vision of the future. It will come only when they are happier causing pain than relieving it; or, if this statement be too strong, when their own happiness is of greater moment than that of the men who have undertaken to protect them..."

She felt poignantly that she was but a spot of mist on the vast window of life—insubstantial, transitory. Some day she knew that the warm winds of time would bring neutrality if not forgetfulness. She thought—

"Even the ghosts of happiness are gray."

A gentle knock sounded.

"Go away, Jennie," she called. "You must learn not to bother me when I'm writing."

"It's only I, my dear," said Arnold, peeping into the room. "I'm not going to disturb you… I just wanted to say that Uncle Toby's out and, as I'm all alone, with nothing to do, I thought I'd make a little notice for you to hang on the door when you are writing, and wish to be free from interruption…"

Thanks to Tanya Finestone, Lauren Perruzza, and Erin Wunker for their contributions to this edition.

Royalties from the print and ebook sales of this edition of *Shackles* will be donated to support the Canadian Women in the Literary Arts (CWILA) critic-in-residence program.

THE THROWBACK SERIES reintroduces public-domain books to contemporary readers, continuing the vital work of keeping Canadian stories alive and available. Our Throwback books also give back: a percentage of each book's sales will be donated to a designated Canadian cultural organization.

INVISIBLE PUBLISHING is a not-for-profit publishing company that produces contemporary works of fiction, creative non-fiction, and poetry. We're small in scale, but we take our work, and our mission, seriously: We publish material that's engaging, literary, current, and uniquely Canadian.

We are committed to publishing diverse voices and experiences. In acknowledging historical and systemic barriers, and the limits of our existing catalogue, we strongly encourage LGBTQ2SIA+, Indigenous and writers of colour to submit their work.

Invisible Publishing has been in operation for over a decade. Since we released our first fiction titles in the spring of 2007, our catalogue has come to include works of graphic fiction and non-fiction, pop culture biographies, experimental poetry, and prose. Invisible Publishing is also home to the Bibliophonic, Snare and Throwback series.

If you'd like to know more please get in touch:
info@invisiblepublishing.com